Midnight with the Marquess

The St. Clairs
Book 2

Alexa Aston

Copyright © 2019 by Alexa Aston
Print Edition

Published by Dragonblade Publishing, an imprint of Kathryn Le Veque Novels, Inc

All rights reserved. No part of this book may be used or reproduced in any manner whatsoever without written permission, except in the case of brief quotations embodied in critical articles or reviews.

Books from Dragonblade Publishing

Dangerous Lords Series by Maggi Andersen
The Baron's Betrothal
Seducing the Earl
The Viscount's Widowed Lady
Governess to the Duke's Heir

Also from Maggi Andersen
The Marquess Meets His Match

The St. Clairs Series by Alexa Aston
Devoted to the Duke
Midnight with the Marquess
Embracing the Earl

Knights of Honor Series by Alexa Aston
Word of Honor
Marked by Honor
Code of Honor
Journey to Honor
Heart of Honor
Bold in Honor
Love and Honor
Gift of Honor
Path to Honor
Return to Honor

The King's Cousins Series by Alexa Aston
The Pawn
The Heir
The Bastard

Beastly Lords Series by Sydney Jane Baily
Lord Despair
Lord Anguish
Lord Vile
Lord Corsair

Dukes of Destiny Series by Whitney Blake
Duke of Havoc
Duke of Sorrow

Legends of Love Series by Avril Borthiry
The Wishing Well
Isolated Hearts
Sentinel

The Lost Lords Series by Chasity Bowlin
The Lost Lord of Castle Black
The Vanishing of Lord Vale
The Missing Marquess of Althorn
The Resurrection of Lady Ramsleigh
The Mystery of Miss Mason
The Awakening of Lord Ambrose

By Elizabeth Ellen Carter
Captive of the Corsairs, *Heart of the Corsairs Series*
Revenge of the Corsairs, *Heart of the Corsairs Series*
Shadow of the Corsairs, *Heart of the Corsairs Series*
Dark Heart
Live and Let Spy, *King's Rogues Series*

Knight Everlasting Series by Cassidy Cayman
Endearing
Enchanted
Evermore

Midnight Meetings Series by Gina Conkle
Meet a Rogue at Midnight, book 4

Second Chance Series by Jessica Jefferson
Second Chance Marquess

Imperial Season Series by Mary Lancaster
Vienna Waltz
Vienna Woods
Vienna Dawn

Blackhaven Brides Series by Mary Lancaster
The Wicked Baron
The Wicked Lady
The Wicked Rebel
The Wicked Husband
The Wicked Marquis
The Wicked Governess
The Wicked Spy
The Wicked Gypsy
The Wicked Wife

Unmarriageable Series by Mary Lancaster
The Deserted Heart
The Sinister Heart
The Vulgar Heart

Highland Loves Series by Melissa Limoges
My Reckless Love
My Steadfast Love
My Passionate Love

Clash of the Tartans Series by Anna Markland
Kilty Secrets
Kilted at the Altar
Kilty Pleasures

Queen of Thieves Series by Andy Peloquin
Child of the Night Guild
Thief of the Night Guild
Queen of the Night Guild

The Book of Love Series by Meara Platt
The Look of Love
The Touch of Love

Dark Gardens Series by Meara Platt
Garden of Shadows
Garden of Light
Garden of Dragons
Garden of Destiny

Rulers of the Sky Series by Paula Quinn
Scorched
Ember
White Hot

Hearts of the Highlands Series by Paula Quinn
Heart of Ashes
Heart of Shadows
Heart of Stone

Highlands Forever Series by Violetta Rand
Unbreakable
Undeniable
Unyielding

Viking's Fury Series by Violetta Rand
Love's Fury
Desire's Fury
Passion's Fury

Also from Violetta Rand
Viking Hearts

The Sins and Scoundrels Series by Scarlett Scott
Duke of Depravity
Prince of Persuasion
Marquess of Mayhem

The Unconventional Ladies Series by Ellie St. Clair
Lady of Mystery
Lady of Fortune

The Sons of Scotland Series by Victoria Vane
Virtue
Valor

Men of Blood Series by Rosamund Winchester
The Blood & The Bloom

PROLOGUE

Winwood, East Essex—1792

EVAN DRAKE, MARQUESS of Merrick, awoke from a nightmare. He whimpered, feeling the damp sheets, knowing he'd wet the bed again. There'd be no keeping it from his father. A year ago, their butler had overheard an upstairs maid mention it. The butler had immediately informed the Duke of Winstead. His father now came to Evan's room every morning before breakfast, regular as clockwork, to check if the bedsheets had been soiled.

If they had, the duke personally saw to his son's beating each time.

Evan shivered as he got out of bed and found a clean nightshirt to wear. He stripped the sheets himself, wadding them up and setting them in a corner. He only wished he could wash and replace them before morning, which was impossible.

The nightmare still lingered, causing his heart to race. Even though he couldn't remember what it was about, it would keep him from sleeping. He trembled, thinking of the beating to come. His thighs and buttocks were still sore from the one three days ago.

Why couldn't he control his bladder? He was six. That was plenty old. Children younger than he did it every night. He worried about it constantly. He'd stopped drinking anything with his evening meal, hoping that would help. It hadn't. His father had warned Evan that if he couldn't get the situation under control, he wouldn't be allowed to go off to school next year with his cousin. Not that he liked Laurence in the least bit. No one did. But he couldn't imagine Laurence getting to go while he stayed home. And when he finally did go, Laurence would no doubt have told every boy in the school why Evan had been withheld from enrolling.

He couldn't let that happen. He had to get away from Winwood.

Even if it meant leaving his mother.

Evan decided to go to her now. Glimpses of the nightmare still came in flashes, making his head pound. Mama would help soothe him. She always did.

He left his bedchamber and crept down the stairs, reaching his mother's rooms without anyone seeing him. Evan didn't bother to knock. He never did. Instead, he slipped into her bedroom and closed the door behind him.

The room stood empty, a single candle burning next to the bed. Evan knew it was late and wondered where she could be. Then he heard a door slam and raised voices coming his way. Fear gripped him. If his father caught him here, the beating would begin immediately. Over and over, he'd complained that Evan was too soft. That his mother coddled him too much.

Knowing he couldn't reach the door in time, he dropped to the ground and slid under the bed. Moments later, two pairs of feet appeared as he peered out.

"You're worthless! You disgust me. Another child lost."

"Have you ever thought it might be *you*, Winstead? Maybe your seed is defective and that's why no baby can grow inside me."

A loud slap sounded. Evan cringed. He saw his mother had been knocked to her knees and crouched on all fours. She pushed herself upright and sat on the ground.

"Think about it," she continued. "I lost two boys at six months. Another two were stillborn. I think something's wrong with you."

Evan shrank, knowing her words would cost her dearly. He closed his eyes as he heard the blows and her gasps. Then the bed above him sank and he figured his father had tossed her upon it.

"At least I have Evan, even if he is your spitting image and I'm reminded of that every time I look at him."

"Have you ever thought he doesn't resemble you for a reason?"

His eyes opened. He listened carefully. Something in his mother's tone made him pay attention.

"What do you mean?" his father growled.

His feet were right next to Evan's face. Suddenly, his mother's bare feet joined them as he dragged her from the bed and across the room.

She laughed. It wasn't her usual laugh, which was high and sweet. Mama laughed all the time when they were together. This laugh frightened him.

"Evan may be yours. Or not. When I couldn't keep a child of yours, I looked elsewhere for satisfaction."

He didn't understand what Mama meant. He dared to look out from under the bed and saw his parents across the room. His father's face held such anger that Evan knew something bad would now happen. He slammed his wife against the wall, his face inches from hers.

"Who? Who?" he demanded.

Mama didn't look scared at all. Evan couldn't understand it. She had to know the beating would get worse.

She smiled. "I'll never tell, Winstead. You'll go your whole life wondering if your title and lands will go to your son—or another man's."

Evan was supposed to be the next duke. That's how it worked. He was the son. He couldn't understand what Mama meant. He wondered if he should ask her.

A guttural sound came from his father, one that might come from some savage beast right before it attacked.

In that moment, Evan knew his father would kill her.

He wanted to slide out from under the bed. Go to her. Save her.

Terror held him hostage, though, and he could only watch in horror.

His father punched Mama in the face several times. She only laughed, blood bubbling from her nose and mouth. He grabbed her shoulders and shook her roughly. The laughter continued. Then his hands went around her throat and he began squeezing. She stopped laughing. Clawed at his face. Latched on to his wrists. Tried to pry his hands from her. His fingers tightened. The animal sounds came more harshly from him. Mama's eyes bugged out. A noise emerged from her, so soft, yet unearthly. Her lips moved as if trying to speak but nothing came out.

Then her body slumped and she stared blankly—at her murderer.

His father released her and she fell to the ground. Evan pushed back under the bed, out of sight. He could see his father's feet now, next to Mama's lifeless body. He forced his fist into his mouth, trying to keep the wail from erupting. His body shook uncontrollably. He begged God to make him be still.

Because he didn't want to die, too.

Evan heard the mattress sag again above him. His father's feet moved about as he mumbled under his breath. Then he crossed the room to the door where Mama's dressing room was. It connected to his father's dressing room and bedchamber beyond.

He was going to leave her. Dead. In bed. Evan put both hands over his mouth to keep a scream from exploding.

"Whore. You got what you deserved."

The door closed.

Evan waited, afraid his father would rush back in and jerk him out from under the bed. Tears spilled down his cheeks. He wrapped his arms around himself tightly, rocking.

After several minutes, he stilled. No one was coming back.

He had to see Mama.

He thrust himself from under the small space and drank in air. Steeling himself, he rose and turned.

Mama lay on the bed, the covers drawn up to her neck. Her eyes were frozen wide open, her bloodied face contorted in fear. Evan trembled as he reached out and pulled away the sheet. Dark bruises showed along her throat where she'd been strangled. He fought the bile that threatened to spew from him. Raising the sheet, he covered her to her chin. Though he was frightened, he leaned over and kissed her cheek, already cooling.

Evan stepped away. He didn't understand everything that had been said. What he did know is that Mama died because of him.

He could only imagine what his father would do to him.

Returning to his room, he saw no one. He huddled in the corner. Sleep didn't come. The rays of morning light finally spilled into his room. Evan washed and dressed and sat in the chair, waiting for his father's daily check of the bedsheets—but the duke never arrived.

Afraid to go but more afraid to stay in his room, Evan nervously ventured to the schoolroom where he ate breakfast every morning. No tray of food was there. Instead, his father awaited him, standing at the window, staring out. Evan gripped the table for support, fearing he might faint.

His father turned and came toward him, his face neutral, his eyes cold.

"Your mother has been ill," he began.

"She was going to have a baby. She told me," Evan managed to say, wondering how the duke would respond.

"Yes. She's had trouble with that in the past. I'm sure you know since you're her only child."

He noticed his father didn't say "our only child".

His father placed a firm hand on Evan's shoulder, causing him to flinch. "Brace yourself. Your mother lost this baby. Because it's happened several times, her body was weak. It gave out on her. It was most likely her heart."

Evan lacked the courage to call the man a liar—and hated himself for it.

The duke sighed. "What I'm trying to say is that your mother died last night. There will be no baby."

"Can I see her?" he asked softly.

"No. No, I don't think that's a good idea." After a pause, he continued. "Once the funeral is done, I've decided you'll stay with your uncle. You and Laurence will be going away to school in a year. It's time to get to know one another better."

"Is it because I look so much like her?"

His words took the duke aback. "You do favor her greatly. Yes, I am very saddened by her death and you would only be a reminder to me. For now, you'll stay with my brother."

Without another word—or any gesture of comfort—the Duke of Winstead left.

Evan vowed once he left Winwood, he would only return when the duke lay dying. He hoped he would be grown by then. If he could summon the courage at that time, he planned to choke the life out of his father.

Right after he told his father that he knew the duke had murdered his wife.

CHAPTER ONE

London—1813

IT WAS THE final night of the Season—and Rachel St. Clair hadn't landed a husband.

It certainly wasn't from lack of trying. She had attended every event to which she'd received an invitation. Balls. Card parties. Garden parties. The theatre and opera. She'd danced practically every dance, sometimes even when blisters formed on her feet. That's how much she'd liked dancing. She'd been on walks and drives and rides with eligible gentlemen. She'd even kissed a few. Three. Almost four.

And nothing.

She'd been sought after by many men of all ages and proved quite popular. Rachel liked people—and they sensed that when with her. She believed she was a good conversationalist. She was outgoing and happy. People proclaimed she was a delight to be around.

So why hadn't any of the men of the *ton* appealed to her?

Maybe she needed a dashing war hero. England's war with Bonaparte still raged on. Perhaps, her one true love was on the battlefield even now, leading men as they charged against the enemy. If so, this bloody war better be over soon because she wanted a husband.

Leah had found one. Almost the very first night. Her best friend had danced with Lord Lock once and had been utterly smitten with him.

If her best friend could find love, surely Rachel could do the same.

But not this Season. After all, how many young women waited until the last ball of the last night to fall in love?

She glanced and watched Leah debating what to wear tonight. They'd been best friends for two years, ever since Leah's sister married Rachel's brother. That was one of her problems. Jeremy and Catherine were so in love, it was almost disgusting. All of society remarked on how the Duke and Duchess of Everton acted as newlyweds. They doted on one another. They constantly told the other "I love you". Rachel couldn't avoid catching them kissing. In hallways. The library. The stables. At breakfast. She wanted what the pair had. It was important to her that a man look at her in the way Catherine did her brother. It was as necessary as air for her to find a titled gentleman who would also worship her as Jeremy did his wife.

Why couldn't she find love?

"Do you think Alex would prefer the sky blue ball gown or the mint green one?" Leah asked.

Rachel pushed herself off the bed. "Alford is mad about you no matter what you wear. In fact, he would probably prefer you wear nothing at all," she said saucily.

"Rachel!" Leah blushed furiously.

"Don't hide it. Celebrate the fact that he's over the moon in love with you, Leah. You've told me what his kisses make you feel like."

That was another problem. Rachel had asked and from what Leah told her, the way Alford kissed was nothing like the gentlemen Rachel had encountered. Leah said her fiancé's kisses sent her to heaven and back. That the more they kissed, the hungrier they both seemed for more.

The total opposite of Rachel's experience.

"I say wear whatever you wish," she continued. "Alford will love you in any color. So you might as well please yourself."

"What are you going to wear?"

"Does it matter?"

Leah came and drew Rachel into a tight embrace. "It will happen for you. I know it will. Just not this Season." She released her and returned to the wardrobe.

"At least Jeremy isn't pushing me out the door," Rachel joked. "He and Catherine sat me down a month ago and asked me if I felt anyone was special. When I told them no, Catherine, in particular, emphasized how I shouldn't feel pressured to wed just anyone in order to be wed. She said her father had also given her permission to take her time and not rush into anything."

Of course, they both knew Catherine would have married Jeremy at the end of her Season if fate had not intervened and kept them apart for five years. Rachel supposed that's why they were so open in their affection. They'd lost those years and probably tried to make up for it even now.

"Wear the green," she suggested. "It makes your eyes a deeper shade of green."

"Very well. It is one of my favorites."

They both dressed, Rachel donning a lavender ball gown that complemented her St. Clair coal black hair and emerald eyes. They sat and gossiped about different people who would be present at tonight's ball as the maid arranged their hair.

She picked up her reticule and slid it onto her wrist as Leah did the same.

"Promise me you'll be open tonight," Leah instructed. "Even if you've danced with someone before or he's brought you flowers or escorted you to the park. Don't shut anyone out. Give every man there a chance."

"I will," Rachel promised easily, knowing she had little to no chance of falling in love tonight. No one new would appear on the scene. It would be the same men she'd spent all Season with.

They went downstairs, where Alford awaited them. He'd taken to walking around the block and riding to events in the Everton carriage ever since his and Leah's engagement was announced two weeks ago. They would be married in mid-October at Eversleigh. It struck Rachel how lonely she would be with Leah gone. They spent practically every waking moment together.

And what if another Season came and went and she still didn't fall in love? Would desperation set in? Would she become one of those women who were on the shelf and never wed? An unmarried woman who served as an aunt, going from house to house and mothering other people's children since she had none of her own?

She shuddered at the thought. Why couldn't she do what most every other young lady of the *ton* did during their come-out and simply set her cap for the highest title and wealthiest man? Most everyone married. Love rarely had anything to do with engagements and marriages. Joining family fortunes and uniting family names were the games played. Leah was merely one of the lucky ones who'd found her soulmate.

"You look beautiful, my dear," Alford said with admiring eyes as they reached the bottom of the staircase. He captured Leah's hand and kissed it. Being a true gentleman, he turned to Rachel. "That lavender is quite lovely on you, Rachel."

"Thank you," she said sweetly although she doubted the earl heard it. He'd already turned back to Leah.

"Come along, Duchess."

She looked up and saw her brother and his wife coming down the stairs. Rachel wished, for a moment, she could have her sister-in-law's striking auburn hair and bright blue eyes. Maybe that would have gained her attention from the right man. No, the right man for her would be attracted to her and no other.

"I don't need to hurry," Catherine admonished. "The twins are in bed asleep. Finally. I read to Jenny and she, too, is now in bed. We have all the time in the world, Duke. Let me savor it."

Rachel chuckled. They were the only two she knew of that used their titles in such a teasing manner. That was another thing. She'd absolutely have to find a man who possessed a sense of humor. Laughter was a way of life in the St. Clair household and she refused to go anywhere gloomy. She would also need someone intelligent. Charm was definitely a plus. She didn't care much about looks but her future husband definitely needed to be a good kisser. If she was going to kiss him as much as Catherine and Leah seemed to kiss their men, he better be skilled at it.

"I see you're already here, Alford," Jeremy said. "You seem to be underfoot all the time."

"If you'd allow me to sleep on your stairs, Everton, I'd do so. That way I could see Leah first thing in the morning when she came down to breakfast."

Her brother snorted. "You're already *at* breakfast every morning when she arrives, eating me out of house and home."

Catherine swatted Jeremy with her fan. "Go easy on him, Duke. He can't help being in love with my sister." She smiled at Leah, her happiness at the match between her sister and Alford obvious.

Barton handed Jeremy his hat and opened the door. "Have a pleasant evening, Your Grace."

Rachel was last out the door and Barton said, "If he's not there tonight, Lady Rachel, the right one will turn up when you least expect it."

"I know," she said with more confidence than she felt. "Thank you, Barton."

In the carriage, Alford said, "I've had a brilliant idea."

"You may not marry Leah earlier than October," Catherine cautioned. "Too much planning is going into this wedding and too much is left to be done."

"I understand, Your Grace." He smiled at his fiancée and then said, "It's ten weeks until our wedding. I don't think I can go that long without seeing Leah at least a few times."

"You're welcome to come visit at Eversleigh," Jeremy said. "We would not keep the two of you apart deliberately."

"Thank you, Your Grace. What I had in mind was a way to introduce Leah to Fairfield since she's never seen it. I've decided to hold a house party in three weeks. That way, Leah can come to know Fairfield and some of our neighbors before we wed. I've already begun to draw up a list of names to invite. We can hunt and play games and enjoy music."

Leah beamed. "That is a magnificent idea, Alex." She looked to Catherine. "Would it be possible for Rachel and me to go? I don't want to leave if you need me for the wedding planning."

"Actually, I think it would do you good. After three weeks away from London and Alford, I'm sure you'd be moping about. We'll already have done your first dress fitting. We can do another once you return. Of course, you'll need a chaperone since Alford's parents are no longer with us. I'm sure Cor would be happy to accompany you two." Catherine turned to the earl. "How long are you thinking it will run?"

"I think two weeks would be a perfect amount of time. That would put us at the halfway mark until the wedding by the time the house party ended."

"Then you could come visit Eversleigh two weeks after that," Leah said. "I think that would be splendid." She looked at Rachel. "What do you think?"

"I'm eager to see Fairfield. It will be nice to have in my mind what it looks like so I can picture you there."

"Fairfield will be your second home, Rachel, won't it, Alex?" Leah asked.

"I expect Lady Rachel will visit often," Alford concurred.

"Maybe you'll find someone at Fairfield," Leah said hopefully.

Rachel doubted it but smiled. "You never know. It's when you least expect it."

CHAPTER TWO

Peninsular War—Spain

MAJOR EVAN DRAKE finished reading the letter from Alexander Lock, his best friend. He folded and slipped it back into its envelope. Mail came sporadically during wartime, especially during the Peninsular War. Because of this, he treasured every letter he received from Alex. This one, written two months ago, made him particularly happy. Alex wrote to him about a Lady Leah Crawford, who seemed to be an angel set upon earth, according to his friend. It was easy to see Alex was smitten with the young woman. It wouldn't surprise Evan if he opened the next letter and found them engaged—or married.

He returned the letter to his trunk, slipping it in the bundle of letters Alex had written him over the last six years since Evan had been a member of His Majesty's Army. He would need to reply and let his friend know of his own news, attaining the rank of major. It was the only good that had come out of this last, miserable year.

Lying on his cot, he fell into a restless sleep. He woke quickly, the sound of artillery being fired echoing in his head. Evan sat up and rubbed his stiff shoulder out of habit. The bullet had been removed a year ago but the shoulder muscles still tightened up on him after he'd been still for any length of time. Worse, his thigh often ached, causing him to limp slightly. That bullet had been nearly impossible to dig out. The surgeon had thought he might need to take Evan's leg. He'd told the doctor to go ahead, not caring whether he lived or died.

Because of what happened to his men.

Every officer lost soldiers in wartime. He was no exception. The battle that had seen him fall after being struck by two bullets had also been one that wiped out almost every man under his command. He could still hear their shrieks. Smell the copper-tinged blood filling the air. See men collapsing to his left and right.

He shook his head hard, trying to rid his mind of the vivid images.

"Major Drake?"

Evan saw a soldier standing at the flap of his tent. He returned the man's salute.

"Colonel Maddox wishes to see you at once, sir."

"Thank you."

He rose, smoothing his wrinkled uniform and raking fingers through his hair before he placed his hat atop his head. Maddox was his commanding officer. Evan wondered if he would receive new orders with his new rank.

Approaching the colonel's tent, he saw Maddox's right-hand man exit. He gave Evan a curt nod.

Maddox appeared at the entrance to the tent. Evan saluted and was bidden to enter. The tent held a large table in the center with an oversized map of the area. He'd stood around this table many times as battle plans were drawn up and orders issued in the seemingly endless war.

"Have a seat, Major," Maddox said, taking one himself. "Wine?"

"No, thank you."

Though the region had incredible wines, he hadn't drunk any in almost a year. He'd imbibed far too much while recovering from his wounds, trying to dull the pain that lay within him for having lost so many men. Since he'd returned to active duty, he'd shunned strong drink of any kind, preferring to keep his mind sharp and the memories alive.

"You've been an admirable officer during your time in His Majesty's Army, Major Drake. You've displayed leadership in abundance. Intelligence. Courage."

The colonel paused and Evan waited patiently. He'd learned the army was all about hurry up and wait and had taken that lesson to heart, tamping down the impatience he was born with and learning how to be still and listen.

"The problem is that you're taking too many bloody risks."

"Sir?" He frowned, confused by the statement.

Maddox looked at him with sympathy. "I know what happened to your regiment, Son. All officers find that some decisions are very hard ones. You had a tremendous loss on the battlefield a year ago. Since then, you've recovered physically—but you're not the same man. You take chances that imperil your life with every step. You do things that your men should be doing, not an officer of your rank."

"How can I ask my men to go and complete such dangerous tasks without leading them by my own example?" Evan quietly demanded.

"Officers issue orders. Soldiers are meant to obey them. True, we sometimes find ourselves in the midst of battle but our larger role is to plan and strategize. It's up to our men to execute our vision." Maddox sighed. "You've been canny in your suggestions, Drake. I've used many of them and seen excellent results as we claw our way through the mire of this war. What you haven't been for well over a year now is circumspect. I expect my officers to think prudently, not charge wildly into battle alongside foot soldiers, hoping to get themselves killed."

He felt the dull flush of guilt and embarrassment flood his face.

"You once were cautious and alert. You still are, where your men are concerned. Now, though, you're careless and unmindful of your own well-being. I require officers under my command to control their emotions. Manage their conduct. Act not on impulse."

"I understand, Colonel. I'm sorry to—"

"I've given you time and haven't seen any progress. You're only going to get yourself killed. I won't have your death on my conscience."

Maddox rose and Evan followed suit. The older man placed a hand on Evan's shoulder.

"You're a marquess. You have no need to be here. With almost a quarter of a million men serving the king, only one hundred and fifty peers and sons of peers are officers." He squeezed Evan's shoulder. "I want you to sell out. Go home. Take your seat in Parliament. Give up this death wish. Few men in the House of Lords have ever gone into battle as you have." He smiled. "Maybe the next war that occurs, you can make them understand better because of your experience here and prevent others from voting to go to war."

It was as if Maddox struck him a death blow. "You want me to sell my commission? What if I refuse?"

The colonel nodded sadly. "I cannot command you to do so. I can only advise you that it's best. You've been at war for six years, Major. You've become a decorated officer and have the respect of every man who's ever served under you." His tone softened. "It's time to go home, Evan. Make a life beyond this."

"And if I don't?"

Maddox's hand fell. He gaze grew harsh. "I will make it known that you are not fit to hold a battlefield command. I'll pull the strings that it takes in order for you to be sent back to London and work in the War Office there. I know that's not where you want to be. I'm telling you. Sell out and return to England—or suffer the consequences."

EVAN STOOD ON the deck of the ship, wearing his officer's uniform of scarlet coatee and close-fitting white pantaloons tucked into his tall

Hessians. He'd left his trunk behind in Spain. It had contained a few short-tailed coatees and gray pantaloons, along with low field boots that he wore on campaign, things he'd no longer need now that he was returning to civilian life. He wondered what titled gentlemen wore these days since he'd been gone from England such a long time.

The only things he'd brought with him were the letters he'd received from Alex and three Bancroft had sent. Winwood's head groom, who'd taught him to ride as a boy, always had a soft spot for him. He'd written to Evan once a year after his father banished him from home. In the infrequent letters, Bancroft kept him up on local gossip, telling him it was important he be kept in the know for the day when he returned as the new duke. Evan knew Bancroft wrote to him in secret. If the Duke of Winstead learned what his head groom did, the man would be out of a job with no references.

He spied land and knew they'd reach Hastings soon. Edgemere, his estate, lay twenty miles north of the coastal city. Once he'd turned thirteen, he'd gone to Edgemere instead of returning to his uncle's between school terms. As Marquess of Merrick, he set out to learn everything he could about his estate and had spent many hours with the land manager going over estate records. He'd also gotten out on the land and met every tenant. Before going to war, he was proud to know all of them and their families by name.

When he left to fight, he drew up papers with his solicitor that granted Mitchell Finfrock, Edgemere's estate manager, full power to run the place as he saw fit. Finfrock had been a kind, father-figure to him while still being a hard-nosed businessman who made sure the estate always turned a profit.

The house itself he'd closed up, letting the staff go since he had no idea how long he'd serve in the army. Only Finfrock, who lived in a small cottage near the stables, and the tenants remained. Evan supposed he'd have to see about hiring new servants to get the house up and running again. The thought depressed him.

The ship docked an hour later. With the only luggage being his satchel, which he carried on his good shoulder, Evan disembarked and went into town. He walked the streets for a bit, familiarizing himself with the city again, and then found a man who loaded his cart with goods. After a brief conversation, where he ascertained the man headed north, Evan offered to pay him to take him to Edgemere. The man readily agreed, only too happy to help an officer from the war return safely home.

The miles went by quickly. It was August in England and everything was green and peaceful in the countryside. He wondered what it would be like adjusting to such a quiet life, with no shells exploding and no men moaning as they lay dying. He'd been so used to having thousands of soldiers around him every day. Now, he would be alone—and dreaded it.

As they drew close to Fairfield, he told the man, "I've changed my mind. Let me off here and I'll walk to the gates. I'm an old friend of Lord Alford and haven't seen him in years."

The man did as requested and stopped the cart. Evan had to insist the driver take the money and then climbed from the vehicle. He waved goodbye and started down the long drive to what had always been his second home.

Arriving half an hour later, he knocked at the front door. Alford's butler recognized him at once.

"Come in, Lord Merrick. It's grand to see you. You look splendid in your uniform."

"I know I wasn't expected, Jones."

"It doesn't matter. Lord Alford will be delighted to see you."

"Evan? Is that you?"

Alex Lock raced down the stairs and wrapped him in a bear hug. "I can't believe you're here, in the flesh." He looked to Jones. "Have tea brought to my study."

They went to a large, comfortably furnished room. In the past, when he'd been a visiting schoolboy, this room had been off-limits. Of course, that was before Alex had become the Earl of Alford.

"Brandy?" his host offered.

"Why not?"

Alex poured them both a drink and passed a crystal tumbler to him.

"What shall we toast?" he asked his friend.

"That's obvious. Your safe return to England."

A dark shadow crossed Evan's soul as his thoughts turned to his men who would never come home to their loved ones. Still, he wouldn't press his conflicted mood upon his closest friend.

"To being home in England," Evan said, mustering as much enthusiasm as he could.

They drained their glasses and set them aside. Alex gestured for him to sit.

"By what you're wearing, I'm assuming you recently arrived in Hastings."

"I did. I paid a man in a rather rickety cart to bring me this far. I meant to go to Edgemere but confess I didn't want to face it. The furniture throughout the house is covered in sheets. I'm sure everything could use a good airing after the house being locked up tight for six years. I'll also need to hire a staff again."

"You can do all of that from here. There's no need to return to a home that's not a home yet. Besides, I must insist you stay. I'm hosting a house party. It just began today." Alex beamed. "It's in honor of Leah."

"Ah, the sweet, earthly angel of your recent letters," Evan remarked, seeing how Alex lit up simply mentioning the woman's name.

"You never received my last correspondence, I'll wager. Leah and I are engaged. We'll wed at Eversleigh, her family's home, come mid-October."

The good news made Evan smile. "My heartiest congratulations."

"Now that you're back, you'll have to stand up with me," Alex insisted.

"Of course. I wouldn't miss it for the world."

"And promise you'll stay for the house party."

Doubt filled him. "I'm not certain that's a good idea, Alex. I think it's going to take some time getting used to being in Polite Society again. I'm not much of a conversationalist. What do I have to talk about? How many cannons were fired at a particular battle? How many soldiers were wounded or killed in action?" He gestured to his clothing. "Besides, this is all I have to wear. I doubt anything will fit me at Edgemere. I have filled out some during my army days."

Alex waved his protests away. "We've always been of a similar size. I insist you stay at Fairfield until Edgemere is up and running. My wardrobe and valet are at your disposal. Let's go upstairs. I'll order you a bath and you can try on some things to see what fits."

The tea cart arrived and they delayed going upstairs for several minutes. Evan relished the first decent cup of tea he'd had in years and gobbled down several scones.

They went upstairs and Evan had to admit that the bath was the best he'd had since he'd left England. Alex pulled numerous items out for him to wear. As he'd suggested, they still were close in size and Evan could make do with what Alex provided until he saw a tailor.

"Seeing these items gives me a better idea what I might request as I have a new wardrobe made up. I suppose I'll need to return to Hastings for that."

"Nonsense. We'll have my tailor from London come in order to outfit you," his friend insisted. "You're a marquess, after all. You have to look your title. I have your old room ready. Lady Rachel was supposed to use it but, as usual, she and Leah are thicker than thieves and demanded they be placed in the same chamber."

"Who is this Lady Rachel? I don't recall you mentioning her."

"Leah's sister, Catherine, married Rachel's brother, the Duke of Everton. Everton took guardianship of Leah and the two are closer than sisters." Alex paused. "I think you'll like Lady Rachel quite a bit."

Evan held a hand up. "No," he said firmly. "No matchmaking, Alex. Just because you've found the love of your life doesn't mean every single man wishes to be in a wedded state. I've only set foot in England a few hours ago. I prefer remaining a bachelor."

"Lady Rachel is an interesting woman. If you find you have no romantic interest in her, she would still be a good friend to have."

The thought of becoming friends with a woman seemed foreign to him. After spending years in the company of men, with only the occasional camp trollop to satisfy his urges, Evan couldn't fathom making friends with a lady of the *ton*. Especially an unmarried one. Those were the ones always on the lookout for a husband.

He yawned, the lack of sleep of the past several days finally catching up to him.

"I was going to say that dinner will be served soon but you look too weary to sit and make polite conversation. Why don't I have Mrs. Dunnavant send up a tray for you instead?"

Evan grinned. "The old girl's still kicking around? After eating camp food for longer than I'd like to remember, anything from Mrs. Dunnavant would be much desired."

"I'll have my valet move some of these clothes to your room. I'm letting you off the hook tonight, Evan. Tomorrow, when you're rested, I expect you to be your usual charming self to my houseguests." Alex hugged him again. "It's good to have you back home."

"It's good to be here."

Evan went across the hall to the room he'd often stayed in. He and Alex had gone to Eton together and become fast friends. The Earl and Countess of Alford had invited Evan to Fairfield several times over the years. When he began staying at Edgemere during school breaks, he came even more often since only five miles separated the two estates.

The room seemed familiar, despite having new drapes and carpeting. He sat in a chair by the window and became lost in thought until a knock sounded at the door. A maid brought in a tray filled to the brim.

Mrs. Dunnavant followed behind her.

"I had to see for myself that it was truly you, Lord Merrick."

Evan hugged the cook. "If I would've known you were still here, I would've sold out and come more quickly. No one can make roast pheasant or apple pies as you can, Mrs. Dunnavant."

The cook blushed. "It's good to have you here again, my lord. I've got to get back. It's almost time for dinner to be served."

"Thank you for coming to see me, Mrs. Dunnavant. I will return the favor and lurk around your kitchen during my stay at Fairfield."

He ate every delicious item on the tray. His belly full, sleep seemed a possibility. Once he rid himself of his boots, lethargy blanketed him and he climbed on the bed, fully clothed, promptly drifting off.

As usual, a nightmare woke him. Evan sat up in the dark, his heart pounding furiously, darkness surrounding him. It took him several moments before he realized where he was. He rose from the bed and went to the window. Moonlight shone across the lawn. Restlessness filled him. He was also thirsty.

Not bothering to pull his Hessians back on, Evan went downstairs to the kitchen. A fat tabby sat next to the hearth. He found some cider and drank it. Now wide awake, he decided to go to the library. Maybe if he could find something boring, such as a seed catalogue, that might help put him back to sleep. He went to the library as a clock chimed midnight. Since he'd seen no one, he supposed all of Alex's guests had gone to bed, keeping country hours.

He lit a single lamp and browsed the shelves. Nothing jumped out at him. He went to a chair in the far corner and turned it so it faced the window. A strong breeze blew clouds across the night sky and the moon peeked out several times. The movement lulled him and his eyes started drooping. He closed them, thinking he would get up in a minute and go back to bed.

The next thing he knew, he heard voices. Feminine voices.

And their conversation was most interesting.

Chapter Three

"THERE'S NO WAY I can sleep now," Rachel declared to Leah as they entered the library. "After staying up hours past midnight for months during our Season, I'm having trouble adapting to going to bed by ten o'clock."

"I know what you mean. We'll need to, though. House party guests usually rise early and go to bed early," Leah replied.

They went and sat on a plush settee. Rachel pulled her bare feet up under her. Both women were in their night rails, covered by dressing gowns. Since everyone at Fairfield had gone to bed, she hadn't seen the need for them to dress when they came downstairs.

"What do you think of your soon-to-be new home?" she asked.

"I love everything about it," Leah said. "The rooms are large and airy. The gardens are beautiful."

"Don't forget the stables," Rachel reminded. "Alford has quite a bit of decent horseflesh."

"You're the rider. Not I."

"I plan to ride often while we're here. Alford showed me which mount he thought would be most suited to me."

Leah touched her arm. "And have you found any of the guests suited to you?"

Rachel laughed. "Not in the way you think. You know me. I adore meeting new people and learning all about them. I did know five of the gentlemen from our London Season. Three others were new to me, though, all neighbors of Alford's. I enjoyed speaking with them and several of the women in the neighborhood. As to what you're asking? No, I didn't find any of them interesting in a romantic kind of way." She sighed. "No sparks like what you've said you felt when you and Alford met."

Leah smiled dreamily. "I do think it was love at first sight, Rachel. Even from across the room, Alex caught my eye that night. That first time we danced? It was magical."

"I remember Jeremy harping on you to give other men a chance when every sentence you uttered began with 'Alford says this or Alford says that'."

"I did try. I danced with anyone who asked. I allowed other gentlemen to come to visit. But it was always Alex, from the beginning. And when we kissed? I knew for certain."

Rachel snorted. "The kisses you describe with Alford are nothing like my experience."

"What men have you kissed, Rachel? I'm curious."

"Three that count. One was a very attractive viscount. The moment his lips touched mine, it was as if I rubbed against a cold fish. A rakish duke came after that. He was far too good-looking. You know how men can act when they're handsome and they know it. Since their looks came to them with no effort, they think everything should come to them easily. He pressed his lips against mine and then did nothing. Surely, there has to be more than that!"

"Oh, there is," Leah murmured. "And the third?"

"You'll know him. It's that terribly sweet earl. I always forget his name but he's the one who constantly steps on your toes when you dance with him."

Leah shuddered. "My feet were bruised for a week after we danced. How did he kiss?"

Rachel laughed. "He put his lips on mine and then started sucking on them. It hurt. I jerked away and gave him the death stare that

Jeremy taught us to use when we wished for a man to be gone."

Leah laughed. "I'll admit I used it a few times myself when I received unwanted attention."

"There was a fourth time but I don't really count it. Another earl, not very handsome, but he was quite decent. He told me that I looked as if I could use some fresh air and escorted me out to the terrace. Then he lunged at me. I knew it would end in a kiss so I turned my head, thinking his lips would merely graze my cheek. Can you imagine my surprise when his *tongue* slid across my face? Whatever did he have it hanging out for, like some panting dog?"

She watched Leah place both hands over her mouth and shake with laughter.

"What? What did I say that was so humorous?"

Her friend calmed. "You have a few things to learn, Rachel. One is that kissing often involves tongues."

"It does?" Surprise filled her. "Why? Do you and Alford use *your* tongues?"

Leah blushed. "We most certainly do. Sometimes, you want to be as close as you can to the one you love. You want to taste him as well as touch him. That involves tongues. And not always in your mouth." She leaned forward, her voice lowered, as she said, "Sometimes, those tongues enjoy running over skin."

"Really? This is fascinating. Why hasn't anyone told me this before? Maybe if one of those gentlemen had known how to kiss me properly, I might have experienced some type of romantic feelings for them."

"Well, it's not quite proper to first kiss using your tongue," Leah said primly. "I would say it's reserved for when you have true, deep feelings for a man."

She sniffed. "I doubt that will ever be the case with me."

"Rachel, you're too hard on yourself. You were the prettiest girl who made her come-out this Season. You had scads of men fawning over you."

"Then why, out of all of those men, did I not feel any sparks like you did with Alford? Like Jeremy and Catherine did?"

"Because that man wasn't present," Leah determined. "You have yet to meet him. That's why I want you to be open at this house party. Alex said two more gentlemen will arrive tomorrow, as well as three more ladies close to our age. The party will be complete by then. Who knows? Maybe one of them will catch your interest."

Rachel doubted it but kept silent, not wanting to dampen Leah's optimism.

Leah yawned. "I'm off to bed. Are you coming?"

"No. I'm wide awake now. I'll find something to read and be up later."

What she wanted to do was think on what Leah told her about kissing and tongues. The prospect interested her greatly. Maybe she could try it out with one of Alford's houseguests to see if it was something that pleased her. How to go about asking a man to kiss her that way would need some thought, though. She did her best thinking when she walked. She would take a long one tomorrow and mull over how to approach one of the men present with her unusual request.

Rachel rose and went to the bookshelves, skimming her finger along the spines of the books. Once, Eversleigh had a great library and she could find any book she desired in it. That was before Jeremy became Duke of Everton. Once he did, all of the volumes were immediately sold. Rachel understood why. She'd learned through eavesdropping on conversations between Jeremy and Cor that her father had gambled away the St. Clair fortune, leaving her brother a huge mess to deal with when he became the new duke.

Somehow, Jeremy had managed to fill the family coffers. She didn't question him about it. Gradually, he was building a new library, often taking her suggestions as to what he should add to it. Rachel read voraciously and was pleased that Jeremy listened to her opinions. She knew money must no longer be a problem since he'd lavishly outfitted her and Leah for their Seasons. Many of her dresses had only been worn once. She decided that since she would undergo a second Season next spring, she wouldn't ask for a new wardrobe and simply wear what she already had. A few petty girls might comment among themselves but she doubted any of the gentlemen would realize she hadn't updated her clothes. Besides, it shouldn't matter. A man should want her for herself and not care if she wore last year's dresses.

Rachel finally found a volume that might interest her and pulled it from the shelf.

"Finally find something to read?" a deep voice asked.

She jumped and the book fell to the floor. From the shadows of the far corner of the room, a man stood in silhouette. He moved toward her. As he came into the light, Rachel saw the stranger was tall, with dark blond or light brown hair. He had broad shoulders and slim hips and wore no boots, his stockinged feet an odd contrast to being fully dressed. His face was tanned from long hours in the sun, making his azure eyes stand out.

Bending, he retrieved the book and handed it to her.

"I believe you dropped this."

EVAN HAD THOUGHT he should stand and let the two women know someone else was present in the room. He quickly realized who they were and found their conversation hard to interrupt. It was obvious they were close and comfortable sharing with one another. He already could picture Lady Leah in his mind from the description of her in Alex's letters.

Lady Rachel, though, remained an intriguing mystery as he stared out the window and listened to her speak. Her low-pitched voice was deeper than most women possessed. When she laughed, it sent tingles down his spine.

Then the topic of kissing came up and Evan knew it was too late to interrupt without totally embarrassing the two women. Instead, he sat back and held in his laughter as they discussed which men of the *ton* Lady Rachel had kissed and her obvious inexperience when it came to the process. Lady Leah insisted tongues were only put into play when love occurred.

Evan would beg to differ.

The more the two women spoke, the more he longed to see what Lady Rachel looked like. She seemed lively and intelligent and more than a tad curious about kissing. Alex's fiancée mentioned how popular and pretty her friend was. It made Evan wonder why she hadn't been deluged with several offers of marriage by Season's end.

He listened as Lady Leah left and then rose, facing the room's occupant. Lady Rachel had her back to him, perusing the shelves for a book. She was taller than most women of his acquaintance and had a long braid of midnight black hair that hung to her waist. He couldn't tell much about her figure because she wore a dressing gown. Evan got a glimpse of her ankles as she reached for a book. The sight of them and her bare feet caused a hunger to rise within him.

He wanted to talk to her.

He needed to see her face.

More than anything, he wished to kiss her.

"Finally find something to read?" he called out and started toward her.

She jumped, the book tumbling to the floor. She didn't scream or faint as most women would have done. Instead, Lady Rachel stood her ground and eyed him with interest as he crossed the long room.

Evan reached her and knelt, picking up the book and placing it in her hands. The moment their fingers brushed, that spark she had referred to ignited between them.

"I believe you dropped this," he said huskily, his eyes falling to her full, bottom, very kissable lip. He wanted to suck on it, much as one of her fumbling suitors had tried to do—and failed.

"Thank you." She turned and placed the book back on the shelf and then regarded him with interest. "Who are you? You weren't present at dinner tonight. Are you one of Alford's houseguests who arrived late?"

"An uninvited one," he said, fighting the urge to take her into his arms. "I'm Evan Drake, an old school friend of the earl's."

She brightened. "Are you Merrick? Alford mentioned him a few times."

"I am he. I only returned to England today, having sold my commission."

"Does it look as if this bloody war will ever end?" she asked.

He laughed at her boldness. "I believe we—and the Russians—have Bonaparte on the run. It's only a matter of time before his troops are defeated."

"That's certainly good news." She paused. "Would you like to sit? I'd be interested in hearing your views on the war. Over here."

She moved to a dark brown settee and sat, pulling her feet up under her and placing one arm on the back so she could face him. Evan sat.

"You haven't told me your name."

She sniffed. "Well, you *were* eavesdropping. I assumed you picked it up in our conversation."

"Lady Rachel," he responded. "No last name given," he teased.

"I am Rachel St. Clair."

"Ah. An unusual name. Is your older brother Jeremy?"

"Yes. He's now Duke of Everton. Do you know him?"

"More of him. He was a couple of years ahead of me at Eton. I remember him quite well. His brother, too. A shame that he drowned as he did. The St. Clairs were known for their intelligence and charm." He eyed her appreciatively. "I see you have both."

Instead of blushing as a young miss might, Rachel St. Clair merely smiled. "Thank you. I must apologize for being in my night clothes. Leah and I thought no one would be lurking downstairs. Everyone was in bed before ten o'clock tonight."

"That would explain your bare feet. And the dressing gown," he noted.

She shrugged. "You were going to tell me about the war."

"Was I?" he asked lazily, longing to trace circles along her back with his hands and around her nipples with his tongue.

"Well, I assumed you were because I asked."

"Does everyone always do what you say?"

She grinned. "Usually. Not that I'm spoiled. Please don't think ill of me. It's just that St. Clairs are known for their charisma. I suppose we do charm most people so we often seem to get our way. Please, tell me about the war, Lord Merrick. Why did you purchase a commission when you are a peer?"

"Because I thought I had something to prove," he admitted, something he'd never told another soul.

"Was it your father who inspired this brash action?"

"You're not only charming but perceptive, Lady Rachel."

She sighed. "It's well after midnight. I think we could relax the rules of society. Call me Rachel."

"And I am Evan."

"The reason I asked about your father is that mine was horrid. He rarely spent time with any of his children. All three of us came from different wives, by the way. He'd rather drink and gamble and consort with others who enjoyed the same than give two figs about his family. When I was young, I wanted to please him. As I grew older, I decided what was important was pleasing myself."

She had revealed a great deal about herself. It gave him the courage to do the same.

"My father banished me from Winwood after my mother died. I

was six."

Her face grew distressed. "What a beast! You deserved comfort and love."

"Love wasn't something I associated with him. He beat me regularly for wetting the bed. It took getting away from him before I finally stopped."

She placed her hand over his to soothe him. Once again, that unseen electricity rippled between them and she removed it, a crease forming on her brow.

Moistening her lips, she asked, "Where did you go?"

"I was sent to my uncle's. His son was my same age and we were headed off to school the next year. I returned during holidays to my uncle's house sometimes. Often, I was invited here, to Fairfield, because of my friendship with Alex. This became more of a second home to me. My own residence, the seat of the Marquess of Merrick, is only five miles north of here. It became my primary dwelling starting at age thirteen."

"So young? With no adult supervision?"

He shrugged. "I received a letter from my father's solicitor. Father didn't write to me directly. I was told that I was of an age to start learning about my estate." He shook his head. "I think my father wanted me to fail miserably and lord it over me."

Her gaze bored into him, her emerald eyes blazing in anger. "Why did he hate you so?"

It was something Evan could never tell her—or anyone.

"I wish I knew. I suppose part of it had to do with the fact that I resembled my mother. I reminded him of her after her death."

It had taken him several years to understand what had happened in his mother's bedchamber that night. The conversation between his parents had been etched into his mind. He knew that his father thought Evan might be another man's child and the sight of him sickened the duke. That was the true reason Winstead had washed his hands of his son.

"That's no reason at all," she proclaimed. "Who is your father?"

"The Duke of Winstead. Winwood lies only ten miles to the west of Edgemere, my own country estate."

"Winstead?" she said, her nose crinkling in disgust. "I actually met him this Season. I didn't like him at all. He was full of himself and quite condescending to me."

Evan chuckled. "That doesn't surprise me. I once overheard the Earl and Countess of Alford discussing him on one of my frequent visits. They said Winstead had no respect for women and treated them all with little regard. Even his countless mistresses."

A smile played about Rachel's lips. "So, do you make a habit of eavesdropping? I doubt the earl and countess knew you were within earshot." Before he responded, she said, "It's quite all right. I've done a bit of it myself. Sometimes, it's the only way to learn about something."

"I don't think you'll be able to learn anything about kissing through eavesdropping," he observed.

Her cheeks pinkened. "Oh, that. I'm sorry you had to listen to me prattle on about kissing." She stopped and studied him. "I really think I should learn how to kiss properly, though. Are you interested in teaching me?"

CHAPTER FOUR

RACHEL COULDN'T BELIEVE she'd actually voiced the words to a man she'd only known for a quarter-hour.

Lord Merrick's face revealed shock—then intrigue.

She found herself saying, "I'm sorry, Evan. I never should have asked that of you. You know from overhearing my conversation with Leah that I haven't been able to attract a husband. I thought if I learned how to kiss properly, it might help. Please, disregard my request."

He held a hand up and she fell silent.

"Since you mentioned my eavesdropping, I have to say that Lady Leah mentioned how popular you were with the men of the *ton*. And despite what you're wearing now, you are a most beautiful woman. It's hard to imagine you received no offers of marriage, the issue of kissing set aside."

Rachel huffed. "I did receive several. Within the first two weeks of the Season. Can you imagine that? Men whose names I could barely remember were lining up, offering for me. It was ridiculous. I put a stop to all of that nonsense."

"How?"

"I made it known that I would entertain no offers of marriage unless I fell in love. Of course, that didn't stop the constant stream of men. Our house was overrun with flowers. I took more rides in carriages and on horseback in the park than I thought possible. I danced every dance when I attended balls. I went to so many events that they became a blur. Men wooed me as if there was no tomorrow."

"And yet you didn't fall in love with any of them?" he asked.

"No—not a one!" she declared.

"You do realize that love rarely has anything to do with marriage," he stated. "Most couples find tolerating one another to be adequate. Some actually grow to like each other and a few others become fond of one another. I suppose a rare handful, such as Alex and Lady Leah, do fall in love. Surely, you could have chosen the man with the best qualities and—"

"And what?" she demanded. "*Marry* him?" Rachel shuddered. "If I'm to spend a lifetime with a man, it better be someone I love. Of course, I expect to like him a great deal, too." She sighed. "I know, I seem to want the impossible. Is it too much to ask that I find one man who is kind, intelligent, and possesses a sense of humor? I don't think so."

"What of looks? Titles? And wealth? Most women would put those first on their lists. Not attributes."

"I'm not most women," she said firmly. "I want a man who's at least as smart as I am. One who will make me laugh whether I'm twenty-two or ninety-two. It would be good to have some things in common, enough so we'd get along. But, at the same time, I'd want us to be different enough so that we would have new things to share with one another every day."

Rachel cracked her knuckles as she spoke. "See? If Cor were here, she'd cringe. Not that I'm speaking to a man in my night clothes and calling him by his Christian name, but that I'm cracking my knuckles in front of him. I want a man who'd love me—and like me—despite the fact that I have this disgusting habit."

"Who's Cor?"

She dropped her hands to her lap. And then laughed. "You *are* different from most men I met this Season, Evan. You haven't run from the room screaming because of my honesty." She tilted her head and eyed him carefully. "I like that about you. As to Cor, she's my grandmother. She raised Jeremy, Luke, and me because all three of our mothers died in childbirth. Cor is the St. Clair rock."

"She's done a fine job of raising you, Rachel. You're bright and curious and a delight to converse with. I'm usually averse to conversation but I've enjoyed ours tremendously."

Evan reached and took one of her hands in his. His touch made her forget to breathe for a moment. She gazed into his blue eyes, mesmerized by them.

"As far as kissing you goes, I will be happy to teach you," he promised.

"When? Now?" she asked eagerly.

"Kissing is a part of flirtation," he said. "You don't quite appreciate it as much unless you build up to it. We shall start slowly."

"You disappoint me, Evan. You're putting me off."

"Am I?" he asked softly and entwined his fingers with hers.

Rachel swallowed, suddenly feeling overwhelmed by merely holding his hand. She licked her lips nervously.

"Stop that," he chided.

"Stop what?" she asked, clueless as to what he needed her to quit doing since she wasn't doing anything annoying. "I'm not cracking my knuckles anymore," she said defensively.

"You licked your lips."

"What if I did?" she challenged.

"That's a part of flirting," he said.

"It is?"

"Most definitely," he assured her. "It calls a gentleman's attention to your mouth." He stared at hers so intently that butterflies exploded in her stomach. "And it makes a man want to kiss you."

"It does?" she asked breathlessly.

He nodded. "It does. So, that's your first lesson tonight. If you do feel that spark with a man and want him to kiss you, you may lick your lips."

Rachel did it again, testing him.

Evan laughed. "Stop. We're going to work up to it."

"How long will this take? The house party is only two weeks long," she complained. "At the rate you're moving, it will be Christmas before you even think to kiss me."

His fingers tightened on hers, causing her to stop breathing again. Evan lifted their joined hands and pressed warm lips to her knuckles. A good kind of chill rippled through her. He released her hand and then his fingers lightly touched her wrist, turning her hand over so it faced palm up. Slowly, he moved his head toward it as Rachel watched in fascination. Just before his lips touched its center, he gazed up at her.

She swallowed. The heat in his eyes stole her breath. He lowered his gaze and brushed his lips against her palm. She thought they'd be warm but, instead, they were scorching hot. Then he pressed a long, lingering kiss directly onto her palm. Rachel was glad she wasn't standing for her knees would've given out and sent her tumbling to the floor.

Evan lifted his lips and stared at her. She couldn't help but stare helplessly back at him.

Then his mouth touched the underside of her wrist. Rachel froze. He pushed up the sleeve of her dressing gown, his lips trailing up her arm. Odd sensations ran through her. He stopped at the crook of her elbow and pressed a final kiss there before sliding the sleeve back down.

"That's your first lesson in kissing," he said softly. "Kisses come in many forms and on many places. Not just your mouth."

He placed her hand back in her lap as she looked at him wordlessly.

"Will you meet me again at midnight for another lesson?"

"Yes," she whispered.

"Good."

He leaned over and pressed a kiss to her forehead. Rachel closed her eyes, breathing in the scent of clean soap and warm man.

"Until tomorrow night," he said and rose.

When he reached the door she called out, "Wait. Won't I see you during the day?"

His smile melted her heart. "You'll meet Lord Merrick tomorrow, Lady Rachel. He will be distantly polite to you. But it will be Evan, your tutor, tomorrow at midnight."

Rachel dressed with care, knowing Evan would be present in the breakfast room. She'd finally fallen asleep shortly before dawn, thinking of his lips scorching her palm. Even with only a few hours of rest, her body thrummed with anticipation.

"Are you ready?" Leah asked.

"You know me. I'm always famished."

Together, they made their way downstairs as the clock chimed nine. Only a few guests from last night were up this early, though she knew more would stream in during the next hour. It didn't matter. The only guest she was interested in sat talking with Alford.

The earl saw them and rose. Evan did the same. She and Leah went over to them.

"Good morning, ladies," Alford said brightly. "I'm very pleased to introduce to you my best friend, the Marquess of Merrick. Evan, this is Lady Leah Crawford, my fiancée."

Evan bowed to her and smiled. "Alex wrote to me about you, Lady Leah. I can see why he was so taken with your angelic beauty."

"Thank you, Lord Merrick. I'm so glad to make your acquaintance. Are you on leave from the army?"

"Actually, I sold out a few days ago and have returned to England for good. My estate is five miles to the north of Fairfield. I will be living there once the house party ends."

"Then you must come to our wedding," Leah insisted.

"I plan to." He turned to Rachel. "And who might this be?"

"This is Lady Rachel St. Clair," Alford told him. "Leah's other half. They are inseparable."

Evan bowed politely. "It's a pleasure to meet you, Lady Rachel."

"I feel the same," she replied coolly. "Shall we get something to eat, Leah?"

They went to the sideboard. Rachel piled her plate with eggs, ham, toast, and jam and joined Leah, who already sat across from the two men.

"Are your eyes larger than your stomach?" Evan asked as she sat and a footman poured tea for her.

Alford chuckled. "I've eaten breakfast many days with Lady Rachel. She can out-eat any man I know."

Leah spread strawberry jam on her toast. "While I eat very little. I can look at food and become bloated. Rachel eats to her heart's content and stays slender. I don't see how she does it."

"I'm more active than you, Leah. I walk daily and enjoy gardening. You're more interested in sedate activities, such as needlework and letter writing."

"What about reading?" Evan asked her.

"I do enjoy a good book. In fact, I perused Alford's library late last night," Rachel said nonchalantly. "It's quite good. You should visit it while you are here. I'm sure you could find something to interest you."

"Thank you for the recommendation."

"I find there's so much to be learned in libraries," she continued. "I think one should go on learning new things throughout life."

Evan smoothly said, "It's a fine philosophy to live by, Lady Rachel.

Provided you can find the right tutor to learn from."

They chatted about some of the guests. Alford informed his friend of who had come and told him about those he was unfamiliar with.

"What activities do you have planned for us?" Rachel asked. "This is the first house party I've ever attended. I'm curious as to what we'll be doing."

"Since Leah loves to picnic, we'll do that twice. One will be held down by the lake, where we can use the rowboats. The usual carriage rides and walks. Lawn tennis. Croquet. Since it's shooting season, the men will take part in that several days, starting today." He looked to Evan. "I'm sure you're a crack shot after your army years. You'll put us all to shame."

"I think I'll beg off today, Alex. I'm in the mood to ride." Evan looked to the two women. "Do either of you enjoy riding?"

Rachel couldn't believe how innocent Evan looked as he spoke. She knew he'd overheard them talking about the stables last night and how Leah didn't care much for riding—but Rachel did.

"I merely tolerate it, Lord Merrick," Leah said. "If you want a riding companion, Rachel loves horses."

"Is that so?" He turned and gazed at her intently.

"Yes. Alford has already advised me on which mount to use during our visit at Fairfield," she replied.

"Excellent. When would you like to go?"

"Give me time to change into my riding habit," Rachel said. "I'll meet you at the stables in a half-hour."

"I look forward to it."

She and Leah excused themselves and returned to their shared chamber. Once they were inside and the door closed, Leah grabbed her hand.

"Isn't Lord Merrick engaging? And he seemed most interested in you, Rachel."

She shrugged. "I suppose so."

"No, don't give me that," Leah warned. "You said you would give everyone a fair chance. This is Alex's best friend of many years. Please, be nice to him. For me?"

Rachel squeezed Leah's hand. "Of course, I'll be nice. He did seem to be a decent fellow."

"Good."

She changed into her riding habit and returned downstairs to the kitchen, where she claimed a carrot. Stepping outside, she saw the day was partly sunny. A few clouds blew across the pale blue sky.

When she arrived at the stables, Evan stood outside it, holding the reins of a horse in hand. He wore his regimental colors.

"Are you back off to war so soon?" she asked teasingly.

"These fit better. Riding puts a strain on clothes. While borrowing some of Alford's clothes will do for a few days, I didn't want to return to Fairfield with my pants split."

"Well, you look quite dashing." Actually, better than dashing. His white pantaloons fit him like a second skin, revealing muscular thighs and calves. The snug scarlet coat emphasized his broad shoulders.

"My lady?"

Rachel tore her eyes from him and saw a groom leading out another horse.

"I took the liberty of having your horse saddled. Alex told me which one he recommended to you. May I help you mount?"

"Yes, please."

Rachel went to the solid black horse and stroked its nose. "I have something for you, my beauty," she said, holding up the carrot and letting the horse munch on it.

When he finished, Evan asked, "Ready?"

She moved to the side and the marquess took her by the waist and hoisted her into the saddle. Rachel tucked her leg around the horn, hoping those unforeseen butterflies going wild in her stomach might calm. They scrambled her thoughts and being on a new horse, she needed to keep her wits about her.

Evan mounted his horse and said, "Follow me."

He cantered away and Rachel followed. As they reached the lane that led up to the house, he paused and she rode up next to him.

"Where should we explore?" she asked. "Since you're familiar with Fairfield lands and the area, I will leave it to you."

"Would you mind if we rode to Edgemere? It's been six years since I've seen it."

Rachel saw the eagerness in his face and replied, "I'd enjoy seeing your home, Lord Merrick. Lead the way."

CHAPTER FIVE

EVAN HAD SURPRISED himself by inviting Rachel St. Clair to ride with him. If he were wise, he would have joined the other male houseguests and gone shooting.

He'd never claimed to be a wise man.

The second surprise had been when he spontaneously asked her to ride to Edgemere with him. He'd wanted to visit his estate in the next day or two. With the pleasant weather and a beautiful companion, now seemed the time to go. She'd readily agreed and they'd struck out on the main road that would pass by his estate.

"Can we ride faster?" Rachel called to him. "This horse is chomping at the bit. I want to see what he can do."

Evan nodded and she took off on the coal black steed, its coat as dark as her luscious, thick hair. He decided tonight's lesson might extend to touch for he very much wanted to run his fingers through her dark locks.

As he urged his horse forward, he wondered if she would show up at midnight tonight. He thought she would. If anything, Rachel St. Clair was curious. She would want to see how the next lesson unfolded. Evan could kick himself for offering to teach her how to kiss. He didn't want to become involved with any woman at this time. He was still nursing a bruised ego from practically being kicked out of the army, plus he had much to do in order to get Edgemere up and running again. More than anything, he wanted total quiet after years of the noises of war. He believed a solitary life would suit him well.

Truth be told, he was a little afraid of this woman. She was independent, spirited, and opinionated. He'd always preferred docile women, who did as he asked and then went away when he wished, no commitment between them. Rachel was idealistic enough to believe in love.

Evan didn't think it was possible for him to love.

He blamed his past for it. He'd been so young when his mother was killed. He supposed she'd loved him but it was hard to even remember what she looked like. His only interaction with his father had been when the duke gleefully beat him, only to send him away, never speaking to him again. His uncle paid very little attention to Evan, favoring his son in every instance. Laurence had no use for Evan, much less showed him any family love. Instead, Laurence tried to bully him. When Evan stood up to his cousin, Laurence resorted to telling outrageous untruths about him to the other boys at school.

Thank goodness Evan had made friends with Alexander Lock. Alex's parents had been warm toward him every time Evan visited but he doubted they loved him. The army had made it clear that fear and discipline were the only factors that guaranteed success. Living for years in a war zone, Evan had never truly relaxed. He became self-contained and self-reliant.

Except for his men. He'd tried his best not to become too attached, knowing that death was only a shot or bayonet away. And when, after years, he finally did open his heart to them, he'd gone and gotten most of them killed. The lesson he'd learned was to lock his heart away. Keep to having no emotions. It was safer that way. If he didn't feel, he wouldn't hurt.

The trouble was, Rachel St. Clair had stirred feelings within him, ones that threatened to escape faster than a team of runaway horses. He needed to watch carefully and not become involved with her. He'd still tutor her so that, one day, when she did find that man she determined to be her soulmate, she'd have a leg up on how to please him. Evan would show the young beauty what she needed to know—but even when things turned physical, he would need to divorce himself emotionally and keep his distance from her.

He caught up to her, astonished at how well she handled her mount. When they reached the turnoff for Edgemere, he signaled and she turned her horse as they headed to the east.

Her cheeks were flushed and those emerald eyes sparkled as they slowed their horses to a canter.

"I haven't ridden so fast in months!" she exclaimed. "Rotten Row is terribly sedate. I would have been proclaimed a pariah if I'd ridden this way in London. Thank you, Evan. This was wonderful!"

"Merrick," he corrected.

"Oh, bloody hell. We're alone. I'll call you whatever I want." Her mouth set in determination and she took off again, flying down the lane.

His heart jiggled in his chest.

Evan knew he was in trouble.

He chased her down again and she finally slowed as they approached the main house.

Rachel tugged on the reins, bringing the black horse to a halt. "Oh, this is beautiful. It's even larger than Fairfield." She grinned at him. "Of course, you *are* a marquess. I suppose you should own a larger house than an earl."

He looked at it with new eyes. The last time he'd seen his home, he'd been twenty-one, a young man fresh out of university. He returned now war-weary, his life experience resting solidly on his shoulders. Yes, the house was beautiful. Much needed to be done, though, to make it livable again.

"I let all but one gardener go," he told her. "I'll need to hire more to help him clean up the landscaping. I'm sure the gardens are in atrocious shape."

"What about your household staff?"

"I dismissed them. I didn't know how long the war would last—or if I would even come back."

"And your tenants?"

"They remained, along with my estate manager, Mitchell Finfrock. I saw no reason to displace them. Finfrock sent me brief reports. The estate has thrived in my absence."

"Which would you rather do first—visit with Finfrock or see the inside of the house?"

"The house," he determined. "The stables are empty. Let's take the horses to the pond and let them drink their fill. They deserve it after being ridden so hard. This way."

They rode to the pond and he dismounted. Walking to her, he held his hands out and captured her waist in them. Evan lifted her from the saddle and placed her on the ground. Reluctantly, he released her. She licked her lips and he thought of last night's first lesson. He decided she did it unconsciously and ignored her.

After the horses drank, they took the reins in hand and led them back toward the house. Evan hitched both to a nearby rail and approached the door. He didn't have a key. It had been ages since he needed one.

She sensed his hesitation. "Either it'll be open or you can simply break a window. After all, you own the place."

He tried the handle and found it unlocked. "I remember that Finfrock was going to keep using the office while I was away. He may even be in here now."

"Let's look around first," she suggested.

Evan left the front door open as they entered. They wandered from room to room, sheets covering all of the furniture, giving it a ghostly look.

"Everything looks in good condition," Rachel noted. "No apparent cracks. No peeling paint. No broken windows. Of course, you'll need an army of servants to get it ready for you to inhabit. They'll need to beat carpets and clean drapes and air out all of the rooms. You'll most likely need new sheets."

They reached the kitchen and she began lifting pans and examining mixing bowls and whisks. Evan watched her as she mentally catalogued things.

"Your kitchen is dusty but has most of the goods you need."

"If only I can find my Mrs. Dunnavant," he said.

"Who?"

"She's the Fairfield cook. I've always been partial to her food."

"Last night's meal was excellent," she agreed. "Why don't you ask her? She might know of someone who is available to take the position. If she doesn't, you might have to go as far as Hastings. Especially to find a good butler. They are worth their weight in gold."

"Do you know anything about hiring cooks and maids?"

She eagerly asked, "Are you asking for my help? If you are, I'd certainly like to get Edgemere up and running. This is the thing women are prepared for all of our lives." She paused. "I'd first check with Finfrock. He will know of people in the local village and if any could be used as maids or footmen. Grooms, too. You'll definitely need to restock your stables. I know horses. We could go to Tattersall's and choose some," she said excitedly.

"Not so fast. Let me stick closer to home before you have us journeying to London."

"When we return to Fairfield, I'll compose of list of what you need to do. Hiring staff. Restocking your wine cellar. Things of that nature." Rachel rubbed her hands in glee. "Oh, I do love a project."

He frowned deeply. Edgemere was *his* house—not hers—yet she already ordered him about as if she were its countess and he a mere servant. Yet how was he supposed to stop such a force of nature as the very audacious Lady Rachel St. Clair?

Before he could think of a diplomatic way to rein her in, he watched her face fall. All enthusiasm that had been present fled. In fact, she looked as if she might burst into tears at any moment.

"I'm sorry, Evan," she began, blinking rapidly. "I've always jumped in wholeheartedly when something's caught my attention. I apologize for being so presumptuous. Telling you what servants needed hiring and what to buy. Demanding you purchase horses at Tattersall's. Giving you advice about your cook. That was arrogant of me."

Rachel paused. "I'm not usually so high-handed. I realize it's not my place to act as if I am in charge. Edgemere needs your touch. Not mine. I'm sorry I became carried away." She looked miserable now.

What had bothered Evan mere moments ago changed with her words. Rachel was right. She knew about so many things that he'd never thought to consider—and how to right them.

"No, Rachel. I would appreciate your help in getting Edgemere livable. More than livable. I want it to shine as both a house and a home. Being a soldier didn't prepare me for this day. I could use all the advice I could get." He smiled reassuringly. "Especially from someone as knowledgeable as you."

He watched the tension which had filled her body leave. She relaxed and rewarded him with a brilliant smile. One that made his heart flutter wildly. One that made him want to kiss her.

Lessons be damned.

"We should find Finfrock," he said gruffly, tamping down the desire that had sneaked up on him. "Come."

Evan hurried out of the kitchen. Seeing her excitement was doing odd things to his insides.

Like wanting to move up tonight's lesson. To now.

He strode toward the office and found Finfrock laboring over ledgers.

"Good morning, Finfrock."

The bespectacled man started and then smiled. "Lord Merrick. What a surprise!" He looked to the side. "And who is this?" he asked with interest.

"This is Lady Rachel St. Clair."

"Good day, my lady. I am Mitchell Finfrock."

"I returned yesterday," Evan said. "I'm staying at Fairfield for a few days. I know there are several things to do in order to open the house again. Lady Rachel had a few ideas to share with you."

She took a seat and began firing away questions at Finfrock. He hurriedly wrote down everything she mentioned. They discussed hiring a few servants to begin with from the local village and what cleaning needed to be accomplished right away.

"If you could have several candidates gathered in two days' time, Lord Merrick and I could return and interview them. I know he's eager to live in his home again."

"Of course, my lady. I can ride into the village this afternoon and put out the word. What time is convenient for you?"

Rachel looked to him. "Would ten o'clock suffice?"

Evan nodded.

"Then we'll see you the day after tomorrow, Mr. Finfrock. I can interview the potential help while you and Lord Merrick discuss the status of the estate. I'm sure you'll want to go over ledgers with him and talk about crops and livestock."

"It's a sound plan, Lady Rachel. I'm eager to share with the marquess what's gone on during his long absence."

She rose and offered her hand. "It was delightful meeting you."

"The same, my lady."

"Merrick? Are you ready?"

"I am if you are," he replied, impressed by her efficiency.

Even as he tried to keep his eyes from her mouth.

"Give me a few minutes to look over the upper floors," Rachel said. "It will give me a better idea of the number of staff to be hired and the tasks they must accomplish to make Edgemere presentable again."

He was her shadow as she went in and out of various chambers.

They came to the master suites and she spent more time in it as she wandered about his bedchamber and dressing room.

"It's quite dated. You'll need to totally refurbish it."

"What's wrong?" Evan looked about and didn't see what she meant.

"Never mind," she said impatiently. "I'll put it all in my report."

"Oh, so it's gone from a list of recommendations to a report?" he challenged.

Rachel sniffed. "Men. You have no idea what goes into running a household."

Evan caught her elbow as she started from the room. Her eyes went wide.

Damnation. She licked her lips again.

"It's not midnight yet. But I could be persuaded to join in another lesson," she purred.

He dropped his fingers. "We should be getting back."

Quitting the room, he hurried down the hallway to the stairs. Once down them, he went out into the fresh sunshine and gratefully inhaled the clean air. After breathing in the musty rooms, he much preferred the outdoors.

Rachel must have taken her time. She finally arrived.

"Back to Fairfield?" she asked sweetly.

His hands encircled her waist. Large, green eyes stared at him intently. He swallowed and lifted her to the saddle and then untied her reins. Once he gave them to her, he repeated the process and mounted his borrowed horse.

With a mischievous smile, Rachel said, "Race you to the main road."

She took off, the horse's hooves thundering along the lane.

Evan had always enjoyed a challenge. He spurred his horse on and set out to beat her, closing the gap between them seconds before they reached the road. Digging in his heels, his horse crossed from the lane onto the road by a head's length. He pulled up.

Rachel turned and kept riding.

She continued at breakneck speed the five miles to Fairfield. Evan joined her but she never glanced in his direction the entire way back. They rode straight to the stables and without waiting for him, she slid from the horse's back, breathing hard.

A stable lad hurried out and took the reins from her.

"He's been ridden hard," she said, her words coming in spurts. "Give him an extra measure of oats."

She turned for the house and he leaped from his saddle and tossed the boy his own reins. His strides were much longer than hers so he easily caught up. Latching on to her arm, he forced her to stop.

"Do you always ride so recklessly?" he panted.

"When I have the chance." Her eyes gleamed at him in amusement.

Evan wanted to kiss the life out of her. The look on her face dared him to do so. Instead, he released her arm and backed away a few steps.

"I will see you at midnight," he ground out.

Rachel smiled. "I wouldn't miss it for anything, Merrick."

Chapter Six

EVAN STRIPPED OFF his coat and waistcoat and tore at his cravat, tossing it to the floor.

Rachel St. Clair infuriated him.

He waited half an hour and stole down to the library, taking the same chair he did last night. This time, it faced the doorway so he could see her enter.

And decide whether he should strangle her or not.

She'd done an excellent job of ignoring him since they'd returned from Edgemere. At afternoon tea, she spoke animatedly to everyone present. He could see why Leah had called her popular. Everyone vied for her attention. She truly listened when others spoke, slightly tilting her head and nodding along. She asked interesting questions. She made astute comments. Moreover, she made a point to draw others into the conversation, making sure no one was left out.

Except him.

Oh, she had spoken to him. Twice. Once, she asked him to pass the cream. The other time, she looked around and saw raisin cakes on a plate near him. Sweetly, she asked him to pass the plate in her direction. He had—and then watched her take a forkful and slip it between those luscious lips. Evan forced himself to look away after that.

Dinner was no better. He found himself at the opposite end of the table from her, seated on the same side. He couldn't see her but he could hear her tinkling laughter. Apparently, she had an utterly amusing dinner companion.

After the men smoked their cheroots and drank brandy, they joined the ladies in the drawing room. Alford suggested a few of them sing and one woman got up right away, eager for attention. She had a tolerable voice. Then Leah urged Rachel to play and sing. She insisted her dinner companion come and turn the pages for her, batting her long lashes at the man. Evan thought her pianoforte skills merely adequate but she sang remarkably well. Her singing voice was low, just like her speaking voice. While she would never be able to hit the high notes of others, her rich tone washed over him, warming his insides.

After that, everyone began claiming how tired they were and retired as the clock chimed half-past nine. If she came tonight, it would be part lesson and part punishment. He'd make certain he didn't kiss her on the mouth. That would show her.

He now sat. Waiting. Wondering if she would show. He listened to the clock in the foyer as it marked each quarter-hour. Finally, midnight arrived. By the sixth chime, he worried she wouldn't come. By the eighth, he was certain she wouldn't. By the tenth, he resigned himself to returning to his room. Evan sighed as the last muffled chime rang out.

Suddenly, the door swung open and closed quickly. His heartbeat sped up.

Rachel looked to where they had sat last night. Disappointment flashed across her face. Though she'd hurt him with her behavior, he didn't want to do the same and stood.

"Rachel?" he called softly.

She raised her chin and searched across the room as he moved toward her.

"I thought you weren't coming," she said as he reached her.

"I thought the same," he admitted.

Taking her hand, he led her to the settee.

"I see you changed after dinner."

"Leah was getting ready for bed so I thought I should do the same."

"Did she ask where you were going?"

Rachel chuckled. "Leah has always needed more sleep than me. She was snoring when I left. I'm the one who's always been a night owl. I used to come downstairs when I couldn't sleep. Jeremy was often there. We'd talk. Sometimes, he'd warm milk for me."

She fell silent and he let it stretch out, his army patience in full bloom.

She broke first. "Well, are we going to have our second lesson?"

"That's why I'm here."

"Good. I'm ready for us to kiss on the mouth tonight. Jeremy and Catherine are constantly kissing, even after being married two years and having had twins. Leah goes on and on about Alford's kisses. It's time I learned what it's all about."

"Not yet," he cautioned.

"Why?" she demanded. "You know the house party only lasts two weeks. Not only do I need to learn how to kiss but I need time to practice. We need to start tonight," she insisted.

"Who's in charge of your lessons?" Evan asked softly.

"You are," she admitted sullenly. "Maybe I should ask someone else."

He froze, hoping she didn't mean it. When she didn't speak, he continued.

"Tonight, you'll learn about other places you can be kissed. And that *you* can kiss."

Rachel looked more interested now.

"Close your eyes."

She did as he asked and he took a moment to drink in her beauty. Then he slipped his hands around her upper arms and softly kissed each eyelid. His lips moved to her temple and glided along her cheek. Rachel let out a sigh. Evan kissed the tip of her nose and then jumped to her jaw where he pressed quick kisses and nibbles along it. He tightened his fingers and slid his lips to her ear. Gently, he sank his teeth into her earlobe. She shuddered in pleasure. He continued playing with it and then used his tongue to circle her ear.

Now, she sighed loudly. He nibbled and tongued along it and then went back to her jaw, taking his time to reach her other ear and repeat the process. When she began to squirm, he moved to the slender column of her throat and kissed and licked and nipped at it. Little moans escaped her lips. Her breathing grew quick and shallow.

He took a risk now. As he continued to press his lips against her throat, he untied the sash on her robe and parted it. The second it opened, he trailed hot kisses along her collarbone.

"Lower," she murmured, starting to move her body.

Evan complied and reached the curve of her breast. He let go of her arms and pulled the night rail down slightly for better access, then glided his tongue along the upper curve.

"Oh!"

Rachel stretched toward him and Evan pushed the gown down further, baring her breast. He kissed his way to her erect nipple and circled around it with his tongue. She whimpered, her hands gripping his shoulders as she moved closer to him. He kissed around it with his lips and then brushed them on the nipple itself.

"Yes," she sighed. "Oh, yes."

Evan took her breast into his mouth, his tongue pleasuring her as she made lovely sounds in the back of her throat. Then he eased away and pulled her nightgown back up.

Rachel opened her eyes. They were dazed—and full of heat.

"You said that I could also do some kissing."

"I did," he agreed.

Her smile looked both innocent and wise at the same time.

Rachel St. Clair proved to be an astute learner. She repeated back to him everything he'd done to her, starting at his temple. A deep longing rose in him as she kissed and nipped at his throat. Then her fingers slid down his chest and opened the three buttons. Before he could stop her, she'd pushed his shirt aside and her lips scorched his chest.

Desire shot through him. Without thinking, he ran his fingers through her unbound hair, something he'd unconsciously longed to do. The silky strands felt cool and smooth to the touch. Then he stilled. He'd promised to tutor Rachel in the art of kissing. Not respond to her kisses. He should stop her. Now.

But he let her go on a little longer.

Anticipation built in him as she worked her way down and, good pupil that she was, used her tongue to circle his nipple. She then grazed it with her teeth and licked at him.

Evan thought he might die from the pleasure. And it was that thought that told him he must put a stop to her actions now. Before he reacted—and things ended badly.

He latched on to her shoulders and pulled her away.

"I think our second lesson has come to an end," he said with more control that he felt.

Her bottom lip thrust out in a pout.

"You're not a two-year-old child," he said brusquely. "Pouting will get you nowhere."

Rachel gazed at him. "Did I do all right?"

He cupped her cheek. "You did very well, Rachel. Very well."

With that, he kissed her brow and then stood.

"Midnight tomorrow?" he asked.

"Midnight tomorrow," she agreed.

RACHEL AWOKE, SURPRISED she'd slept any at all, since Evan's second lesson had kept her tossing and turning. She'd never imagined all the places one could be kissed. He stirred incredible feelings within her. She closed her eyes and imagined his lips grazing her jaw. His tongue tracing along her ear. His mouth on her breast. She didn't even touch her own breasts, except to run a quick washcloth over them. It seemed almost taboo to even do that. Quietly, she raised her fingers to one and squeezed it slightly. She allowed her thumb to brush across the nipple, causing it to pebble. Not only did it make her breath quicken but it also caused other places on her to come alive. She squeezed her nether region, another place she didn't linger when she washed.

She wondered if that, too, was a place that could be kissed. For a moment, Rachel imagined Evan lifting her skirts and pressing his mouth against it. The wicked thought caused her body to heat.

How could she face him at breakfast this morning?

She would. She'd never been a coward. Besides, he wouldn't know she'd thought something so terrible. At least she hoped not.

Leah began to stir so Rachel sat up and swung her legs from the bed. They washed and dressed for breakfast and went downstairs. The room was more crowded than yesterday, probably because of the picnic that Alford had announced at dinner last night. It would be served by the lake at one this afternoon and she figured more people rose early to eat a little something now to tide them over before the picnic commenced.

Rachel went to the sideboard and gathered her usual hearty breakfast. While Leah went to sit with Alford and Evan, she decided to eat with Cor.

Taking a place beside her grandmother, she asked, "Are you enjoying your stay at Fairfield?"

"It's a very pleasant place. Leah is going to be happy here."

"I think she could be happy living in a hovel if Alford lived there with her."

Cor chuckled. "She is quite in love with the boy, isn't she?"

"I'm very happy for her," Rachel said. "Though it's starting to hit me that I will miss her terribly once she's married and gone."

"I know she'll want you as a frequent guest at Fairfield. At least until you marry yourself," Cor said, eying her. "What do you think of Merrick, Alford's friend?"

She took a sip of tea, hoping no blush rose on her cheeks.

"He's very nice. We went riding yesterday."

"I know."

Cor fell silent and Rachel knew why. Every time she wanted to get information from someone, her grandmother would start a conversation and then grow quiet. The other person usually felt obligated to fill the gap and thus spilled to Cor whatever she was after. It had worked on Rachel as a child.

Not anymore.

Instead, she attacked her meal with gusto. Cor eventually returned to her own food and others sitting nearby included them in their conversations.

"Since the men are not shooting today, is anyone up for a ride this morning?" Alford asked.

Several people agreed with enthusiasm. Rachel didn't say anything. She waited to see what Evan would do.

Her dinner companion from last night, Lord Merrifield, turned to her. "Are you up for a ride, Lady Rachel?"

"I think not," she said. "I'm eager to see Alford's gardens."

"I'd be delighted to show them to you," Merrifield replied enthusiastically.

Two other gentlemen chimed in, both wishing to escort her. Rachel politely agreed and then looked down the table. Evan arched one eyebrow at her and turned back to his coffee.

Rachel excused herself in order to collect her parasol. Not only would it keep her hands occupied, but it would provide a slight buffer so none of her escorts could get too close to her.

She met the three gentlemen in the foyer and they retreated across the wide expanse of green lawn and then took their time meandering through the gardens. Rachel noted the placement of shrubs and the variety of flowers. They passed several Chippendale seats along the various paths and two fountains. She thought her favorite thing might be the bridge they crossed over until they arrived at a gazebo. The eight arches reached high to an Italian-styled roof. A low fence encircled the structure. Three benches and several single chairs rested inside.

"Oh, let's sit for a bit," she told her escorts.

Lord Merrifield guided her to a bench and sat next to her. Rachel closed her parasol since they were in the shade. The men discussed yesterday's shooting and that Alford would finish the house party off with a country ball for his guests and neighbors.

"I suppose we should get back," she said. "I hate leaving here, though. It's so peaceful. Wouldn't it be lovely to take tea here some afternoon?"

Immediately, all three gentlemen assured her they could arrange for it. She had to bite back a smile, thinking how Evan would point out how easily she'd charmed the trio into doing her bidding.

Merrifield offered his arm and, this time, she strolled next to him. When they returned to the house, she thanked them for their escort and went to her room to change into a fresh gown for the picnic. Leah had gone riding with the others and wasn't back yet. Rachel found herself pacing restlessly. She decided to go to the library and find something to read.

Once there, she retreated to the wing chair in the far corner.

Evan's seat.

She wondered what tonight's midnight lesson would entail. She hoped it would finally include kissing on the mouth. Rachel desperately longed for Evan to kiss her. She also hoped she could also incorporate some of last night's kisses. Little had she known her kissing him was as delightful as him kissing her. Rachel remembered pressing soft, butterfly kisses along his strong jaw. Teasing his earlobe. That had been a wonder, that kissing involved not only tongues but teeth. She recalled grazing her lips along the strong column of his throat, thanks to the fact that he'd discarded his cravat. His smooth skin had been slightly salty as she tasted it. Inhaling the sandalwood soap on his skin, along with that musky, masculine scent she associated with him, had only enhanced the kisses she bestowed upon him.

And that chest. Oh, his muscular chest, or at least what little she'd seen of it, was a thing of beauty. She smiled, remembering the sounds he made as she kissed it. It pleased her that she affected him so. The trouble was, he also had a profound effect upon her.

No man during the Season had intrigued her as much as Evan did now. None of them had been as handsome or interesting. She'd been happy when he accepted her request for tutoring her in kissing. Now, she wasn't so sure it had been a good idea. Although she was enjoying every minute of her lessons, she feared she enjoyed them a little too much. Rachel longed to be in his company because he was constantly in her thoughts. That's why she kept trying to put distance between them. She didn't think he felt the same way about her.

Her greatest fear was that she might fall in love with him—and he wouldn't return her affection.

Rachel heard the clock chime and hurried to the drawing room so she wouldn't be left behind. As she entered, she determined to put her heart under lock and key as far as the Marquess of Merrick was concerned.

CHAPTER SEVEN

EVAN WAS DETERMINED to spend time with Rachel today. Not just at midnight tonight. She'd avoided joining the large group that went riding earlier, preferring to walk the gardens with three men. He noted one was her dinner companion of last night. Evan watched not Rachel during breakfast—but Merrifield. The earl definitely had intentions toward her.

And Evan didn't like it. At all.

The best way to Rachel St. Clair was through her friend. Because of that, he joined Lady Leah and made small talk with her as others began arriving to walk together to Fairfield's lake. When he heard the chimes ring out and still no Rachel in sight, he steadied himself. She'd made a last-moment appearance last night.

He could only hope for the same now.

Sure enough, she slipped into the room and hurried toward Leah. When she arrived, he saw her look of dismay at spotting him chatting with her friend. Alex announced it was time to head toward the lake and claimed Leah. Evan and Rachel fell into step with them, leading the pack of twenty or so houseguests.

The two women walked together, with the men on the outside. Rachel peppered Alex with questions about his gardens. Some he readily answered, while others he admitted he hadn't a clue.

"How could you not know about your own gardens, Alford?" Rachel admonished. "Don't you ever give them any thought?"

The earl only laughed. "That's why I hire gardeners, Lady Rachel. So they can do the thinking—and pruning—for me."

They continued walking at a brisk pace, leaving the others behind.

Evan said, "You seem to know quite a bit about gardens, Lady Rachel."

"I love getting my hands in the dirt. Fortunately, Cor is not one of those women who might chastise me for dirtying my hands or gown. She always encouraged me to pursue whatever activities interested me."

"What did you like about Alex's gardens?"

"They're very well laid out. The thickets are nicely balanced with flowers. He had some beautiful trellises. The most outstanding feature is a large gazebo. I can just imagine sitting inside it at night, once the sun has set and the moon has risen. I'd close my eyes and inhale the perfume of the flowers. Late at night and early mornings are the best times to smell blossoms."

"Perhaps, it would be interesting to hold a lesson in the gazebo some midnight," he said quietly.

She stumbled and Evan grabbed her arm. Each time he touched her, he sensed something move between them. Something wild and utterly delicious.

"Thank you, Merrick," Rachel said, pulling her arm away.

He made no more mention of their lessons and, soon, they arrived at the lake. Several tables and chairs had been set up, along with large blankets scattered near the water. A large tent had been erected, closed on three sides, with the open flaps facing the lake. Tables ladened with platters of food abounded.

Alex seated Leah at a table while Evan and Rachel headed straight to the food. Before he could tease her about her voracious appetite, she went to Jones and Mrs. Dunnavant, who stood in the center behind the tables.

"This looks sumptuous," Rachel exclaimed. "Mrs. Dunnavant,

your food looks almost too good to eat. And Jones, I know how much work went into bringing all of this down for us to enjoy. Thank you both for your efforts on our behalf."

With those words, Rachel chipped off a huge chunk of the armor surrounding Evan's heart. He could think of no lady who would have given a second thought as to the time and effort it had taken to create this picnic for such a large group. Rachel not only appreciated it, she had sought out those responsible and complimented them for it.

"What is your favorite thing you made, Mrs. Dunnavant? I shall make sure it's the first item on my plate."

The cook blushed. "It's hard to say, my lady."

"Then I'll answer for you, Mrs. Dunnavant," Evan declared. Looking at Rachel, he said, "Go for the apple pie. If none is to be had, then find the apple tarts. No one makes them as well as Mrs. Dunnavant."

He picked up two plates and handed one to her. Rachel looked at the table and cried, "There they are!"

The cook herself placed one on each of their plates.

"May I have two, Mrs. Dunnavant? Cor didn't come with us today. It's a little too far for her to walk at her age in this heat. I'd like to be sure she eats one."

"I'll save one for her and see that she gets it," the cook said.

"What makes your tarts so special?" Rachel asked.

"I use not only cinnamon but nutmeg. It brings out the flavor of the apples better," Mrs. Dunnavant confided.

By now, the others had begun to arrive. Evan suggested he carry both of their plates while Rachel placed items on them. They went through the line and by the time she finished, he wasn't certain he could eat everything she'd chosen.

They left the shade of the tent and he asked, "Would you like to join Lady Leah?"

She sniffed. "It's a picnic, Merrick. That doesn't mean eating at a table. It's only a picnic if you sit on the ground and stretched out your legs." She pointed. "Over here. That's a nice spot. That tree is shading the blanket a bit."

Rachel led him to where she wished to be and seated herself. Evan handed her both plates and situated himself before claiming his again. A footman scurried over and provided them each with a lemonade. She took a sip and declared it delicious. Then with gusto, she attacked her plate, trying the apple tart first. After one bite, she moaned in pleasure.

Evan wished he'd been the one to draw that sound from her.

"You were right about Mrs. Dunnavant's cooking. It will be hard to find you a cook of this caliber. Remember, we should ask her if she knows of one you might hire."

"Are you ready for tomorrow's interviews?" he asked.

"Of course."

"We didn't look at Edgemere's gardens while we were there. I'd appreciate you taking a look at them while we're there. I'd be open to any suggestions."

Her eyes lit up. "Don't get me wrong, Merrick, but I hope they're in abominable shape. I'd love to draw up plans and start from scratch."

"I'll bow to your good judgment."

"I hope Finfrock found a few men who'd be interested in hiring out as gardeners. We should go an hour earlier tomorrow so I have time to view the gardens. Is that possible?"

"I'm an early riser thanks to my army days."

"Mrs. Dunnavant seems sweet on you," she said. "Perhaps you can talk her into having a light breakfast ready for us earlier since we won't be able to partake in the usual buffet."

Another couple asked to join them and the conversation turned to other things. Both newcomers were interested in hearing that he'd recently sold his commission, and begged for war stories. Evan shared a few humorous ones about camp life, keeping everything light. He'd discovered that people really didn't want to know about the horrors of war.

He set aside his plate, having managed all but two items. Rachel finished every bite and signaled a footman. She collected Evan's plate and hers and passed it to him, once again thoughtfully thanking him.

With her eyes closed, she leaned back, her hands braced behind her, and raised her face to the sun. If no one had been present, he would have stolen a kiss—and more.

"Would you care to go rowing?" he asked.

She opened her eyes. "Yes, thank you." She grinned. "As long as you do all of the work."

They excused themselves from their companions and walked to the boathouse, finding several canoes and oars inside. He handed her a pair of oars and lifted a green canoe from where it hung, dragging it down to the shore and partway into the water.

Rachel climbed into it and gracefully moved over several boards, despite the canoe rocking slightly. She turned and seated herself so she'd be facing him. Knowing how well she rode, it didn't surprise him that she moved with such feline grace.

Evan rotated his shoulder several times, trying hard not to wince. He shoved off the boat and jumped into it, taking his seat on the bench across from her. Rachel handed him the oars and he slipped them through the oarlocks. Gripping the end of each oar, he placed the blades into the water and pulled. After several long strokes, they glided across the water.

"Is your shoulder bothering you?"

"It tightens up on me sometimes. If I stretch the muscles properly, it behaves. For a while, anyway."

"Did something happen to it?"

"A bullet went through it."

Concern filled her face. "I'm sorry, Evan. I didn't know you'd been injured in battle. Did it take long to heal?"

"Longer than I would've liked. At least it went straight through so there was no bullet to retrieve. Of course, that left a scar on both sides. Most soldiers have many of them."

"Were you also shot in the leg?"

He drew in a quick breath. "Is it that obvious?"

"Only to me. I enjoy observing people. I doubt anyone else has noticed. You hide it well. On occasion, I've seen an almost imperceptible limp. Just a slight favoring of your right leg. Was it from another bullet?"

"Yes," he said brusquely, not wanting to think back on that time, especially on a picture-perfect day with a beautiful woman seated in front of him.

Rachel, however, was not one to let things go. "I imagine it was quite painful. Did both injuries occur during the same action?"

He saw she was genuinely interested and not morbidly curious, as others might be and found himself opening up to her.

"They did. I wasn't as lucky with my leg. The bullet remained. A surgeon had to dig it out."

Her nose scrunched up. "That sounds terrible."

"He almost didn't find it. For a few hours, I thought I might lose the leg."

She placed a hand upon his knee and he stopped rowing. "That must have been awful. To be so far away from home. Hurt and in agony. Hundreds of other men also injured and lying about you. No one to comfort you." She smiled. "I wish I could have been there to kiss it and make you feel better."

His breath caught in his throat.

Quickly, she removed her hand. "I'm sorry. That sounded like flirting, when all I meant was that I wish I could have consoled you. Soothed your pain. My apologies."

Evan wished she had been there, holding a cool cloth to his hot forehead and bathing his fevered body. Giving him sips of water. The infirmary had almost been as hellish as the battlefield as he listened to the groans and muffled cries of grown men, many whom didn't live to see another day. He knew he was fortunate because he had survived. Not only to fight another day.

But to be here. Now. With this woman.

Evan cleared his throat, pushing aside the emotions welling within him.

"It would have been nice to have you bringing me solace. When you've been shot and carried from the battlefield, waiting for a surgeon to check your wounds and see if it's worth his trouble to save you, it can be the loneliest place in the world. I was one of the lucky ones. An officer is always seen to before enlisted men. The shoulder was easy to stitch up. But even after they found the bullet and removed it from my thigh, I was left alone for long stretches of time. I've never felt so isolated, so desolate, so lacking in hope, as I did during those dark days."

Rachel touched his knee again, squeezing it, empathy in her eyes.

"I won't claim to know what you went through. I can only thank you for your service to king and country." She glanced to the shore, where others were pushing boats into the water. "If we were alone, despite my lack of experience, I would kiss you on the lips. Not in passion or desire. Merely to thank you for your bravery."

Evan smiled. "And I would most certainly let you."

"Will you meet me at midnight tonight, Merrick?"

"I will, my lady. In fact, I look forward to our next lesson."

CHAPTER EIGHT

RACHEL CREPT DOWNSTAIRS well before midnight, eager to partake in her third lesson from her brilliant tutor. She went to the wing chair he favored and waited for him to arrive.

What he'd revealed about his war injuries today brought her heartache. Evan wasn't a man to talk about his accomplishments. She doubted anyone here, beyond Alford, knew he'd been severely wounded. Then again, as humble as Evan was, maybe even his best friend hadn't known the extent of the injuries. It awed her that he'd trusted her enough to reveal some of his past to her.

Of course, he'd also done so the night they'd met in this very library. The night he became her tutor. Both of them had shared confidences. She still ached for the lost, lonely boy whose father cruelly beat him and then turned him out after his mother died. Evan hadn't mentioned if her illness had been drawn out and death was expected or if it had occurred suddenly. Either way, it would have strongly affected a boy of six. She couldn't imagine growing up in a household away from Cor, Jeremy, and Luke, much less being sent to a house as large and rambling as Edgemere to live on her own. Why the Duke of Winstead had behaved so brutally to his only son and heir remained a mystery.

At least his father's behavior hadn't influenced Evan. He was a fine man and would make an excellent duke someday. His sterling character was a testament to him bringing himself up.

The clock chimed a single time as the door to the library opened. Evan came in fully dressed. A flare of disappointment shot through her. She'd looked forward to stroking that lovely, tanned throat of his with her fingers and tongue. Maybe she would be daring enough to untie his cravat and slide it from his neck.

Rachel stood. "I'm here," she said as she moved toward him.

Evan closed the door and met her. His hand reached for hers and he entwined his fingers through hers possessively.

She liked it. She liked him. She liked what they were about to do.

"We're going to stand tonight," he informed her, leading her back to the far end of the room. The shadows enveloped them and she could hardly make out the features on his face.

"Most first kisses come in the dark, like this, standing up. Taking air on a terrace. Walking in a moonlit garden. Stepping into a darkened alcove. These are the usual places your first kiss with a gentleman will occur. Because of that, we need to mimic the situation so you'll be prepared."

"Are we going to kiss on the mouth tonight?"

Rachel thought the corners of his mouth turned up but she couldn't be sure.

"We are. No tongues, though."

"No tongues? But Leah said that is the best part," she complained.

"It is, but we will work our way up to that. You don't want to be a hoyden, Rachel, and use your tongue the first time you kiss a man. And he if tries to use his that first time with you, he is no gentleman. No, you need to learn something about chaste kisses to start. They will help you determine whether you like a man enough to use your tongue later. Are you pouting?"

"No," she said stubbornly, pulling her bottom lip back.

"An innocent, sweet kiss can be very special. Even sensual. As I said, it's the start of getting to know someone. If you have feelings for a man afterward, then you'll need to consider pursuing those feelings.

If after a chaste kiss you aren't moved in any way, you know he's not the one for you."

"Hmm. Are you telling me after an innocent kind of kiss that if I feel something stir within me, that is the man I'll fall in love with?"

"No. Only that the potential to fall in love is present." He brushed a stray lock from her face. "You can enjoy kissing someone without being in love with him. It's done all the time. Many women marry and find they enjoy the physical aspects of marriage, whether they love their husband or not. Men can become aroused and easily make love to a woman without love being present. It's been done for hundreds of years."

"What makes a man aroused?" she asked, very curious now.

"Sometimes, beauty alone can do it. A fondness for a certain color of hair. The scent of a woman's perfume. The feel of her breasts." He chuckled. "It doesn't take much for a man to want to have sex with a woman."

"Are women the same?"

"I think in some ways, they are. They may be attracted to a man's looks or his build. They may like that he's powerful or wealthy. They may simply enjoy how it feels when he touches them. A women's arousal isn't as obvious as a man's."

"Can you show me yours?"

Evan sputtered, "No. Stop asking so many questions. We need to proceed to our third lesson."

"Kissing. With no tongues," she added.

"Ever the good pupil," he said, a smile in his voice. "All right, let's pretend that we've been dancing at a ball."

"The waltz?" she asked quickly.

"Does it matter?"

"I think so. I'm trying to create a picture in my mind. The waltz is a very sensual dance. If that's what you and I danced to, I'm already aware of you as a man. Your touch. Your scent. If I'm to go out on a darkened terrace with you, it's because I already find I somewhat like you."

"All right, a waltz it is. We've danced. I've held your hand. My arm has been around your waist. Perhaps I've even held you a bit too close as we've danced and your breasts have brushed against my chest. You're anticipating something will soon occur. We've now stepped out for some air and walked to the far end of the terrace. It's dark but we can see one another's silhouettes, like now."

Rachel pictured it in her mind. How Evan linked his hand with hers. How she smelled the sandalwood soap he'd used. How intimately they'd moved, almost as one.

"No more talk. Our lips will now do the speaking."

She waited, her heart racing. Evan released her hand. His strong hands cupped her face, ever so gently. He bent, his mouth approaching hers. Anticipation ran through her.

Then his lips softly brushed against hers.

A fire lit insight her. Instinctively, her hands went to his shoulders and gripped them. He continued touching his lips to hers as his thumbs stroked her cheeks. Rachel stepped closer, her breasts making contact with his chest. Evan's lips stilled. He lifted them from her slightly and then pressed his mouth against hers. He kissed her, over and over. Soft. Hard. In the corner of her mouth. Fully against her lips. His hands released her face and slid down her neck, his thumbs again stroking it as he had her cheeks.

Then they slid down her back, sensually moving up and down. She moved her hands around to the back of his neck and pulled him to her, her fingers locking so he couldn't escape. When she did that, his hands ceased to move. Instead, his arms pinned her to him. His kisses became more heated. They came harder. Faster. He'd break the kiss and then lean back in hungrily, kissing her over and over.

Rachel had no idea how long this went on. Time ceased to exist. All she could think of was his mouth on hers. Her body crushed to him as if he'd never let her go. Wonderful tingles electrified every part of her body, especially in her most private place.

Then she became aware of something hard pressing against her and realized it was his arousal. Curiosity overcame her. She relaxed her hold and dropped her arms. Her hand moved between them and she gripped his member.

Evan tore his mouth from hers. "Stop," he ordered quietly and stepped away from her.

Rachel panted heavily, feeling as if she'd been cut adrift at sea.

"Did I do something wrong?"

"You most definitely did. When you're kissing a man for the first time, it is not appropriate to touch him in that manner."

"What if it's for the second time? Or third? Frankly, I lost track of the number of our kisses."

Evan grabbed her shoulders roughly. "Don't play games with me, Rachel. I'm trying to teach you about men. If you do what you just did to a man, he will expect that you are more experienced than you are—and that you want him to make love to you."

He grabbed her elbow and walked her across the room to where they were in the light.

"Look," he said.

She looked down and saw how his member strained against his pants and how tight his features were as if he were doing everything he could to hold back.

"This is the sign that a man is aroused. That he wants you. Many men lose their heads when this happens. They can't think straight. Even if they are a gentleman, that goes out the window. They aren't thinking with their heads. They don't remember that there are consequences. All they want is satisfaction with the woman in front of them."

Rachel bit her lip. "You're saying . . . that some men might force themselves upon me?"

"Exactly. You don't want to put yourself in that position. Think what might happen. He could deflower you and you might find yourself with child. Someone might discover you in the act. You say you want to marry for love. What if you'd already decided you didn't believe you could fall in love with this man?"

He grabbed her arms roughly. "It wouldn't matter," he ground out. "You would be forced to wed. And then you'd be stuck with a stranger. Angry that he had taken away the choice from you."

Evan loosened his grip. "I don't mean to scare you. I'm only trying to warn you that there are consequences in kissing a man. Especially if it becomes too heated. I recommend that you keep your tongue in your mouth and don't even think of using it until you are in love and properly engaged. You'll get into less trouble that way."

"You haven't waited," she accused. "You know how to use your tongue when you kiss."

"It's different for a man. I've told you. People—men in particular—don't need to be in love to have sex. Arousal comes easily for a man. He's likely to do it with numerous women."

"As you have."

"As I have."

Rachel stared at him, understanding that he had kissed many women. Had relations with them. And never made any kind of commitment.

It frightened her. Even more because she could see herself falling in love with Evan Drake. Yet she was just another woman to him.

"I think my time as a tutor has come to an end."

No!

"You promised you'd teach me how to kiss properly," she calmly reminded him, her pulse jumping. "I assume you are a man of your word. I promise you that I will keep my hands off your member. Off any man's member. At least until I am married. Then I suppose it's expected for me to touch it. Frequently."

Evan glared at her. "One more lesson," he said, no room for bargaining present.

"One more," she agreed, raising her chin a notch. "Here. Tomorrow. At midnight."

Before she knew what was happening, he yanked her to him. His mouth came down hard on hers, bruising her. Then just as quickly, he pushed her away and stormed from the room.

Rachel's fingertips came to her lips.

Something had changed between them with that kiss.

The question was . . . what?

Chapter Nine

Rachel dressed quietly, not wanting to disturb Leah, and crept from the room. She went straight to the kitchen in order to find Mrs. Dunnavant. The cook sat at a table, having a cup of tea, as she called orders out to a few scullery maids who made preparations for the morning's breakfast buffet.

When she saw Rachel, her jaw dropped and she leaped to her feet.

"Please, have a seat, Mrs. Dunnavant. May I join you?"

The cook looked baffled at the presence of nobility in her kitchen. "Of course, my lady." She snapped her fingers at a passing girl. "Tea for Lady Rachel."

"Yes, Mrs. Dunnavant."

Rachel took a seat. "I have a favor to ask. Would it be possible for Lord Merrick and me to have tea and toast in the kitchen this morning before the breakfast buffet begins? We have plans to go to Edgemere and begin interviewing workers today to staff his home."

"I'll make you whatever you'd like, my lady. How about a poached egg on your toast and some fruit?"

"That would be lovely."

"I heard you were hiring people from the village today. Everyone's quite excited."

A servant placed a cup of tea in front of Rachel and she thanked the woman. "Yes, we are. What I'm most worried about is finding a good cook. Lord Merrick is so fond of your cooking, I'm afraid no one will quite live up to your standards."

Mrs. Dunnavant slowly smiled. "What if it was someone who learned to cook right beside me? Now, mind you, every cook puts her own mark on what she makes, but my sister would be an ideal choice as Edgemere's cook."

"Would that be possible? Oh, Merrick would be so happy."

"She's engaged now as a cook at Townsend Hall, Viscount Thatcher's seat. It's two miles west of North Stony."

"Oh, the village between Fairfield and Edgemere. That's where Mr. Finfrock was to put out the word that we would be interviewing for positions today." She paused. "If your sister is already gainfully employed, I'm afraid that wouldn't work out."

Mrs. Dunnavant held up her chubby hand. "Elsie is most unhappy. Anyone who works for Lady Thatcher is, forgive me for saying so."

Rachel immediately understood. "You're saying we could possibly lure Elsie away?"

"I'm sure of it."

She picked up her saucer. "I'm going to write a brief note to your sister, Mrs. Dunnavant. When Lord Merrick and I leave this morning, I'll have one of the grooms deliver it to her. What is her surname?"

"Bridges. Mrs. Elsie Bridges. She wed Mr. Bridges at seventeen but has been a widow for many years."

"I'll ask if she has an immediate reply to let the messenger know. If not, she can think on it but not for too long."

"There'll be no thinking, my lady. Elsie will come. I've spoken fondly of Lord Merrick for over fifteen years. She knows who he is and that he's a particular favorite of mine." The older woman hesitated.

"What is it, Mrs. Dunnavant?"

"There have been several cooks before my sister at Townsend Hall. I'm afraid once she gives her notice that Lady Thatcher will give her the boot. Would it be possible to send the groom with a cart? In case Elsie is asked to leave? That way, she could gather her few possessions and depart immediately."

"Lady Thatcher would throw her out before finding another cook?" Rachel asked in amazement.

Mrs. Dunnavant snorted. "You'd be surprised what that woman is capable of. Sorry for being indiscreet, my lady."

"Don't worry about it, Mrs. Dunnavant. I'll go write Mrs. Bridges the note and return for breakfast. Lord Merrick should be downstairs by then. Would you like to add anything to the letter?"

The cook shook her head sadly. "I cannot write, my lady. I'm sure your note will suffice. Be sure to mention Lord Merrick's name in it."

"I will," Rachel promised.

She went to Alford's study, knowing he wouldn't be up yet, and dashed off a quick letter inquiring if Mrs. Bridges would care to become Lord Merrick's cook at Edgemere. If she was available immediately, the messenger would bring her and her things to the estate. If not, she only had to send word to Lord Merrick at Fairfield and he would arrange transportation for her. She thanked the woman for considering the offer and included that her sister, Mrs. Dunnavant, thought she would be the ideal person for the position.

When Rachel returned to the kitchen, Evan was already seated at the table with tea and toast in front of him. Mrs. Dunnavant took the cup and saucer Rachel had brought back and replaced it with fresh tea as she seated herself.

"Mrs. Dunnavant was telling me about our new cook," Evan said. "Or I should say, I hope Mrs. Bridges will take up the offer to come to Edgemere."

"It does sound promising," she agreed, thinking Evan sounded perfectly normal this morning and she had imagined something changing in their relationship the previous midnight.

They ate quickly so they could be off. When they arrived at the stables, Evan spoke to the head groom, who allowed Robby, one of the younger grooms, to take a cart in order to deliver the message to

Mrs. Bridges.

"You know where Townsend Hall is located?" questioned Evan after Robby had been summoned.

The young man frowned. "I do, my lord. I worked in the stables there before a position opened up here at Fairfield. Mrs. Bridges is a lovely person and an even better cook. I'm pleased she'll go somewhere she's appreciated."

Robby promised to wait for a reply or convey Mrs. Bridges to Edgemere before returning to Fairfield.

Evan assisted Rachel in mounting her horse. She tried to ignore the flickering feeling in her stomach as she inhaled his cologne and felt his hands briefly clasp her waist. They rode at a steady clip to Edgemere, where Mr. Finfrock met them.

"You're early, Lord Merrick," the estate manager said. "I asked the women coming to interview to be here at ten and the men at eleven-thirty. I thought it would be easier separating them into two groups."

"Very wise, Finfrock. We're going to tour the gardens for now. Lady Rachel has some ideas about what might be done and wanted to see them in person before she hires any gardeners."

"They're a bit wild, Lord Merrick," Finfrock warned. "With only Stanley on staff, he's worked on keeping up the landscaping along the lane and surrounding the house in good condition. He hasn't had much time to spend on the gardens themselves."

Evan laughed. "That's fine, Finfrock. Lady Rachel is hoping they'll be in abominable shape. She has grand ideas for ripping things out and deciding what new items should be planted."

They excused themselves and Evan led her around the house and across a wide expanse of lawn. Discovering an entrance to the gardens took some minutes to locate. The brambles had run wild. Hedges needed to be trimmed. Trees begged to be pruned. They walked through as best they could.

"I must apologize," Evan said. "I had no idea things were in such dismal shape."

Rachel waved a hand. "You've been gone for years, Evan. No one expected things to remain pristine, especially with only one man on staff."

"Do you have any ideas now that you've seen them?"

"I do. Once we return to Fairfield, I'll draw up a plan. We can talk about various shrubberies and trees to plant. What flowers you enjoy. I'd love to scatter some benches throughout so that family or visitors could pause on their walks and enjoy the nature surrounding them."

"What about a gazebo? You'd mentioned the one at Fairfield so I went to look at it last night."

She wondered if he'd done so before or after their midnight lesson.

"What did you think of it?" she asked.

"I liked it. Quite a bit. I think I'd want one larger, though. And no fence around it. I'd like to be able to step up from any of the portals to enter it."

"Anything else? Do you have particular flowers you're fond of?"

He shrugged. "Not really. I'll leave that to you and Stanley to decide."

They returned to the house and saw a group of women had gathered outside the entrance.

"Please, come in," Rachel told them. "Come with us, Lord Merrick."

Rachel led everyone to the library and asked that the bedsheets be removed from the furniture. Dust flew everywhere as the sheets came off and were tossed into a corner. She had the women take a seat and told Evan to address them.

He frowned. "What should I say?"

She sniffed. "Men." Turning the group, she said, "I am Lady Rachel St. Clair. As you know from Mr. Finfrock, Lord Merrick has returned from the Peninsular War and will be opening Edgemere immediately. He's in need of a large staff to maintain it. As a bachelor, I'm afraid

Lord Merrick doesn't know the first thing about running a household, which is why I'm here to help him hire his staff."

The women chuckled.

"I do know his lordship wanted to welcome you, however." She turned to Evan. "Lord Merrick?"

"Thank you, Lady Rachel." He looked to the expectant women. "I've been away a good while and am eager to return to living at Edgemere. Some of you may have worked here in the past. Others of you may be new. What I'm interested in are hard workers who will support one another. I want this to be a happy household. You will be paid fairly, according to your experience. Lady Rachel is more aware of what positions will be available. Be honest in your answers to her. I hope to meet those she decides to hire later today. Thank you for coming."

He excused himself and Rachel announced, "I'll be conducting interviews in the kitchen." She gave directions on where it was located. "Once we've spoken, I ask that you return and invite the next candidate to where I'll be and accompany them so they arrive in a prompt manner. Is anyone present that intends to apply for the position of housekeeper?"

One woman stood. "I would like to, my lady. My name is Mrs. Kent."

Rachel saw a woman in her early forties with a competent, calm air about her. "Please come with me, Mrs. Kent."

The woman accompanied Rachel to the kitchen. She'd decided to speak to the prospective employees there because a kitchen was smaller and held an air of intimacy. All of the other rooms at Edgemere would be too intimidating. She wanted to work quickly so as to hire as many qualified people as possible today.

She indicated for the woman to take a seat and Rachel did the same.

"Tell me of your experience, Mrs. Kent."

"I began in service as a laundry maid when I was eleven. I worked my way up to chamber maid and then downstairs parlor maid. Eventually, I earned a place as housekeeper when I was twenty-six to a viscount. I remained in that position for ten years before I left. I can offer you references." She withdrew a folded page from her reticule and handed it to Rachel, who skimmed the glowing letter of recommendation.

"Why did you leave?"

"I fell in love with a shopkeeper in North Stony. I'd never thought I'd fall in love at my age, much less marry, but Mr. Kent was a very special man." She paused. "He had heart troubles, though, and passed away two months ago."

"I'm very sorry to hear that, Mrs. Kent. Do you have children?" Rachel asked.

"No. We weren't blessed with any. I suppose I was too old by then. I sold the shop last week to a man from London, wishing to bring his family to the country. Naturally, they will take over not only the business on the bottom floor but the family abode upstairs. They arrive in two days and I was going to leave and move in with my sister."

"You'd rather come to work at Edgemere instead?"

"I would, my lady. My sister isn't a pleasant person. I'm afraid I would be treated more as a servant than family. Though I'm not afraid of hard work, I suspect she would view me as little more than slave labor. I would rather make it on my own. I believe I would be an asset to Lord Merrick because of my previous experience."

Rachel had always read people well and she knew this first hire would be one of her best.

"I would be delighted to offer you the position of housekeeper, Mrs. Kent."

The woman's face brightened with a smile. "Thank you, my lady. I can start as soon as you'd like."

"Then I think it best if you help me complete the interviews this morning. After all, it will be you that supervises the staff, along with whatever butler we hire."

"May I be so bold as to make a suggestion, Lady Rachel?"

"Of course, Mrs. Kent. Your opinion is important to me."

"My brother-in-law, Charles Kent, has served as a butler for a good number of years in London. His employer is getting up in age and decided to close his town residence and reside strictly in the country. He already had staff there and released his London servants with an extra month's salary. Mr. Kent is looking for a job. He is as hard a worker as my husband was and of good moral character. Might I suggest you interview him?"

"You make a good case for hiring Mr. Kent, Mrs. Kent," Rachel said. "Please give me his address and I will write to him once Lord Merrick and I return to Fairfield."

"Thank you, my lady."

"Anytime you have an idea, you'll need to share it with Lord Merrick."

The new housekeeper asked, "Are you and Lord Merrick . . . what I mean is . . ."

She laughed. "No, we are not engaged. I won't be Lady Merrick anytime soon. We are merely friends and so I am helping him out."

"I see."

"Let's start the process, then," Rachel said. "If you'll bring our first candidate in, we'll see what kind of staff we can assemble today."

Mrs. Kent left and they spent two hours speaking to all of the woman who'd shown up. By then, the men had gathered and Rachel took a break to summon Evan from where he and Finfrock discussed estate records so that he could give another brief speech to those gathered. After another hour and a half, she and Mrs. Kent had seen everyone who'd turned up. The two women decided on which hires to make and made a list of tasks to be performed and the order they should occur.

Evan wandered in at that point, finished with his business with Finfrock. Rachel introduced Evan to Mrs. Kent and they discussed how Mr. Kent would most likely become Edgemere's butler. By then, Finfrock escorted in a woman who greatly resembled Mrs. Dunnavant and Rachel knew they'd found Edgemere's cook.

They discussed the number of staff who'd been hired and Evan gave Mrs. Bridges free rein to go into North Stony and purchase whatever she needed to stock the larder so as to feed the servants who would report the day after tomorrow.

Evan was able to show Mrs. Kent which room had belonged to the previous housekeeper and she asked if she could remain and walk through the house to familiarize herself with everything. Evan agreed and she said she would be back tomorrow to help Mrs. Bridges establish the kitchen and prepare the house for the incoming staff.

Rachel and Evan rode back to Fairfield and went straight to tea. She was famished and had to force herself to slow down and not gobble up every morsel on the tea tray. Evan was called away because Alford's tailor from London had arrived to take his measurements and show him various cloths. All of the men wound up excusing themselves in order to give their opinion as to the new wardrobe being created for Evan.

After dinner, the houseguests indulged in several rounds of charades. Rachel paired with Cor and Lord Merrifield and they were the winning team.

She went upstairs with Leah to their bedchamber and readied herself for bed. As usual, Rachel got under the covers and waited for Leah to fall asleep so she could sneak downstairs for her last midnight lesson with Evan. She'd enjoyed herself today—breakfasting with him, riding to Edgemere, and then walking the gardens together. She believed she'd gathered the foundation of an experienced staff for him, though he'd still need to hire some gardeners and stable hands, as well as purchase horses.

Suddenly, she awoke with a start and cursed herself for falling asleep, knowing the long day had been partly to blame. She crept from the bed and slipped downstairs as the clock chimed half-past two. Opening the door to the library, she saw the lamp had been extinguished. No one was there.

Rachel had missed her lesson—and didn't know if Evan would be forgiving enough to hold another one in its place.

CHAPTER TEN

Evan awoke, wondering how he was going to face Rachel St. Clair today.

After missing their last lesson.

He'd wanted to go but didn't think he should. He was far from objective where she was concerned. His feelings for her had continued to grow and he wanted to squelch them. She needed someone younger. More idealistic. A man who believed in love as much as she did.

That's why he hadn't gone downstairs last night for their midnight rendezvous.

Evan wondered how long she'd waited for him in the library. If she'd become upset. Angry. Disappointed. Hurt.

He knew he'd done the right thing, though. After the last kiss he'd given her the night before, one going beyond the scope of their lesson, something was different. He refused to attach a name to it. He certainly didn't need to be kissing her anymore. She was an apt pupil and when she found the right man, nature would certainly take its course. Rachel St. Clair and her titled gentleman would do just fine on their own with no more lessons from him.

But the thought of tasting her lingered in his mind.

He washed and dressed and went downstairs. She was already present in the breakfast room, talking quietly with her grandmother. Her eyes met his for a brief moment and Evan nodded cordially before taking a plate and joining Alex at the buffet. They collected their breakfast items and then joined Rachel and Cor.

"What did you think of my tailor?" his friend asked, slathering jam on his toast.

"He's very competent. In fact, I'm riding into London today. He wanted me to stop by his shop to examine a few more sets of materials. I also need to see about having some new boots made and I have a butler to hire."

"If you're going to London, are you thinking about looking at horses?" Alex asked eagerly.

"I suppose I should while I'm there. It would save a return trip. With all I have to do, I think I'll stay overnight and come back to Fairfield tomorrow."

Leah seated herself next to Rachel. "You're leaving the house party, Merrick?"

"I do need to go to London. Ask Lady Rachel. We have a solid lead on an outstanding butler. I can't let Mr. Kent slip through my fingers."

"I may go with you," Alex said. "There's nothing better to do than examine good horseflesh."

"You'd leave your guests?" Leah asked, huffing. "No. You will stay, Alex."

Evan chuckled. "I see who'll rule the Fairfield roost in the future."

"Leah's right," Alex said, giving his fiancée a contrite look. "It would be wrong to abandon my guests. I wasn't thinking properly."

"I wasn't even invited to your house party to begin with so no one will miss me," Evan said lightly.

He could sense Rachel deliberately ignoring him throughout this exchange and chose to do the same to her.

"As long as you're back in time for the ball," Leah said. "I would hate for you to miss it."

"I'm not much of a dancer, Lady Leah," Evan admitted.

"Still, I expect you to conclude your business by tomorrow and return tomorrow night, Merrick," Leah said. "A guest shouldn't interrupt his stay at a house party, invited or not."

Her eyes twinkled at him with a smidgeon of mischief and Evan decided Alex would have his hands full with Leah Crawford as his countess.

Rachel said nothing.

"As you wish, Lady Leah," he replied.

Evan concentrated on eating as the others spoke of casual things. When he finished, he hated leaving without saying a single word to Rachel. Guilt still played heavily upon him. He looked at her and noticed she played with the food on her plate.

Definitely un-Rachel-like.

"Lady Rachel? Would you accompany me to the stables? I'd like to get your input on what to ask Mr. Kent when I meet with him."

Looking almost bored, she said, "Certainly, Lord Merrick. If you'll excuse me?"

They left the house and headed in the direction of the stables.

"I must apologize to you," Rachel began. "For missing last night's lesson."

He managed to keep his jaw from dropping and simply shrugged. "I assumed you'd decided you'd learned everything you needed and I had nothing more to offer," he lied.

Rachel stopped in her tracks and faced him. "On the contrary, I believe we were going to have a last lesson using our tongues. I'm still unclear as to how they factor into the kissing process. Remember, I want to be prepared as I look for my future husband. Tongues may very well have something to do with falling in love. I won't know unless I have some experience with them."

Evan almost retorted that tongues had nothing to do with love—but then again, he'd never been in love. They did, however, have much to do with pleasurable kissing.

"I fell asleep," she said sheepishly. "I got into bed and waited for

Leah to start snoring and the next thing I knew, I'd missed our engagement."

She began walking again and he fell into step with her.

"When I arrived, it was long past our lesson. I'm sorry that you waited for me, Evan." Her voice was low, her tone sad.

He should tell her.

But he didn't.

"Don't trouble yourself. It was nothing," he said brusquely.

They walked the rest of the way in silence. When they reached the stables, she turned to go.

"Rachel?"

Those amazingly green eyes met his.

"Yes?"

"I'm still willing to complete our last session if you are."

Evan saw hope spring in her eyes.

"That would be nice," she said primly.

"I won't be back tonight. But we can meet the midnight after that."

"All right. Have a safe journey."

He watched her move away, the subtle swing of her hips calling to him as loudly as any siren's song.

EVAN REACHED LONDON and stopped first at his solicitor's offices. Mr. Bowkey was shocked to see him.

"Lord Merrick! It's been several years."

"Six, to be exact, Bowkey. I've sold my commission and have returned to England for good."

"Please, have a seat. What can I do for you, my lord?"

He ran through a list of things he wished to be done and concluded with asking about his London townhouse, which he'd only seen once, almost fifteen years ago. Even at the tender age of thirteen, he'd recognized he had no need for the place and had Bowkey arrange to lease it at a substantial profit. Now that he was back for good, he decided the time to take ownership again had arrived.

"The lease ended only last week, Lord Merrick. The couple staying there launched their daughter for the Season, successfully, I might add. She is engaged to be married come November. They have since returned to the country and no other tenant has been found."

"Take it off the market," he ordered. "I plan to make use of it from now on. Does any work need to be done on it?"

"No, my lord. After each lease, I personally go over it with a fine-toothed comb. It was painted throughout only last autumn. It's clean and in excellent condition." Bowkey paused. "Will you move in immediately? Hire a staff? I can recommend the agency I used for temporary staffing. Perhaps some of those employees might suit your purpose."

"I'm readying Edgemere at the moment and have my hands full with that. Any servants I require in London can travel with me from there in the foreseeable future. If I decide to spend any length of time in the city, that may change. For now, I'll simply need the keys."

"Of course." Bowkey opened a drawer and fished out a keyring. Presenting it to him, the solicitor said, "Everything is here, from the main entrance to the wine cellars."

"Thank you."

Next, Evan stopped at his bank. He'd already thoroughly studied the ledgers with Finfrock but wanted to see how much he had in his holdings. The amount revealed was very satisfying, especially since he had horses to buy and a bevy of servants to pay.

After quick stops at his new tailor and former bootmaker, his next errand led him to a rented room. The door opened quickly after he knocked.

"Mr. Kent? Mr. Charles Kent?" he inquired.

"Yes, my lord," said a tall, lean man approaching forty. "How may I help you?"

"Inviting me in would be a good start. I'm the Marquess of Merrick. My country home, Edgemere, lies near North Stony, where your brother's store was located."

Kent stepped aside and allowed him entrance. The room was shabbily furnished, with only a narrow bed, washstand, and single chair. Evan took the chair and Kent perched on the edge of the lumpy bed.

"I've recently sold out of the army after several years and plan to make Edgemere my home. Yesterday, I hired your sister-in-law, Mrs. Kent, to be my housekeeper. She explained that you were searching for a position."

Kent's eyes brightened. "I am indeed, Lord Merrick. Although I've recently served as a butler for four years, I'm happy to do any job available—assistant butler, valet, driver. I've worked at all of those positions in the past and am willing to work in whatever capacity you might have available."

Evan liked that the man had experience in various areas, especially since he'd manage a large portion of the household. He was of a good age, too, and still had many years of service left to give.

"I'd prefer you as my butler if that's satisfactory."

Kent's smile lit up his face. "That would be my preference, my lord. When shall I start?"

"I could use you immediately. Tomorrow, the new staff members I've hired will arrive. I still have need of a few more. I'm off to Tattersall's now, in search of horses and, hopefully, a few grooms."

"I'm available now, my lord. I think it's important for me to be there to greet the new staff members with Mrs. Kent."

Evan withdrew a good amount of banknotes and handed them over. "Consider this an advance on your monthly salary." He named the year salary and saw Kent swallow. "Find a mail coach heading to North Stony and go today. Mrs. Kent may or may not be there. Mrs.

Bridges, my cook, has already taken up residence. Be sure to order plenty of feed, both oats and hay, for a good number of horses that will be arriving with me."

He stood. "I know you've worked in London most recently. I hope you will find the country to your taste, Kent."

His new butler also rose. "Working for a decent man is all I ask. You seem to be that man, Lord Merrick. Might I inquire about your family?"

"It's only me. I'm a confirmed bachelor."

"Very good, my lord."

Evan left and headed straight for Hyde Park Corner. Tattersall's had the best horseflesh in all of England. He introduced himself when he arrived and told the two staff members selected to accompany him that he was looking for a horse for himself, another four to six to pull his carriage, and between six and eight other mounts for guests to use in hunting and riding. Over several hours, he decided on a matched team of Cleveland bays for the carriage and chose several others for the stables after riding them.

Then he came across a magnificent beast. Coal black and frisky, the horse seemed to look him in the eye and dare Evan to try and ride him.

"What's this one's name?"

"Goliath. He's seventeen hands—and a handful."

"I want to test him—and see if he'll test me."

Evan enjoyed every moment on Goliath's back. He left Tattersall's and let the horse have his head. The black was full of speed and looked to have great stamina. He returned to the yard.

"I'll take him."

Choosing two more horses, he thought he was through when he spied a dapple gray horse as he was ready to finish negotiating prices.

Drawn to the horse's color, he asked for it to be removed from its stall. Evan ran his hands over the horse's graceful lines.

"What's this one's name?"

"That's Calypso. She's a bit hard to handle but an excellent horse for a knowledgeable rider. The trouble is, she's not large enough for a man. She'd require a lady who had a subtle hand and plenty of experience."

He asked to mount and ride the mare and found her spirited and agile. The horse reminded him of Rachel in many ways. Beautiful lines. Energetic. Challenging. Evan had no need to purchase this mount—but he wanted it.

For Rachel.

He concluded his business, purchasing saddles for each horse, and arranged for the entire group of horses to be brought to Edgemere. He would personally lead the caravan to the country. As far as a new carriage went, he'd see to it on his next trip to London. The old one hadn't been used in years and he wanted something more modern which would be safe for travel. When he asked about hiring grooms, he was sent back to the stables and talked with several men. Three were willing to accompany the horses and remain at Edgemere, while a fourth had more experience and would serve as his head groom. He might need more stable hands in the future but these four would suffice for now.

By now, it was very late and Evan found a nearby inn to stay at. The innkeeper's wife brought him a large bowl of hearty stew and half a loaf of brown bread as he washed it down with a couple of tankards of ale. The owner showed him to his room and Evan stripped off his clothes and climbed into bed. Sleep didn't come even though he was weary. He thought back to Calypso and wondered if Rachel would accept the gift from him. She would look perfect atop the horse, flying down the road, her braid bouncing merrily.

Of course, Rachel always looked perfect to him, whether in her riding habit or her dressing gown. He thought about the final time he'd spend tutoring her tomorrow night and fell asleep dreaming of her kiss.

CHAPTER ELEVEN

Rachel went down to breakfast with Leah and saw several servants placing items on the buffet. The room was empty except for Cor and Alford on one side of the room and four gentlemen on the other. She and Leah joined Cor and Alford.

As they began eating, Rachel said, "I think I may go to Edgemere today since the new servants are arriving."

Leah sighed dramatically. "Rachel, I don't even think you've enjoyed this house party at all. All you've done is put in work at Edgemere for Merrick. You even spent all afternoon drawing up plans for his garden yesterday instead of picnicking with us. *He* won't even be at his estate this morning. Why should you go?"

Cor patted Leah's hand. "Rachel is doing something she enjoys, Leah. She has always loved creating and organizing things. To her, it's just as much fun as what you've been doing to pass your time while at Fairfield. Though you two are similar in many ways, Rachel is different from you in some of the activities she enjoys."

"Like riding," Rachel reminded her best friend. "You do it when it's expected. I would spend most every day in the saddle if I could. You are talented with a needle. You can while away an entire afternoon creating a lovely sampler. All I would do is stick my finger enough times to bleed all over it and ruin it in the long run."

"I suppose so."

"If you're truly interested in riding over to Edgemere this morning, you'll need an escort," Alford reminded Rachel. "Evan has been with you on previous occasions." He turned to his fiancée. "What say you and I accompany Lady Rachel this morning? I think you'd enjoying seeing Fairfield. With Evan back in England now, I'm sure we'll be spending plenty of time there in his company."

A pang of jealousy shot through Rachel. The time would soon come when Leah and Alford would be wed. This would be her friend's home. They would naturally socialize with Evan since they were so close in proximity.

She wondered if he would ever commit to a woman. She didn't expect it to be her but surely, as a marquess, he had to think of leaving his title and estate to an heir. It hurt her more than she imagined, thinking of him with another woman. Kissing that woman. Fathering her children. Anger swelled within her.

Rachel wouldn't admit it to herself. Not yet. She forced Evan Drake from her mind.

"That's sweet of you to volunteer to escort Rachel, Alex. Of course, I'll go with the two of you," Leah said. "Rachel, let's go change into our riding habits."

They met at the stables and rode to Edgemere. As they cantered up the lane and the house came into view, Leah exclaimed how wonderful it was.

Several pieces of furniture rested outside and two maids beat upon a rug, dust kicking up in the air. Rachel greeted both by name, having a sharp memory, and they curtseyed and smiled.

Alford led them inside, where a whirlwind of activity prevailed. Mrs. Kent spied them and came to welcome them. Alford introduced himself as the closest neighbor and the marquess' oldest friend.

"Would you mind if my fiancée and I have a look about? I told her we'll be frequent guests of Merrick's once we marry."

Mrs. Kent offered to accompany them but Rachel told the housekeeper to remain with the staff. She'd be happy to take the couple around. They ran into Mr. Kent and introduced themselves to the new butler, who informed them that the marquess would be returning sometime today with the horses he planned to purchase.

"I ordered quite a bit of feed in the village. I've got two footmen who'll help out if Lord Merrick doesn't bring back any grooms with him," Mr. Kent said.

They toured the entire house, which was larger than Fairfield. Rachel could tell Leah was suitably impressed. Rachel made their last stop the kitchen, where Mrs. Bridges greeted them warmly and offered some refreshment. They took her up on the offer and sat around the kitchen table, drinking lemonade and eating freshly-baked scones.

Once they'd finished, Rachel took them outside to the gardens and walked them through, explaining some of the things she had in mind.

"I'm impressed, Lady Rachel," Alford said. "You have a keen eye. Hopefully, Evan will use your ideas. It would make his gardens remarkable."

They made their way back toward the house and saw the horses had arrived from London. Rachel caught sight of Evan, sans his coat and waistcoat, showing off his lean yet powerful frame. He'd removed his cravat and rolled up his shirtsleeves, revealing strong, tanned forearms. His shirt was also unbuttoned and she longed to press her lips against the column of his throat. She had to force herself not to run to him and make a fool of herself. She gazed at him longingly, wishing he could love her as . . .

No!

She refused to think it. If she didn't think it, it couldn't possibly be true, could it?

The three of them headed in his direction and Evan greeted them with enthusiasm.

"You're just in time. I can't wait for you to see what I've bought, Alex. Ah, here they come."

Rachel turned and saw beautifully matched bays being led into the stables.

"Are those Clevelands?" Alford asked, envy obvious in his voice. "These I've got to see." He strode toward the stables and Leah followed after him.

Leaving her alone. With Evan.

"I'm surprised to see you here," he said.

"I thought it would be wise to put in an appearance and see how your new help was working out."

"Is everything to your satisfaction?"

"Quite. Mr. Kent and Mrs. Kent have everything under control. They both have a calm but firm manner about them. I'm sure they'll manage your staff to perfection."

"Come see my new horses," he said.

Rachel accompanied him to the barn, where he showed off the carriage horses and others that he'd purchased for riding. Then they came to a stall with a huge black. The horse had powerful haunches and a sleek coat. Alford and Leah stood admiring the large mount.

"That's Goliath," Evan said with evident pride.

"I want him," Alford said. "I'll double whatever you paid for him."

Evan laughed. "I'm afraid not, old friend. He's mine—and he's magnificent."

The horse came near and Rachel stroked his muzzle. "You're certainly a handsome fellow and you know it, don't you," she said softly.

The men chatted for a few minutes about what Evan had seen at Tattersall's and what horseflesh he'd purchased. Leah didn't bother to hide her boredom.

Finally, Alford said, "You've seen everything at Edgemere, my love. Are you ready to head for home?"

"Yes." She glanced to Rachel. "Are you coming with us?" Her eyes flicked to Evan and back.

"I think Lady Rachel was going to show me what she plans to do with my gardens," Evan said easily. "I'll be sure to see her back to

Fairfield."

They said their goodbyes and the couple left to retrieve their horses, leaving Rachel alone with Evan.

"It seems your trip to London was successful. You have a qualified butler and now a stable full of horses."

"And grooms. I brought back a few. And something else."

His words piqued her curiosity. "What?"

"Come and see."

Evan led her around the corner and stopped in front of a stall. Rachel looked inside—and lost her heart.

A horse of dapple gray stood inside. It looked at her with intelligent eyes and neighed softly. She reached out a hand and horse came to her. She let it sniff her first and then took both hands and stroked it lovingly.

"That's Calypso."

She lowered her head to the horse's muzzle and pressed against it softly. "Like the sea nymph in Homer's *Odyssey*."

"Yes. She held Odysseus prisoner for seven years, capturing him with her song. Though he was enthralled with her, eventually he yearned to return to Penelope, his wife."

Rachel kissed the horse. "I can why you were enthralled with this Calypso and purchased her."

"Would you like to ride her?"

"Of course!"

Evan saddled the horse for her himself and then went to do the same with Goliath. Together, they led the pair from the stables and he helped her to mount.

"I rode her before buying her. She's more suited for a smaller rider than I am. Watch, though. She's definitely a challenge to handle."

Rachel patted the horse. "Not for me."

With that, she was off.

Riding Calypso was the closest she would ever come to soaring as a bird. Evan soon caught up to her on Goliath and they let the horses thunder across the estate. He signaled for her to slow and Rachel eased Calypso to a stop.

"There's a stream just through that copse. Let's take the horses to it."

She followed him, hearing the running water before seeing it. They led the animals toward it and both drank their fill.

"You are a phenomenal rider," he complimented.

She laughed. "It's not hard when atop such a magnificent creature." She looked from Calypso back to Evan.

And saw the heat in his eyes.

Rachel glanced quickly at the horse, suddenly feeling cowardly.

"No, it takes a special rider to control a horse of that breeding," he continued. "You are special in many ways, Rachel."

She wanted to kiss him. She wanted him to kiss her. It wouldn't make a difference, though. Evan always held himself slightly apart from others. If they kissed, she would only want more from him. More than he was willing to give.

"Come along, Calypso," she said, tugging gently on the horse's reins. "You've had your fill."

Rachel led the horse away from the stream and back through the wooded area. She knew Evan followed with Goliath for she could hear them behind her. When they reached the open meadow again, she stopped.

Evan appeared and placed his hands on her waist. She started to lick her lips and thought twice.

"Are you ready for tonight's final lesson? With tongues?" he teased.

She thought, for a moment, he might start the lesson here. Now. She swallowed, desperately wanting him to and afraid if he did, she might shatter.

With a braveness she didn't feel, she met his gaze. "I am. I intend to learn a lot in our last session."

A lazy smile turned the corners of his mouth up. "There's a lot of material to master. We may be at it a good while."

With that, Evan hoisted her back into the saddle and they returned to Edgemere.

EVAN DECIDED TO remain fully dressed as he made his way downstairs to the library. Tonight was his last lesson with Rachel.

He didn't want the lessons to end.

He understood that his time at war had damaged his soul. If anyone could heal him, it would be Rachel St. Clair. He didn't want to want her—but he did. He was almost ten years older and felt thirty more, due to his war experiences. Life hadn't really seemed worth living beyond fighting for his lost men. When he'd been forced out, Evan had thought he would retreat to Edgemere and live a quiet life of solitude.

Now, he wanted more. He wanted Rachel. And would do whatever it took to have her.

He didn't think he loved her. He'd never known love, that ephemeral feeling that poets waxed about and women longed for. Yet he'd seen the heated looks exchanged between Alex and Leah. Was that merely passion? Or did the two truly love each other? It made Evan question everything he knew.

If he could ever fall in love, it would be with someone like Rachel. No, no one was like the dark-haired beauty. If love came to him, it would only be with her.

She'd said she wouldn't marry unless she loved the man. Would it be enough for her to love him—and him to only desire her?

Tonight's lesson would reveal a great deal.

Evan had wanted to give Calypso to her this afternoon but thought better of it. A gift of that magnitude, bestowed upon a woman from a man not her blood relative, would be more than frowned upon by society. It would put Rachel in an awkward position of having to refuse his gift. Perhaps, even refuse him.

Instead, Evan would make the horse a wedding present to her.

He reached the library half an hour before their scheduled rendezvous, eager to begin what would be the beginning of a lifetime of lessons. He would indoctrinate her into the physical ways of love, of passion and deep desire. He wanted children from her. He wanted to be her world. Now that he'd determined to wed her, nothing would stop him.

Nerves flared within him. They were almost as bad as the ones which had come when it came time to lead men onto the battlefield. Evan reached for the decanter of brandy and poured two fingers, hoping by sipping the alcohol, it would calm him. Of course, it would be what Rachel tasted when they first kissed. He smiled at the thought.

He sat on what he thought of as their settee and took a drink. The brandy burned going down his throat, trailing a hot wave until it hit his belly. He closed his eyes and let it soothe him.

In the stillness, he heard the door handle turn and smiled.

She'd come early.

It warmed him even more than the brandy, knowing Rachel looked forward to what would pass between them tonight.

Evan opened his eyes. Dismay filled him as Merrifield entered.

Chapter Twelve

Rachel and Leah readied themselves for bed. Leah was in a chatty mood and took her time, making Rachel all the more jittery since she was eager to meet Evan.

Leah unpinned her hair and held out her brush. "Would you mind, Rachel? I love when you do it for me."

Knowing how brushing Leah's hair soothed her, Rachel readily took the brush in hand. She stood behind her friend and pulled it through her long, blond locks.

"At least one hundred strokes," Leah murmured, closing her eyes.

Rachel counted in her head. When she reached thirty, Leah opened her eyes and began chatting.

"Oh, this has been a wonderful house party. I've enjoyed getting to know some of Alex's friends and neighbors. And then the ball will be two nights from now, with many more of his neighbors in attendance. I'm so glad Catherine and Jeremy are coming for it. I can't wait for them to see Fairfield."

"It is a beautiful estate. I know you'll be happy here."

Leah laughed softly. "I would be happy anywhere Alex was. I'm so glad I had a successful Season and found the man I was meant to be with for eternity." She paused. "Your future husband is out there, Rachel. You'll find him when it's meant to be."

"I hope so." She counted ten more strokes before asking, "Do you think kissing with your tongue had anything to do with falling in love with Alford?"

Leah gasped. "Rachel! Only you would dare to ask me something like that."

"Well ... did it? I'm merely curious since I haven't used mine before."

"Hmm." Leah thought a moment. "I believe I fell in love with Alex the first time I saw him from across that crowded ballroom. Although I will admit that kissing him—with my tongue—did confirm that my feelings for him were true."

Leah looked over her shoulder. "Is there someone here at Fairfield that you particularly want to kiss in that way? I know Merrifield and Merrick have paid you special attention, more so than the others."

"They are both very nice," Rachel said noncommittally.

"Merrifield is quite handsome. He seems to dote on you. In fact, he—and two other gentlemen—have a special surprise planned for you tomorrow."

"Let me guess. They've talked Jones and Mrs. Dunnavant into holding tea in the gazebo."

Leah frowned. "You already know?"

Rachel shrugged. "I suggested it when we first toured the gardens. Merrifield said he would make it happen. Frankly, I'm surprised it took him so long to arrange it."

"Well, please act surprised. I know he's gone to a great deal of trouble for you."

"I will smile graciously," she promised.

"What of Merrick? You've spent the most time with him."

"What about him?" Rachel said casually, continuing to brush Leah's hair.

"You seem to verbally spar with him quite a bit. And enjoy it."

"Merrick is interesting. Possibly because of his war experience. He's been places and done much more than most men of my acquaintance."

"Alex would be very pleased if something stirred between the two of you." Leah turned and removed the brush from Rachel's hand and took it. "I would, too. As much as I love Alex and can't wait to marry him, I regret leaving you behind."

She laughed. "You're not leaving me behind, silly. First, you will be busy settling in as Alford's countess. In fact, it wouldn't surprise me if this time next year, you'd already birthed his child."

Hope sprang in Leah's eyes. "You think so?"

"You will be a wonderful mother, Leah."

"I know I'm supposed to get an heir and possibly a spare but I know nothing about boys. I want a girl first. Is that selfish of me?"

Rachel squeezed her friend's hand. "Not at all. Why don't you have some of both? And I do know what you mean. Having two brothers, I always longed for Father to wed again so that I might have a sister. Instead, Jeremy brought me you and Catherine. It's as if I have two now."

"I feel the same, Rachel. Catherine's so much older than me. She's been more of a mother than sister, at times. With us being of a similar age, it's been ever so much fun, being an honorary St. Clair."

"Soon, you will be a Lock—and Countess of Alford."

Leah frowned. "Still, we'll be miles apart."

"I will come visit. Besides, you'll come to London each year for the Season. I'll see you there."

"I will do my best to find you a match next year. If not sooner." Her friend paused. "Answer me truthfully. Don't dodge my question this time. Do I sense something between you and Merrick?"

"I thought it possible at one point," Rachel said, knowing she would reveal this only to Leah. "I'm afraid, though, that the Peninsular Wars affected Merrick in ways he may never share. Do you know he was shot—twice in the same battle?"

"No. How awful."

"I don't think he's told anyone, not even Alford. I'm surprised he revealed it to me."

"That's something, isn't it? Sharing confidences with you."

Rachel shook her head. "We have been friendly. Possibly even friends. I don't see anything coming of it, though. I think it may be a long time before Merrick wishes to commit to a woman. At least that's the impression he's given me."

"I'm sorry. I know that must disappoint you." Leah squeezed Rachel's hand again and then released it.

They climbed into bed and her earlier eagerness melted into sadness. It was true. She finally admitted it to herself.

She was in love with the Marquess of Merrick. And absolutely nothing would come of it.

Instead of pitying herself, Rachel determined to continue with tonight's lesson. Learn what she needed to move on. Just because she loved Evan didn't mean there wasn't another man out there that she might fall in love with. One who would love her back.

To make sure she didn't fall asleep, Rachel pinched her thigh. She counted to ten and pinched it again. By the time she reached forty, Leah's breathing had softened. When she made it to seventy, the subtle snores had begun. As she slipped from under the covers, Rachel wondered what Alford would make of his wife's snoring. Leah was perfect in absolutely every single way, except for this tiny flaw which Rachel found endearing. Knowing how Alford felt about his fiancée, he would probably love Leah even more once he discovered it.

She shrugged into her dressing gown and instead of knotting it, she tied a bow on the left side of her waist. It would be easier for Evan to slip it off her. Just in case he chose to. She knew tonight's lesson involved kissing with tongues but she remembered the delicious way Evan's tongue had caressed her neck and breasts. Maybe after they'd kissed for a bit, he'd want to combine the various lessons.

Or so she hoped.

Rachel made her way down the corridor and reached the stairs. By now, she knew the two which squeaked and avoided both of them. As she passed the grandfather clock, it chimed half-past eleven. She was very early. She paused in front of the library's entrance and took several deep, calming breaths. Anticipation built within her as she turned the handle on the library's door and slipped inside, closing it behind her. When she turned, she froze in her tracks.

Evan was already here.

With Merrifield.

"Lady Rachel," called the handsome earl. "What a pleasant surprise."

He rose to his feet and Evan followed suit. Rachel masked her shock and moved across the room, noticing both men held crystal tumblers in their hands.

"Forgive me, my lords." She sensed her cheeks reddening with embarrassment. "I would never have come down in my dressing gown if I'd known someone was awake and in the library."

"We'll forgive you," Merrifield said cheerily. "I found myself restless and came down for a drink. Imagine finding Merrick here, doing the same."

She finally glanced in Evan's direction. His face gave nothing away.

"I had trouble sleeping," he said. "I thought some brandy might be the very thing to help me relax."

"I was unable to fall asleep," Rachel began, "especially since Leah snores. I thought if I found a boring tome, it might help me grow sleepy."

Merrifield laughed. "Go for something about agriculture. Any time my estate manager wants to talk crops, it puts me quite to sleep. Boring as anything I've known. Here, I'll help you find something tedious and tiresome."

The earl set his brandy down and moved toward the shelves of books. Rachel quickly glanced to Evan, nerves shooting through her as she felt her cheeks continue to burn. He shrugged and gave her an encouraging smile.

"Ah, yes. This might do." Merrifield turned and motioned for Rachel to join him.

She somehow managed to put one foot in front of the other and reluctantly came to stand next to him.

He handed her a large volume and said, *"The History of Manure Use in Farming.* This is a strong possibility." He turned back to the shelves and removed an even thicker volume. "Or how about this one? I'm sure reading about grain production in Essex County would knock you straight out. In fact, you might sleep straight through breakfast and beyond."

Nervously, Rachel licked her lips as she accepted the book. "I'll think about which one to choose, my lord."

She stood rooted to the spot, wishing he would leave. Instead, Merrifield stared at her a long moment, a glint of amusement in his eyes.

Finally, he turned to Evan, who now drained his glass. "What say you, Merrick? Shall we leave Lady Rachel to her reading?"

Evan set the tumbler down. "Good night to you both."

He nodded deferentially as he passed Rachel. Merrifield followed closely behind and did the same, though he winked at her as he passed. They exited and she replaced both volumes from where Merrifield had taken them and placed her palms against her face, feeling the fire in her cheeks.

What if Merrifield had walked in on them?

Horrified by that thought, Rachel realized how risky their behavior had been. If anyone had caught them together . . .

She moved to the shelves and grabbed the first book her hand landed upon. Holding it tightly to her chest, she made her way back to her room. Just before she reached it, Merrifield stepped from the shadows. He joined her, slipping the book from her hands.

"Poetry? I would have thought this would be something young

ladies adored reading. All those verses about unrequited love." He smiled. "Or the power of love—when it is fulfilled."

Rachel managed to chuckle. "I find all poetry bland. All those tedious rhymes being forced. Especially if it waxes on about love."

"You aren't romantic in nature?" he asked, lifting the braid that fell over one shoulder and toying with it.

"Not especially." She stepped back, enough for him to drop it. Holding out her hand, she said, "May I? This isn't appropriate."

"No," he said huskily. "It isn't. But then again, I've never found being proper very interesting. I feel we may be kindred souls in that regard, Lady Rachel."

She felt the pulse beating in her throat and her mouth grew dry. "I assure you, my lord, I am most interested in conforming with Polite Society's rules. Not flouting them. And those rules don't involve standing in a darkened hallway having a discussion with you at this time of night."

"Especially in your night rail and dressing gown," he said softly. "It's a very pretty color on you. In fact, everything looks good on you, Lady Rachel. And probably off, as well."

He took a step forward and she sensed the possibility of a kiss. For a moment, the thought thrilled her. She could put to practice what she'd learned in her midnight lessons.

But Merrifield wasn't Merrick. Though Merrifield was a remarkably handsome man, intriguing and full of fun, it would be a betrayal of Evan. Even though Evan wouldn't have cared. She deliberately moved back a foot, putting distance between them again.

Their gazes held for a moment and then she lowered hers to the book. Snatching it from his hands, she said, "Good night, Lord Merrifield."

Rachel entered the bedchamber and closed the door quietly. She leaned against it for support, her breath coming rapidly.

Why had he deliberately waited for her? Was that flirting? Had

Merrifield truly wanted to kiss her? More importantly, should she have let him? Evan had made it clear he had no interest in pursuing a relationship with her. At some point, she would have to explore kissing with other men. Merrifield was interested in her. Perhaps she should reciprocate that interest—and see where it went.

She went to the bed and placed the book down on the table beside it. Climbing into the bed, she raised the sheet over her and curled up on her side, wondering if she would ever be allowed to partake in her last kissing lesson with Evan.

Maybe it was for the best. If she did, she might lose her heart to him. For good.

And be miserable the rest of her life.

Chapter Thirteen

The men went shooting the next morning so Rachel spent time perfecting her plans for Evan's garden and then visited with a few of the other ladies who'd come to the house party. She read to Cor for an hour and then they went to the drawing room for tea. Alford announced that tea would be held in the gardens in the gazebo. Rachel smiled in Merrifield's direction as the others oohed and aahed over the special treat.

As she'd expected, the earl came directly to her.

"May I escort you to the gazebo, Lady Rachel?"

"Yes. If you would also help Cor," she insisted.

"I can accompany the duchess."

She turned and saw Evan had approached. He took Cor's arm. "Go ahead with Merrifield," he urged.

Rachel did as he said and allowed Merrifield to walk with her to the gazebo. Everything looked lovely.

"Are you pleased?" he asked.

"Yes. I'm sure everyone will enjoy taking their tea here. It's a beautiful spot."

"I didn't do it for everyone. I did it for you."

"Thank you."

Merrifield fetched her a cup and saucer and then servants delivered plates of food. Rachel spoke to everyone present, her frustration growing. She hadn't had a moment alone with Evan and hoped to arrange a midnight rendezvous with him. Several of the men fawned over her and she despised them for it. Evan never did that. If anything, he argued with her. Or challenged her. Or spoke of interesting things. Rachel found herself bored and restless from keeping her smile in place.

"You know what we haven't done?" Alford asked. "Croquet."

"Let's play now," Leah cried. "The weather is perfect."

The earl signaled a footman, who immediately left. Rachel assumed the servant would see that the wickets were set up and mallets and balls put out by the time they arrived at the house.

The group set aside their dishes and slowly made their way through the gardens, everyone remarking on their beauty. Rachel had allowed a viscount to escort her back, knowing Merrifield was dismayed. She didn't care.

As she expected, the game had been set up once they returned. She teamed with Leah. They were both croquet fiends and often beat any men who challenged them. Today, though, Rachel's game was off. She couldn't seem to concentrate.

"What's wrong, Rachel?" Leah asked.

"I think it's how you're holding your mallet, Lady Rachel," Evan said, appearing at her elbow. "Here. Let me assist you."

He stood closely behind her, causing her to hold her breath. His arms went around her and he leaned into her, placing his hands atop hers and adjusting them slightly.

Then he murmured into her ear. "Midnight. The schoolroom."

Evan moved the mallet to the right and then struck the ball. It sailed through the wicket. He released her and, immediately, she felt the loss of his body heat.

"Well played," Leah cried. "That puts us only two shots from the lead."

"I think I need a lesson, as well, Lord Merrick," a woman said. "Could you please help me?"

Rachel retrieved her ball, keeping her head averted. She did not want to see Evan's arms around another woman. She ignored him after that, concentrating on her game.

When they finished, Leah remarked, "You achieved your old form, Rachel. I'm glad Merrick helped put you back on track."

They waited until everyone finished play and tallied their scores. As expected, she and Leah claimed victory.

"What do we win?" Leah asked her fiancé.

"I hadn't thought about offering a prize." He leaned over and boldly kissed her in front of everyone.

The group chuckled and Leah said, "I've claimed my reward but what about Rachel?"

"I'll indulge in two desserts tonight," she said airily, causing everyone to laugh more.

As they started to break up, Evan stepped toward her. "I've heard from Cor that you finished your plans for my gardens. Would you care to show them to me now? In the library?"

"Of course, my lord. Let me fetch them from my room."

As she left, she saw Merrifield lurking nearby. He must have heard what they arranged. Sure enough, she arrived in the library with her drawings and found the earl there, along with two of his friends, having a drink.

"I hope we won't disturb you," he called out.

"Not at all," she replied evenly.

She sat at a table and waited. Evan arrived a few minutes later, not raising an eyebrow. He seated himself.

"I see we have company," he said lightly. "Chaperones?"

"It doesn't matter." Rachel began spreading out the sheets she'd brought. "Look first. Then I'll walk you through what I've come up with."

He studied each drawing and asked a few questions then asked her to lead him through her plans. She explained the overall feel and then discussed the various places she wanted special groupings of seats or flowers. He offered some suggestions regarding a fountain she'd sketched and agreed with the alterations. Quickly, she redrew it on the back side of the page and saw his satisfied smile.

Then he took the page with the gazebo in hand. She'd drawn it as they'd discussed, with six wide openings that she'd designed in the manner of Roman arches. As requested, she'd left the area surrounding the actual gazebo open, with no fencing.

Evan grinned. "This is exactly what I envisioned when we spoke of it." His gaze regarded her warmly. "You're quite talented, Lady Rachel. In many regards."

"Thank you."

She looked down and began gathering the pages into one stack, hoping the blush would die down. It wouldn't do for the others, especially Merrifield, to see it. Rachel tapped the pages on the table and handed the stack to Evan.

"You'll have to let me know what your chief gardener thinks of these. I can answer any questions he might have."

"I think it's self-explanatory. I also want to give him a free hand to change anything he wishes. Except for the gazebo. I will find carpenters to build it to your exact specifications." He paused. "I hope you will come to visit when it's completed."

"I would like that, my lord."

Rachel rose and Evan followed suit.

"I will see you at dinner, Lady Rachel," he said formally.

All she could think of was midnight–when the marquess dropped all pretension as he kissed the life out of her.

RACHEL UNPINNED HER hair and let it spill about her shoulders and down her back. She picked up her brush and pulled it through the dark curls. Leah had gone to bed minutes ago. Rachel bided her time, running the brush through her hair. She wasn't going to braid it. Tonight, it would be free. She hoped Evan would run his fingers through it.

Setting the brush aside, she rose. Already, Leah had fallen asleep. She envied her friend for having the ability to rest her head on a pillow and immediately tumble into a deep slumber. Rachel had never been able to do that. She pulled the dressing gown around her night rail and, once again, tied it to the side of her waist before leaving the bedchamber.

Alford had taken Leah and her on a tour of Fairfield's rooms the first day they arrived. It was the only time she'd been to the upper floor but Rachel remembered the schoolroom's location. Gripping the rail, she cautiously ascended the stairs. When she reached the top, she paused. Not having a candle, she was stepping into darkness. Rachel took a deep breath and placed her hand on the wall, gingerly placing one foot in front of the other as she ran her hand along for support. She hadn't thought about bringing a candle. If she had, it would stand out like a beacon. They couldn't afford having that kind of attention called to their midnight session.

Slowly, she made her way down the corridor, her heart thumping loudly. She reached what she thought was the correct door and swung it open.

A row of windows ran across the space directly across from her. In the moonlight, she saw Evan's silhouette. Rachel breathed a sigh of relief and quietly closed the door.

"Rachel?" he softly called.

"I'm here." She realized he was gazing into shadows while she had the benefit of the moon illuminating him. "Stay there. I'll come to you."

She skirted the furniture, sticking to the wall, until she reached him. Stepping out, he clasped her elbows.

"I was afraid to bring a candle. With the house in a U-shape, the light, though faint, could be seen from too many places." Evan pressed a tender kiss against her brow. "I'm glad you came."

"And miss my final lesson?" she said lightly, not wanting to reveal the depth of emotion running through her.

His hands dropped away. "We wouldn't want that to happen." His tone matched hers.

"I was thinking once you tutored me a final time, we might merge all of our lessons together. Like a musical piece with several movements."

His even, white teeth gleamed in the moonlight. "First, let's see if you can master tonight's lesson. Shall we begin?"

"I'm ready," she proclaimed, her nerves fraying even as anticipation caused her heart to beat rapidly.

Her eyes began to adjust to the dim moonlight and she could now see Evan's face. He was handsome beyond measure—and for the next hour?

He was hers.

His hands came up to cradle her face. Just his touch caused a quickening inside her, a longing for this man and everything he had to offer. He gazed at her, a trace of a smile playing about his lips, and then he bent and touched his mouth to hers.

Finally.

Rachel had no idea what came next, knowing she would follow his lead as she had in their other lessons. Her palms flattened against his muscular chest to steady herself as he softly brushed his lips against hers. A wonderful tingling rippled through her. In this moment, she felt treasured.

Evan's kiss changed. His hands left her face and glided along her neck, coming to rest on her shoulders. As he lightly gripped them, his tongue slowly outline the shape of her mouth several times, a languid, drugging feeling. A tremor ran through her. Then he ran his tongue along the seam of her lips, teasing them open. The moment she granted what he wished, his tongue swept into her mouth. A thousand feelings came alive inside her as her fingers grasped his linen shirt.

His kisses were playful to begin with and then grew in intensity. Tentatively, she touched her tongue to his and heard a low, satisfied groan. Rachel hadn't known you made noises when you kissed. She'd been holding back. But no longer.

She began matching him, stroke for stroke, as his fingers pushed into her hair. They both began making small sounds to let the other know how pleased they were. He ran his fingers throughout her hair, causing her breath to quicken. Then he tugged on her curls, forcing her head back, giving him better access. The kiss deepened.

Evan's arm went about her waist, pulling her against him, crushing her breasts to his chest. She could feel his heart beating as wildly as hers and sighed with happiness, knowing he was as affected by her as she was by him. His fingers went to the nape of her neck and held her in place, his thumb stroking the side of her neck even as his tongue stroked hers.

Time didn't exist as one kiss blended into another. Not only did her heart pound violently, but at the apex of her core, a primal beat had begun, a throbbing that demanded to be taken care of. By him.

His mouth finally left hers as his lips trailed along her throat, nipping lightly before his tongue soothed where his teeth had been. He found the tie to her dressing gown and loosened it before parting it, revealing her night rail. He walked her backwards until she bumped against a table and he lifted her atop it. His mouth, warm and wet, traveled to her nipple and he laved it through the gown. She felt it grow hard as he put his mouth against the thin cloth and worked his tongue along it, nibbling and sucking greedily. His kisses were driving all reasonable thoughts from her head.

Evan moved to satisfy the other breast and her body began to vibrate all over, humming like a musical instrument's strings being tuned as he played her. His mouth traveled back to hers and kissed her over and over, sometimes hard, sometimes soft, and every way in-between. Rachel's arms went around his neck and she stood, pushing against him, demanding more from him. His hands clasped her waist, the thumbs stroking her ribcage, causing her to tremble.

She finally understood what Leah meant about kissing. Why Jeremy and Catherine couldn't keep their hands off each other, even after being wed and having the twins. Rachel ran her hands along Evan's muscled arms, up and down, and then wrapped her arms about his waist, pressing as close as she could as they continued to kiss. She didn't know where her breath started and ended because it was a part of his.

The back of his hand brushed against her belly and then moved lower. The kisses became more heated as Evan's fingers trailed downward. Then his hand cupped her nether region and Rachel murmured in the back of her throat. He must have understood what she wanted—what she needed—as his hands yanked her night rail up to her waist. Evan slid a finger inside her and she almost exploded from the intimate touch. Slowly, he stroked her, maddening her, fulfilling her, making her gasp. His tongue began to mimic his finger, lovingly stroking her. Another finger joined it, doubling her pleasure.

A sense of something building inside her like a tidal wave caused Rachel to hold on to him tightly. Then the wave erupted, flowing over her like waves crashing against a rock. She whimpered. She panted. She cried out his name but it was lost as he kissed her deeply. Clinging to him, her body quivered with the deepest of pleasure. The waves subsided, leaving her weak and spent. She was afraid she might collapse into a puddle at his feet.

Evan must have sensed this for he swept her off her feet and sat on the table with her in his lap. His kisses softened and then only his lips brushed against hers. He tenderly kissed her cheek and then her brow. She rested her cheek against his chest, his heart bumping against her ear.

They sat that way for some minutes, Rachel cradled in his arms, Evan kissing her hair as he lightly stroked her back. She never wanted this to end.

And then it did.

He stilled his hand and ceased kissing her hair. He rose and placed her on her feet again. Rachel still held on to his waist, reluctant to let go, knowing she was touching him for the very last time.

"You've learned your lessons well," he said huskily.

She wished she could see his eyes but they were hidden now in the shadows. She wanted a glimpse into his soul. Wanted a chance to see if he might possibly wish to make a commitment to her.

Finding her voice, she said, "I had a wonderful tutor. And I've always been an exceptional student."

He cupped her face again. "Remember, my sweet Rachel, this kind of kissing is like playing with fire. You can easily be burned. Kiss a man if you're truly attracted to him. If you think he might make you a good husband. If you feel a spark between the two of you, then by all means try a few kisses with your tongue. That should tell you whether or not you're meant for one another."

Her heart cried out that they were meant for each other but she could already feel him withdrawing from her. The Marquess of Merrick had no intention of wooing her. He'd done as she asked on the night they met—taught her how to kiss.

Rachel doubted she would ever kiss a man the way she had Evan, much less feel all the things she felt for him.

It was her fault. She blamed herself. She'd gone and fallen in love with the one man who would never consider wedding her.

He released her and retrieved her dressing gown. Ever the gentleman, Evan helped her slip into it and belted it snuggly.

"Our midnight lessons have come to an end," he said, a tinge of sadness in his voice. "I've enjoyed getting to know you, Rachel St.

Clair."

Rachel encased her heart in stone, knowing it folly to vocalize her true feelings. "You've been a most excellent tutor, my lord. I'm sure what you've taught me will help me decide upon who my future husband should be. Thank you for taking the time to teach me so well."

With that, she turned and reached out a hand until she found the wall. Using it to guide her way to the door, Rachel held her head high as she exited. She wouldn't give in to tears in front of him. She wouldn't embarrass herself. Or him. Silently, she made her way back to her room and climbed into the bed.

And quietly wept for what would never be.

CHAPTER FOURTEEN

Evan stood and watched Rachel go. The further she moved away from him, the more the shadows swallowed her up. Finally, she vanished into the dark, though the scent of her perfume lingered in the air.

He sat on the desk, trying to get a hold of himself. He'd kissed more than his fair share of women in his twenty-seven years.

None had affected him as much as Rachel.

Even now, he could still taste her. A deep yearning grew within him. It took everything he had not to race after her and claim her as his. Yet doubt flooded him. At the end, when he declared their lessons over, she'd reacted coolly. Dispassionately. As if she hadn't been affected by what had passed between them. At the beginning, Rachel's inexperience was obvious but she was a rapid learner who threatened to surpass him. She'd matched him kiss for kiss tonight, stirring his soul as no other ever had. Surely, she felt what he did.

He hadn't wanted to make any type of declaration to her after the final lesson. He wanted that separate from what they would share in the future. Evan knew her brother and the rest of her family would arrive sometime tomorrow morning. Should he go to the Duke of Everton and ask for her hand in marriage? Or should he make known his feelings to Rachel first and then seek permission from her brother? Conflict filled him. Had she only used him to learn what she wanted and once their lessons ended, she was ready to move on?

No. Please, God. No.

Evan couldn't imagine a life without Rachel St. Clair in it. She made him feel alive again. Gave him a reason to live. He hadn't wanted to return to England. He didn't wish to wed and have a family. It didn't matter to him if his title and lands reverted back to some distant Drake relative. Until now. Now, Evan wanted to marry. He wanted children with Rachel. He wanted to pass down a legacy for those children.

If she would have him.

The ball would take place tomorrow night. Rachel wouldn't lack for partners. Every man at Fairfield during the house party had lavished attention upon her. Evan thought it best if she spread her wings a bit during the ball. Maybe kiss a man or—heaven forbid—two. Just to let her know that something with those men was missing. That what they'd shared together was real. Something lasting. Only then would he declare his feelings for her and ask for her to become his marchioness.

The thought of Rachel being held by another man, much less kissing him, brought agony to him. Still, it would be for the best. She needed something to compare what had passed between them in order to see how genuine their attraction was. God, he hoped she could then love him. Evan knew how important that was to her. She could've wed countless men she'd met during her Season and yet hadn't because she wanted to be in love with her future husband. He would show her how he worshipped her. How he could make her happy. Take her to new heights every time they coupled in the bedroom—and beyond.

Idly, he wondered about traveling to London to obtain a special license. He could bring it to Alex and Leah's wedding. With so many family and friends there, it would be incredible if Rachel agreed to wed him the day after their two best friends tied the knot. Still, he realized most women planned for weeks—if not months—for the ceremony of their dreams, what many considered the highlight of their lives. He would not keep Rachel from writing out the invitations and selecting a wedding gown. He could always tear up the special license and have the banns called for their future wedding date.

Satisfied that he had a plan in place, Evan returned to his own room. When he reached Rachel's door he paused, putting his palm against it, knowing that was what separated them. What he wouldn't give to sneak in and lift her slumbering form from the bed and return with her to his bedchamber. He would make love to her tenderly that first time, initiating her slowly into the ways of love.

With regret, he left her doorstep and continued down the hallway to his own room. Stripping off his clothes, he left them on the floor and climbed into bed. Sleep evaded him for a long time and when it came, his dreams were of Rachel.

RACHEL BATHED HER eyes again with cool water. Twice, she'd gotten up during the night to do the same. She wanted no trace of redness or swelling in them when she came downstairs for breakfast today. Drying them, she set the cloth aside and brought her fingertips to her lips. They'd been swollen last night from Evan's demanding kisses. Even now, they were still tender to the touch.

She closed her eyes and again relived every moment from last night, even the wicked ones. His mouth on her breasts. His fingers inside of her.

How was she supposed to look him in the face after being so intimate with him?

She'd have to. Evan would be back to his aristocratic self in the breakfast room, not giving away a clue as to how the midnight hour had been spent.

At least her family would arrive today. She needed to see them.

She'd missed them terribly.

"Where did I put that shoe?" Leah complained. "I can find one but not the other."

"Let me look."

Rachel rose and went to the bed. She got down on all fours and looked under it. Sure enough, the missing shoe was located far underneath. She had to flatten herself and stretch her arm out in order to snag it.

"Here it is," she proclaimed.

"However did it get there?" Leah asked as she slipped it onto her foot. "Oh, I'm so excited that everyone will be here today. I can't wait for them to see Fairfield."

"Let's go to breakfast," Rachel suggested. "Hopefully, they'll arrive soon."

As they entered the breakfast room, she braced herself. As expected, Evan sat with Alford and Cor, looking immaculately dressed and as if he'd had the best night of sleep in his life. It grated on her as she placed eggs and toast upon her plate and followed Leah across the room in order to join them. A servant poured tea for them.

She pushed her eggs around and then took a bite, finding it hard to swallow. Instead, she sipped on her tea.

"You didn't get any of the ham, Lady Rachel," Evan said.

No, not Evan. She must think of him as Merrick from now on.

"It's quite good this morning." He speared a slice with his fork and transferred it to her plate.

The small gesture almost ripped her heart out, as if his fork had stabbed it and not a piece of pork. She had no idea how she would get it down. Glumly, she sliced a bite and brought it to her mouth, praying she would have the energy to chew and swallow.

"Rachel!"

She turned to the tall figure standing in the doorway and dropped her fork. "Luke!"

Quickly, she pushed her chair back and hurried to him. Her brother enveloped her in a tight hug and then kissed her soundly.

"Is everyone already at Fairfield?"

"No. I rode ahead. The coaches will arrive soon. I wanted to get here first and see you. And Leah."

By now, Leah had risen and joined them. Luke hugged her and captured Leah's hands, holding her arms out.

"You look wonderful, Leah. Happy." Luke grinned. "I'd even say in love."

"I am, Luke. Please, come join us."

Alford and Merrick had risen. Luke knew Alford and greeted him warmly and then the earl introduced Luke to Merrick.

"My oldest, closest friend in the world," Alford proclaimed. "Just back from the Peninsula."

"Are you hungry, Luke? As if I should ask," Leah said. "All you St. Clairs have a healthy appetite."

Luke grinned. "I could eat something." He went to the buffet and filled a plate high with food before returning and taking a seat.

They talked for a half-hour and then a servant came and whispered into Alford's ear.

"The ducal coaches have been spotted," the earl said. "Why don't we go to the drive and greet your family, my love?"

Luke assisted Rachel from the table and they walked ahead of the others.

"So, how has the house party been? How many men fell in love with you?" he teased. Then he grew serious. "Or better yet—did you find love?"

She had spent long hours talking with Luke about how she must love the man she wed. She witnessed the wonderful example of Jeremy and Catherine and would settle for nothing less.

"Oh, I've had several male houseguests interested in me," she said airily. "No one who's truly caught my fancy, though."

"Hmm," Luke said thoughtfully. "Not even Merrick? I liked him for the brief time we spoke. And the fact he's Alford's good friend speaks well of him."

"Major Merrick... that is, the marquess, has recently sold his commission and returned to England this past week. I think he is ready to be alone after spending so many years at war. Possibly, he will marry in the future but I'm not interested in him in that way." Rachel thought her lies sounds quite natural and was proud of herself.

Before Luke could reply, Leah cried, "There they are!"

Rachel watched three carriages come up the long drive. She knew the first would contain Jeremy and Catherine and the second their servants. The third would hold trunks for clothing and provide adequate room when she and Leah returned to Eversleigh. The house party ended tomorrow but they were to stay an extra day before leaving for home.

The first carriage pulled up and came to a stop. The footman opened the door and before he could place any steps down, Jeremy bounded from the coach. He reached and captured Catherine's waist, swinging her to the ground. A pang of envy rose within Rachel. She knew what it was like to have Merrick's hands on her waist. The way it made her breathing shallow and caused butterflies to beat wildly within her belly.

"Darlings!" Catherine cried, wriggling from Jeremy's hold. She raced to both Rachel and Leah and threw her arms about them. "It's wonderful to see you."

"We've only been gone a week," Leah pointed out. "How are the wedding plans going?"

"Everything is on schedule but I will be ready to have you back at Eversleigh. There are so many things I wish to have your approval on before going forward."

Leah tugged on Catherine to come greet Alford. Rachel noticed Merrick had come out with them and quickly turned to her brother.

Jeremy smiled and embraced her. With him being eleven years older, he'd served more as a father figure to her over the years.

"I'm happy to see you, Rachel." His emerald St. Clair eyes twinkled. "Did you and Leah behave yourselves?"

She slipped her hand through the crook of his arm. "I can't speak for Leah. I'm afraid she's already doing all kinds of naughty things with Alford that I've caught you and Catherine at the past two years."

He grinned. "And I hope to be doing those same naughty things with my wife until they place me in my grave. What of you?" He looked at her expectantly.

"No, I haven't fallen in love, if that's what you're asking."

He shrugged. "It will happen, sweetness. Don't rush it. Don't look for it. Love will find you."

As she pulled him away from the coach, her gaze connected with Merrick's. Rachel swallowed and led Jeremy toward Alford. The two greeted one another and Alford introduced his friend to the duke.

"When Alford last spoke of you, he said you were still on the Iberian Peninsula with your regiment," Jeremy noted.

"I was until a week ago, Your Grace. I sold my commission and will live at my country estate, just to the north of Fairfield. Your sister has been kind enough to help me in hiring servants for Edgemere, as well as having a hand in designing new gardens for the estate."

Jeremy laughed and patted Rachel's arm. "This woman should be a general, Lord Merrick. She has the heart of a lion and would gladly ride into battle for a cause she believed in. I'm assuming your household is now up and running smoothly, with the best servants available staffing it."

Merrick nodded. "It is, indeed, Your Grace. Lady Rachel is more organized than any military officer of my acquaintance."

"I'm glad to hear it," Jeremy said.

"Come along, St. Clairs," Alford said. "Let's get you and your things inside."

"I'll show everyone to their chambers," Leah interjected. "And then I want to take Catherine and Jeremy on a tour of the house. Luke, too, if you'd like."

Luke shrugged. "I'd rather see the stables and estate. I'm not much for looking over drawing rooms and kitchens."

Alford laughed. "Then I will allow my beautiful fiancée to conduct the house tour."

Jeremy asked, "Could I join the men? I'm afraid one bedchamber looks like the next to me. I'd much rather see your horseflesh and view your livestock and crops."

Leah sighed. "Very well. You men go do manly things. Rachel, come with Catherine and me. We have so much to talk about."

The men turned to go. Rachel could feel Merrick's eyes burning into her.

"Lady Rachel enjoys riding so much. Perhaps she would rather join the men?" he said.

She gave Merrick a cool look and replied, "I'd rather not ride with the ball happening tonight. I want to conserve my strength for all the dancing I plan to do. I'll accompany Leah and Catherine. Thank you for the invitation, though."

Rachel hurried to catch up with the Crawford sisters as they entered the house. She planned to do more than dance tonight.

She was eager to put her kissing lessons to good use.

CHAPTER FIFTEEN

RACHEL DRESSED WITH care for the ball. Not only would Alford's houseguests attend, but he had invited of bevy of neighbors up to twenty miles away in order to give Leah the chance to meet everyone—and shine. Some of these same guests would attend the wedding between the earl and his fiancée at Eversleigh once October came.

A maid had taken over Leah's toilette while another fussed over how to style Leah's hair. Rachel waited until her friend was completely dressed and sat to have her hair arranged before claiming the maid's services in helping her to prepare for the evening.

She started with her linen chemise. Its open, square neckline fit well with the dress she'd brought for the ball. It was a favorite of hers, one she'd worn twice during the Season. Next, she slipped into her corset, which had minimal boning that supported her breasts. It fell long enough to flatten her stomach, which she didn't really need. Though she possessed a healthy appetite, she got plenty of exercise. Catherine had told her once she had children, things might change. Rachel pushed that thought away as she lifted the shoulder straps and asked for help in tightening the corset enough so that the cups supported her without squishing her breasts together.

Once finished, she allowed the lady's maid to lift her gown over her head and she slid her arms into it before draping and smoothing the dress. It was actually two pieces that she'd had sewn together, the bottom one a soft shade of pale gold satin that dominated the skirt, while the upper layer was a deep emerald green, the exact shade of her eyes. The green was cut away to reveal the gold and Rachel thought the colors blended together beautifully.

She sat in a chair and pulled on opaque, silk stockings in the same unusual shade of pale gold. Her flat, satin slippers of emerald had decorative gold ribbons that laced up her calves. She reached for the cameo that hung from an emerald satin ribbon and fastened it about her neck. Last, she slid on the long, white, kid gloves that went slightly above her elbows.

She remained seated and watched as Leah finished getting ready. Her friend wore a gown of deep green trimmed with gold rosettes. The gown itself brought out her deep, green eyes and looked marvelous with her golden hair, piled high atop her head. Leah's cheeks were already flushed with excitement.

"You look beautiful," Rachel proclaimed. "Alford is a lucky man."

"Your turn," her friend said, instructing the maid how she wanted Rachel's hair to be styled in a similar fashion to hers.

She took a seat and let the maid artfully arrange her hair. Looking into the small hand mirror, Rachel was satisfied that she looked her best. For her. *Not* for Merrick.

"Let's go downstairs so we can join the receiving line," Leah said, slipping her arm through Rachel's and leading her from the room.

"I see no need for me to be in a receiving line."

"Well, I do," Leah said emphatically. "I want all of my family to meet my new neighbors. I've even asked for a chair to be placed at the end so Cor won't have to stand for too long. Besides, it will go quickly. None of Alex's houseguests will go through it. It will only be the surrounding neighbors which I haven't met yet. And who knows? You might be attracted to some wonderful gentleman who introduces himself to us. Wouldn't it be fun, Rachel, if you married someone in the neighborhood? Then we wouldn't have to be parted at all. We could see each other all the time."

She doubted she would be drawn to any man but smiled as Leah continued to babble. She would not dampen her closest friend's happiness. Rachel determined not only to act happy tonight but be happy. She adored dancing, especially country dancing, which was a nonstop whirlwind. Of course, she doubted Merrick would dance. She hadn't noticed him favoring his wounded leg lately but lively dancing would most likely aggravate it. That was a good thing. She wouldn't have to dance with him. Look across and face him. Have their fingers touch. She would be free to enjoy the evening.

Especially kissing someone.

Rachel was determined to try out her lessons tonight. Perhaps, she would meet some eligible bachelor in the receiving line. Or allow one of Alford's houseguests to escort her to the terrace and see if kissing any of them appealed to her. Merrifield had been most attentive. He might be one she decided to kiss. He was very handsome and intelligent. If the opportunity arose, she would certainly kiss him.

They arrived at the entrance to the ballroom and saw Jeremy and Catherine already standing with Alford. Cor was next to them in a chair. Luke rushed in and joined them.

"Sorry. Am I late?"

"No," Leah assured him. "We just arrived."

"Good. I'm looking forward to meeting your neighbors. Especially the pretty ones." Luke grinned. "Any I should be watching for, Alford?"

The earl glanced to Leah. "My fiancée is the only pretty one in this neighborhood. Every other woman is only tolerable."

"Splendid answer, Alford," Jeremy said. "I see Leah already has you well trained."

The arrivals began after that. For half an hour, a steady stream of people who resided in the area came through the receiving line. Rachel found two prospects from the group, both bachelors who looked to be in their late twenties. She hoped she would have an opportunity to dance with both.

Since it was a country ball, no dances would be reserved. Rachel preferred the spontaneity of that. She danced with two of the houseguests and three of Alford's neighbors before taking a much needed rest. She'd partnered with Viscount Michaels for the most recent dance and he led her to the punch bowl, retrieving a cup for each of them. They strolled out the terrace doors once they finished their drinks to get some fresh air.

Rachel decided Michaels was interesting enough to kiss. Not with her tongue. Merrick had warned her of that. She knew only to kiss someone she really wanted to—and then only use her tongue if the attraction was there. She doubted that would happen tonight. Merrick, the bloody fool, still held her heart. It would take time to heal from the invisible wounds he'd caused. In the meantime, she would do her best to recover on her own.

And not look at him across the ballroom. No matter how much she wanted to.

Michaels led her at an easy pace as they spoke. She'd already learned he lived seven miles from Fairfield and that he cared for his elderly parents. That he enjoyed riding and was fascinated by breeding horses.

He was the first one she would kiss.

They reached the far end of the terrace. As the viscount made the turn, Rachel stopped. She licked her lips, something she knew had always quickened Merrick's blood. She hoped her eyes also conveyed her wish to be kissed.

Apparently, Michaels received her wordless message. His hands lightly grasped her shoulders as he bent and brushed his lips softly against hers.

She felt nothing.

He began to pull away and she ordered, "Again, please."

A startled look crossed his face and then he smiled. Michaels had a very nice smile. He also enjoyed riding and lived close to Fairfield. Those were three definite factors in his favor. Rachel doubted it was enough to base a marriage upon—but it was a start.

This time, his grasp on her tightened. His kiss wasn't as chaste. It was firmer. She relaxed her mouth as Merrick had taught her and Michaels actually slipped his tongue in briefly. Rachel kept her own tongue still, not wishing to mate with his, merely interested to see what feelings might be stirred.

Again, nothing.

He broke the kiss, his eyes darker than before. She supposed that was due to passion.

Sadly, she told him, "We won't be kissing again, Lord Michaels."

He smiled ruefully. "I suspected as much, Lady Rachel. I must say, I've never had a woman be so bold before. Why did you ask me to kiss you twice?"

"To make certain. I am searching for a husband. I need to know that I satisfy him as much as he satisfies me. Especially when we kiss. You kiss very well, my lord. I just don't think you're the one for me."

The viscount laughed. "Well, I'm glad we cleared that up."

"You are a most marvelous dancer though. Very light on your feet." She offered him a smile, extending an olive branch to him. "And I very much would still like to dance with you."

He threw back his head and laughed. "You are a delight, my lady. Come. Let us dance again."

They returned to the ballroom and danced another time. Supper was served after that and she went and sat with her family.

"Have you found any beauties that appeal to you?" she asked Luke.

He grinned. "A few. How about you?"

"No one that strikes my fancy, though I have found a few good dance partners."

She noticed that Merrick sat in the corner as he ate. Though he was with several of this week's houseguests, he didn't seem to be adding much to the conversation. Rachel turned away. Merrick was none of her business, just as she was not any of his. She could kiss anyone she wanted without his approval. She could even stay on the shelf and never wed if she chose. It was important that she do what made her happy.

Even if she felt miserable.

It disappointed her that no waltz had been played but she understood that most country residents disapproved of the foreign dance. After supper, Rachel danced several more times until she found herself out of breath. Her current partner, Lord Merrifield, asked if she wanted to rest.

"Or we could step out for a breath of fresh air," he suggested.

He had been one of the candidates that she'd considered kissing. She decided now was as good a time as any to do so.

"That would be lovely," she replied, smiling sweetly at him.

Once again, she strolled with him along the terrace, though two other couples also had the same idea. Merrifield slowly guided her to the far corner. It was obvious what was on the earl's mind.

"Are you going to try and kiss me, Lord Merrifield?" she asked coyly.

"Only if you let me, Lady Rachel," he said smoothly.

He was one of the most handsome men present tonight. He had beautiful manners and had pursued her over the last week. From what he said, his estate was nice. He also had a sister and brother he spoke of fondly. Rachel supposed she might as well kiss him.

She smiled. "I will oblige you in one kiss. No more," she said primly.

"One is all I'll need."

With that, his hands spanned her waist and he stepped close to her. His mouth came down hard, no gentle exploring to start. She started to protest and that gave him the opportunity to slip his tongue inside her mouth.

He was skilled. She'd give him that. Lord Merrifield knew exactly what he was doing. She briefly allowed her tongue to touch his to see if they had a spark. His hands tightened on her waist and he deepened the kiss.

It was a terrific kiss—if she hadn't already known Merrick's.

Merrifield smelled wonderful. He tasted of mint. He was intuitive enough to know what a woman needed. His kiss was much better than Michaels'.

But not as moving as Merrick's.

She had to forget Merrick.

If she could.

Rachel broke the kiss, out of breath. Merrifield's eyes gleamed and his smile showed those lovely, even, white teeth of his.

"Is anyone courting you, Lady Rachel?" he asked huskily, his hands still holding her waist.

"No."

"Hmm. I thought Merrick might be. You've spent quite a bit of time with him this past week. I thought I sensed something between you."

"We have been thrown together. I love organizing things and have helped him get Edgemere up and running. Merrick has no other woman in his life—no mother, no sister—who could aid him. I was happy to help Alford's closest friend because of Leah."

His thumbs began stroking her. "May I court you?"

Rachel's heart still hurt too much to allow any man to grow close to her. Still, Merrifield had great potential. He was kind. He was rich. He made her laugh.

"I won't be having anyone try to woo me until next Season," she said. "I want to help Leah with all her wedding arrangements and then I have several family obligations to attend to." She paused. "Will you be in London next spring when the Season begins?"

"I will . . . if you are."

She smiled brightly. "Then I will look forward to getting to know you better then, my lord."

He released her. "Plan on seeing a lot of me, Lady Rachel. I know you enjoy dancing and riding. What about the theatre?"

"It's one of my favorite things to attend while in London."

"Good. Plan on us going to the theatre the first week."

"Only if Jeremy and Catherine accompany us."

Merrifield smiled indulgently. "That can be arranged." He offered her his arm. "Shall we return inside?"

Rachel slipped her hand through the crook of his arm and accompanied him as they slowly strolled toward the French doors leading to the ballroom. As they entered, she glanced around.

And saw Merrick glaring at her.

Chapter Sixteen

Evan had never been more miserable in his life. Not when his father all but disowned him. Not when he'd fought the enemy in the mud and rain and cold. Not even when he'd lost men in battle.

His dejection was all because of Rachel St. Clair.

She was stunning tonight, in some concoction that made her look alluring and unattainable. She had danced almost every dance, her cheeks flushed with excitement as she moved. He'd enjoyed watching her gracefully wind her way around the ballroom with various partners as he'd stood on the sidelines. Evan had no desire to dance.

At least not with anyone but Rachel.

She hadn't looked in his direction once, blithely ignoring him. He'd avoided being near Alford when the butler announced supper because he knew his friend would encourage him to dine at his table, full of St. Clairs. Instead, he'd retreated to the opposite side of the room and watched her from the corner of his eye.

Rachel had already left the ballroom once with Viscount Michaels. They'd returned a short while later. Evan wondered if they'd kissed and assumed they had. He knew her well enough to figure she would want to test out her new skills. She amiably parted with Michaels after another dance and hadn't danced with him since. Relief had washed through Evan.

Now, though, she'd just finished dancing with that bloody Merrifield, who'd panted after her like a dog in heat all week. He was just the sort of man that Rachel might consider kissing. Evan had no way to stop her because he had no claim on her—but he could satisfy his curiosity. Without drawing attention to himself, he left the ballroom and exited the house by its front door. Making his way around the house, he arrived at the rear of the country home. The terrace sat above him. Knowing Merrifield's type, he waited at the far left end, which seemed to him darker than the opposite side.

Sure enough, he heard the familiar voice that tugged at his heartstrings and knew Rachel and Merrifield approached. He held his breath—and heard Rachel ask if Merrifield was going to kiss her. The bastard said one kiss was all he needed. Rage coursed through Evan as their conversation ceased for a long time. Knowing what they were doing. Knowing the little fool was allowing the earl to kiss her in a way that could lead to other things.

Then Merrifield asked to court her, wondering if Evan already did. Rachel breezily explained that she'd merely helped him get Edgemere up and running.

Her words stabbed in his heart more painfully than any French sabre.

Then she surprised him, telling Merrifield that she didn't want anyone courting her until next Season. Evan wondered why she put the nobleman off, especially since she'd kissed him for so long. Was it her way of letting him down gently? If so, why make plans to attend the theatre with the man next spring?

Rachel St. Clair confused—and exasperated—him to no end.

Quickly, he left the post where he eavesdropped and hurried back to the ballroom. He went to the punch bowl and ordered a cup for himself, downing it quickly and setting the cup aside. Evan turned to watch for Rachel and Merrifield to reappear.

When they did, he did not bother to disguise his fury.

She spied him immediately. Her lips parted as if she would speak to him, even from a great distance. Then somehow, she thought better of it and turned away. A new dance was beginning and Merrifield led her back onto the ballroom's floor, where they joined a line of others.

Evan paced the edges of the ballroom through that dance and several more. He came to stand next to the musicians and asked a man holding a violin how much longer they'd play.

"The next number is our last, my lord," the violinist said. "Lord Alford has requested a waltz. I only hope he won't be vilified by his neighbors when the strains of it begin."

A waltz...

He could waltz. He was a passable dancer. The waltz wasn't nearly as spirited as the many country dances that had played tonight.

Determined to dance with Rachel, he found her on the dance floor again as the music came to an end. She separated from her partner and moved in the direction of her brother and his wife. Evan had studied the Duke and Duchess of Everton off and on throughout the night. It was obvious the pair was madly in love. He knew they had a set of twins and yet the couple still acted as if newly wed. No wonder Rachel's head had been filled with notions of love, having seen the example her brother and sister-in-law set, not to mention how obsessed Alex and Lady Leah were with one another.

Evan strode in Rachel's direction and reached her before the music began.

He bowed. "Would you do me the honor of dancing the final dance with me, Lady Rachel?" he asked formally.

She seemed bemused so he took her hand and placed it upon his arm, immediately escorting her to the center of the room as the strains of the waltz began. He took her hand in his and placed his arm around her waist, inhaling her perfume as he stepped into the dance.

"You look lovely tonight, Rachel," he said.

Warily, she stared into his eyes. "I believe I am Lady Rachel to you, my lord."

"Even after our lessons?" he asked, smiling at her lazily.

"Especially after them," she said dismissively. "No one is to know of those. Ever."

"Have you put them into practice tonight?"

"If I have, it's none of your business," she retorted.

"That means you have. At least with Merrifield. You were gone a long time from the ballroom."

She sniffed. "Merrifield is a gentleman."

"Merrifield is a rutting bastard who's been sniffing around you all week."

Rachel sucked in a quick breath. "You go too far, Merrick."

"Or not far enough," he replied evenly.

She felt good in his arms. Where she was meant to be. Their lessons had ended. It was time he separated the so-called tutoring sessions from their real lives. He definitely wanted Rachel St. Clair in his. Maybe he'd kept her too much at a distance, passionate during their lessons and then cool apart from them. He realized that he'd never given her any indication of how he felt toward her. Perhaps, she pushed him away because she had those same feelings, too, and doubted he reciprocated them.

It was time to act upon them. Now.

The music finished playing. Evan gazed deeply into her eyes.

"We must talk." He left no room for refusal.

He wove through the couples on the dance floor. There would be chaos now as others looked for those they'd come with, saying their goodnights to the earl and either going to their carriages or their bedchambers upstairs. Someone might see them if they headed toward the schoolroom. He couldn't take that chance.

Instead, he swept Rachel out the doors and down the steps of the terrace. As they crossed the wide expanse of lawn, she tried to slow him.

"Where are we going?" she demanded.

"Somewhere quiet. Where we can talk without others listening."

Somewhat mollified, she began walking again.

They reached the gardens, where two lanterns burned, one on each side of the entrance. Evan snatched one and took her down the path. He remembered how fond she'd been of Fairfield's gazebo and had mentioned sitting in it late at night or early in the morning, inhaling the intoxicating blossoms that surrounded the structure.

When they reached it, he stepped inside and pulled her along. Setting the lantern on the ground in front of them, he tugged on her so they sat side by side on a bench.

Immediately, she crossed her arms in front of her. "What is so important, Lord Merrick, that you needed to drag me all the way out to the gardens to discuss it?"

She was being prickly. Evan decided words would never disarm her.

He would show her instead of tell her how he felt about her. How he didn't want a day without her in it. As a man hardened by war, he couldn't use pretty words of love because he still was uncertain if that's what he felt for her or not.

But he needed her as much as he'd show her that she needed him.

His hand went to the nape of her neck to hold her firmly in place. The other stroked her cheek gently. Rachel's eyes widened. Evan lowered his lips to hers and kissed her softly. More kisses followed, each one longer than before, beating back her resistance. He sensed the moment it crumbled and coaxed her lips apart.

She tasted like warm sunshine and everything good in life. She tasted like Rachel.

His arm went around her, his hand running up and down the length of her back. He took his time, not wanting to rush her, gradually drawing her in until he heard one of those little sighs that made his heart quicken. With that, he pulled her into his lap and deepened the kiss. She wasn't an active participant yet but he knew that would come. Her resolve was fading. And then it shattered and

Rachel was kissing him with abandon. Her fingers pushed into his hair and tightened in it, as if she would never let go. Her tongue warred with his as they both sought to dominate the other. Evan tightened his arms about her, promising himself to never let her go.

They kissed until he couldn't breathe unless it was a breath he stole from her. He tore his lips from hers and then nipped at them, licking as he went to soothe her. He kissed the long column of her throat and then the sweet spot where her neck and shoulder joined. Her sigh carried in the night air. His hand cupped her breast, squeezing lightly as he felt it swell. He dragged the pad of his thumb back and forth across her nipple, causing her to whimper. Her fingers tugged on his hair, pushing his head toward her breast and he knew what she desired.

Evan pushed the material covering her breasts down and caught sight of the swell of them. His tongue traced that swell as Rachel's fingers kneaded his scalp and his hands kneaded her breasts. Her bottom squirmed against him, causing his manhood to spring to life. He returned to kissing her mouth as one hand slipped under the hem of her dress and glided along the satin of her calf. Her fingers relaxed and then she wound her arms about his neck, kissing him wildly, with a passion he'd never known from any woman.

His fingers danced up her leg. He stopped just shy of the curls protecting her womanly core.

She broke the kiss, her eyes glazed with need. "Please," she whispered, and then kissed along his jaw.

Hot desire ran through him and he captured her lips again with his as his finger teased the seam of her sex. Rachel moaned as he entered her with two fingers, stroking her, enflaming her. She moved against him, sounds of want coming from the back of her throat. He would satisfy her in every way he could. Physically, they were perfectly matched. She would see the evidence of that tonight—and then he would ask her to become his wife.

Evan toyed with her, teasing with both lips and fingers, withdrawing and claiming her, over and over, until Rachel writhed against him. He sensed her orgasm nearing and caressed her deeply. She shattered in his arms, crying out her pleasure, his kiss muffling it as best as he could. Her pleasure was his one mission in life and Evan knew he had exceeded her expectations. She collapsed against him, her lips parting from his as she placed her cheek against his chest. He stroked her once more, wishing he could fully take her, but knowing that time would soon come.

Suddenly, a voice cried out, "What in bloody hell are you doing to my sister?"

CHAPTER SEVENTEEN

RACHEL PLACED HER cheek against Evan's beating heart, dazed by everything that had just taken place. Then, from out of nowhere, someone shouted and ripped her from Evan's lap, forcefully tossing her onto the bench next to him. She saw Jeremy jerk Evan to his feet. Her brother smashed his fist into Evan's face and a loud crunch sounded. Immediately, blood spurted everywhere and Rachel knew Evan's nose had been broken.

In horror, she watched Jeremy slam his fist into Evan's face, over and over, even as the marquess kept his hands to his sides, refusing to defend himself. She leaped to her feet and jumped between them.

"Stop!" she cried. "You're killing him."

Rage filled her brother's face. Fortunately, he contained it and halted his next blow. If not, she would have been sporting a broken cheekbone. Catherine came and pulled Jeremy back a few feet as Evan collapsed onto the bench.

"You have ruined my sister," Jeremy spat out. "You will leave in the morning for London to obtain a special license."

Rachel saw resignation on Evan's face as he nodded in agreement. Nausea filled her. She loved Evan. Everything about him. But he didn't love her. They had an amazing physical attraction between them but the Marquess of Merrick had never given her any indication that he felt anything beyond that. She couldn't marry a man who didn't love her. She wouldn't see him forced to marry her. If she trapped him in this way, neither of them would ever find happiness.

"No."

Jeremy snapped his head toward her. "No?"

"No," Rachel said firmly. "There is to be no special license. No wedding."

Her brother pulled away from Catherine and placed his hands gently on her shoulders. "Rachel, this man has compromised you. He must wed you, the sooner the better."

Resolve filled her. "I asked him to do what he did."

"What?"

Anguish filled her. "I have seen how madly in love you and Catherine are. How Leah and Alford look at one another. I've barely been kissed, Jeremy. I wanted to see what it was all about. Merrick only kissed me because I asked him to."

Jeremy scowled. "He did far more than kiss you."

"I know. I was curious. I begged him. But rest assured, I am not compromised. Merrick did touch me but we did not have relations."

"Still, he—"

She jerked away, fire blazing within her now. "Listen to me, Jeremy St. Clair. Get it through that thick skull of yours. I *will not* marry this man. Special license or not. If you force me to stand with him in front of a clergyman, I will merely embarrass you for I will remain silent. I'll not take vows with a man I don't love."

Rachel took her brother's hand. "You know I want a love match. It's why I didn't choose any of the gentlemen I met during the Season. Because I wasn't in love. I would rather sit on the shelf and be a doting aunt to all my nieces and nephews than compromise myself by marrying a man I don't love. Would you force me into a marriage that I would be miserable in? Waking up every day to a man I had no desire to be around for decades? Have children with a man I didn't love?"

She crossed her arms. "You won't. You love me too much to do that." She waved her hands in the air. "Look around. No one present at Fairfield saw us here tonight. Everyone is saying their goodbyes to Alford and Leah. They are sorting their way to their carriages or going upstairs and falling exhausted into bed. Only you two saw what happened, I assume because you also had naughty plans."

Her brother flushed but didn't deny her words.

"If every party here promises to bury this, then it will stay buried. No one need ever know what took place tonight. I will be free. Free to find a man I love. I am still a virgin. Still intact. My wedding night with the man I love can take place successfully without anyone the wiser."

She squeezed his hand. "Please, Jeremy. Please. Let us put this incident behind us. Merrick is not the man I love. He's not the man I wish to marry and spend the rest of my life with."

Knowing her brother as well as she did, Rachel saw when he gave in. Obviously, he wasn't happy about it, but at least he could see her reasoning.

"Very well. But not a word to Leah. It would distress her. And she'd only tell Alford. We must agree that this remains between the four of us." Jeremy glared at Evan. "Do you understand, Merrick?"

Rachel finally looked in his direction. Blood covered the front of him. Already, one eye had swollen shut. His nose sat crooked and bruises covered his face. She watched him nod in agreement.

"You're never to speak to Rachel again. Never even be in the same room with her," Jeremy instructed.

"That will be a little hard to pull off," she noted. "He's Alford's best friend and will stand with him at the wedding ceremony."

Her brother's face darkened. "Alford would have too many questions if you refused. I can't have that." At that moment, Jeremy drew himself up as haughtily as any duke who'd ever lived. "You will make some excuse and not come to Eversleigh until the morning of the wedding. You may go directly to the St. Clair Chapel. I'll even grant you admission to the wedding breakfast—but you will stay away from Rachel. Don't look at her. Don't speak to her. Make your wedding toast and then quietly slip away. Is that understood?"

"Yes, Your Grace."

Catherine slipped an arm about Rachel. "Come, Rachel. Let's return to the house."

She led Rachel away from the gazebo. Away from the only man Rachel would ever love. Each footstep that separated them was as a knife plunged into her heart. Jeremy silently followed behind them.

No tears came. She felt numb, as if some great cold had invaded her body and left a frozen Rachel behind. One who could move but had no feeling.

They reached the house and entered through the French doors. Catherine held on to her until they reached the bedchamber she shared with Leah.

"I know how difficult this will be for you," Catherine said. "For your reputation, though, you must follow through and play your part." She framed Rachel's face with her hands. "I know you are hurting but you are doing the right thing by waiting to marry a man you love." She kissed Rachel's brow. "I think it best we never speak of this again."

She nodded in agreement, the effort to form words too difficult.

"Goodnight," Jeremy said. He kissed her brow tenderly.

Rachel couldn't look at him. She entered the bedchamber and closed the door. Leah sat unpinning her hair.

"There you are. I wondered where you'd gone off to. Oh, it took forever to get everyone out the door. I adore Alex's neighbors. They were so welcoming, weren't they?"

Leah had barely glanced at Rachel when she entered. She steeled herself and sat, unpinning her own hair. Leah turned and studied her.

"Are you all right? You look odd."

Rachel mustered a smile. "I'm so tired. You saw me tonight. I danced almost every dance."

Her friend grinned mischievously. "I saw you leave the ballroom.

Twice."

"Yes. I took some air with Lord Michaels."

"He seemed very nice." Leah gave her a hopeful look. "I understand he lives nearby."

She sighed. "He does. He even kissed me. I didn't feel anything, though."

Disappointment shadowed Leah's face. "What about Merrifield?"

Rachel forced herself to smile again. "That is more promising. He also kissed me. It was much better than Michaels' kiss."

"I like Merrifield. He makes me laugh."

She nodded. "He does, doesn't he? He seems interested in me."

"He should be. You are a fascinating person, Rachel. I hope you'll give Merrifield a chance."

"I think I will. I asked if he would take part in next Season and he assured he would—if I did."

"Oh!" Leah exclaimed. "That's an excellent sign."

By now, Rachel's hair was down. She and Leah assisted one another out of their gowns and dressed in their night rails for bed.

Rachel turned away from Leah and soon heard the soft puffs of breath that let her know Leah had fallen asleep.

Only then did she allow her silent tears to fall.

THE FIRST THING Evan did once the trio departed was place his hands on both sides of his crooked nose and yank hard. Tears came to his eyes, but he felt the nose sitting back where it should. He'd had to do the same for others while in the army. The pain from his swelling nose, though, was insignificant compared to the heartache filling him.

Rachel didn't love him.

As hard as it was to admit, the beauty had never loved him. What they had was a grand, physical attraction to one another. He, above anyone, knew not to confuse passion for love. What his heart told him, though, was that he did love her. Evan had never loved anyone.

Until now.

How ironic that he had been the one who didn't want a wife or family. It had been acceptable to him for his title and lands to pass to some distant Drake in the future. He'd come home from the war unhappy—and had found happiness with a divine creature. On his deathbed, he would remember Rachel's kiss. The feel of her satin skin. The taste of her. Always.

And he would spend the rest of his life in love with a woman who didn't return his feelings.

Why had love come now? Like a thief in the midnight hour, Rachel St. Clair had stolen his heart. Evan would never be the same again.

He couldn't blame her, though. She'd spoken of how important it was for her to wed a man she loved. If she experienced none of those feelings for him, she would have become melancholy and dejected being tied to him for life. Evan had to be glad that the Duke of Everton loved his sister so much that he would allow tonight's incident to be swept under the rug, thus allowing Rachel the freedom to find a man worthy of her love.

That was the problem. He wasn't worthy of a woman as magnificent as Rachel. She must have recognized how damaged he was from the war. If anything, she probably pitied him. The thought chilled him. He would rather have her indifference—even hate—than pity.

How was he going to be able to see her again? Everton was right. Alex would do more than question Evan if he refused to attend the wedding and stand with him. They were closer than brothers. No explanation would prove worthy. That meant seeing Rachel again. He would certainly honor Everton's wishes and not speak to her.

But she would be standing at the altar. Next to Leah. Evan wouldn't be able to avoid her. It would take more courage than he'd ever displayed on a battlefield to be in close proximity to her as the clergyman spoke words about love to Alex and Leah. Evan would do it, though. He would soldier on as he always had. Whether it was dealing with being banished by his father to charging onto the battlefield, he would support Alex on his friend's wedding day. Evan would give a toast that all would remember.

Then he'd leave to go lick his wounds in solitude.

He rose, his body aching and his face tender from the blows Everton had landed. The important thing was to be seen by no one. In his condition, too many unanswered questions would be dangling. Evan had nothing of value in his bedchamber at Fairfield, only the borrowed clothes from Alex. His new wardrobe would be arriving soon at Edgemere, within a day or two. He would leave for there now. Once he arrived home, he could compose a note to Alex and tell him he'd returned home since the house party was ending in the morning. That way, no guest would see what he looked like.

Wearily, Evan made his way back through the gardens, remembering the drawings Rachel had done for him. He could leave them behind for he recalled every suggestion she'd made, her sketches burned into his memory. She would never see them but he would bring her vision to its full glory.

Exiting the gardens, he went to the stables and saddled Goliath, leading the huge black outside before mounting it. Enough moonlight shone to light his way home but he would walk the horse the entire way. He'd invested far too much in the animal to be careless.

As he slowly went down the road toward Edgemere, he tried to close his mind and damaged heart to Rachel.

CHAPTER EIGHTEEN

RACHEL LOOKED UP as their butler entered the drawing room. Before he could speak, Leah leaped from her seat.

"He's here!" she cried as she ran across the room and out the door.

Cor grunted. "Young love. I'll wait here and ring for tea."

Catherine looked at Rachel as they both stood. "Shall we take our time going to greet Lord Alford in order for the lovebirds to have a proper reunion?"

She laughed. "My advice is to walk slowly but not give them too much time, Catherine. You know whether we go out in two minutes or twenty-two minutes, they'll still be kissing."

The duchess chuckled. "I'm pleased my sister has found her soulmate. Both Jeremy and I like Alford quite a bit. They will be good for each other."

"I know they'll have angelic-looking children."

The two made their way from the drawing room and went outside. The October day was cool and overcast. Just as Rachel predicted, Alford had enfolded Leah in his arms and the two passionately kissed. A multitude of feelings ran through her. Rachel had kissed Merrick that same way during their midnight hours together. Seeing this happy couple made her sad. A bit envious. Most of all, hurt. She still loved Merrick and hadn't made peace with the fact that he only desired her without feeling any love for her. A tiny part of her almost wished she had let Jeremy force them into marriage. At least then they would have had a satisfying physical relationship. Merrick could also have given her children to love, which would have made up for the lack of his affection toward her.

Yet deep inside, Rachel knew his unhappiness at becoming her husband would have ultimately done them in. She doubted she could have lived with his growing bitterness, being tied to a woman he didn't care for.

Catherine gently cleared her throat and Alford broke the kiss, looking up in astonishment as if he hadn't realized other people existed beyond him and Leah. He released his fiancée and came toward them.

"Your Grace. Lady Rachel."

Catherine clucked her tongue. "We are to be family in two days' time. Don't you think it's about time you called us Catherine and Rachel?"

Alford looked hesitant but said, "Then I am Alex."

"Is something wrong?" Rachel asked, having a good idea what bothered the earl.

"It's just . . . well, when I think . . . I mean, perhaps I could practice calling you Catherine and Rachel in private first. I'm not certain how Everton . . . that is, His Grace, might feel about it."

Catherine laughed. "Oh, Jeremy is a pussycat, Alex. He only glares like a duke should when in public."

Alex nodded. "That's it. It's the glare. When His Grace looks at me, it's as if I'm . . . stealing something valuable from him."

Leah slipped her hand through Alex's arm. "Just think, Rachel. I'm only his sister-in-law. Think how he'll glare when a man wishes to wed his own sister."

Rachel laughed with the others but her smile fell as she turned away and went back into the house. Catherine directed them to the drawing room and the earl greeted Cor.

"Where is His Grace?" Alex asked.

"My brothers are out doing manly things," Rachel said. "They went to examine a horse that's gone lame. Look at a fencepost that might need repair. I also think they were going to ride out to look at a cottage roof that possibly should be replaced."

"So Mayfield has already arrived?" Alex asked.

"Yes, Luke came only last night," she informed him.

He looked to Leah. "The rest of our guests will show up sometime tomorrow?"

"Yes. Then the wedding is the day after. Oh, I can't wait."

The tea cart arrived and Catherine poured for everyone. Cor suggested Alex try Cook's blueberry scones, claiming them to be the best she'd ever eaten.

"I do know my way around a scone. I've had decades of consuming them."

"You are ageless, Cor," Alex complimented. "If I hadn't fallen in love with Leah, I might have decided to woo you instead."

Her grandmother's lips twitched in amusement and Rachel knew Cor, too, was pleased with the match between the couple.

The earl caught them up on all of the local gossip around his estate and the nearby village. Leah hung on his every word and she commented about several of the people she'd met at both the house party and the ball that he'd held at Fairfield. After several minutes, talk turned to Leah's wedding gown and a last-minute change in the lace. Rachel saw Alex's eyes start to glaze over so she decided to engage him in a separate conversation.

"Have you decided on where you will honeymoon?" she asked. "Leah said you are keeping her in the dark about where you plan to take her."

"Are you the spy sent to wring the information from me?" he asked teasingly.

"No, just merely curious. You can tell me, you know. Although Leah and I may be joined at the hip, I do know how to keep a secret."

"I'll never tell," he proclaimed laughingly. Then he grew serious.

"You might be able to help me with something else, though, Rachel."

"I'd be happy to," she said eagerly.

"It's Evan."

She kept her features composed though her gut clenched painfully. "What's wrong with Lord Merrick?"

"I thought with him being home from the war we would see each other frequently. Since the house party, I've only been to Edgemere one time. For dinner. And he hasn't come to Fairfield at all."

"I'm sure Merrick still has much to do to acclimate himself to civilian life and running his estate," she said guardedly.

"It's not just that. He drank at dinner. Evan has never been much of a drinker in the past. Some when we were at university and out carousing but not nearly as much as other students. In fact, he was already tipsy when I arrived and continued to drink heavily during our dinner. It's not like him."

"Maybe the ghosts of his past have caught up with him. The war may have affected him more than you know, Alex. Especially being wounded."

"You know of that?" he asked, his surprise evident. "I didn't think he'd shared it with anyone except me."

"It came up while we were at your house party," she said, wishing now that she hadn't mentioned it for it would make Alex believe she and Merrick were closer than she wanted him to know.

"He must trust you a great deal to have spoken of it."

"I think I caught him in a weak moment."

Alex shook his head. "Weak isn't in Evan's vocabulary. He's had to be strong from the beginning, the way Winstead treated him as a boy. And then when the duke cut ties with him, dumping Evan at Edgemere when he was thirteen. Still a boy—expected to do a man's job and run an estate. Fortunately, he had an astute estate manager."

"Yes, I met Mr. Finfrock."

"I know he's gone through more than most men have. His childhood, for one. Evan was more a second son to my parents than ever the first son of Winstead."

"I met Winstead this past Season. He was cold and arrogant."

"That describes him well, though I have heard he can be charming where the ladies are concerned. The war also stained Evan's soul. That's why I'd hoped that you and Evan might make a good match. Leah, too."

Rachel gripped her hands tightly in her lap. "Leah did mention that to me. I'm afraid Merrick will need to deal with whatever demons have him in their grasps before he ever would be interested in marrying. Frankly, I didn't think we'd ever suit."

Alex frowned, his disappointment evident. "To top it off, I wanted him to come with me today to Eversleigh. He put me off. Sent a message that he had urgent business in London and that he wouldn't arrive until the day of the ceremony. It's so out of character for him."

"War changes men," Rachel said softly. "The Merrick who came home isn't the boy you grew up with. Give him time, Alex."

He nodded. "You may be right. I might be pushing too hard. Expecting too much from him that he's not capable of giving yet." He paused. "Would you at least try to talk to him after the wedding? See if you can break through his walls? He seemed to like spending time in your company when you were both at Fairfield."

Knowing how Jeremy had forbidden Merrick from even speaking to her, Rachel didn't see this happening. She couldn't let Alex know, though, without revealing what had occurred in the Fairfield garden.

"I will see if I can help," she said. "I make no promise, though."

He smiled. "It's enough that you'll try. Thank you, Rachel. I will be happy having you and Catherine as my sisters-in-law."

She sensed Catherine staring and turned. The duchess smoothed out the concerned look on her face and said, "I think we've talked enough of lace and wedding gowns. Alex has grown bored," and once again included them in the conversation for several minutes.

"Perhaps my fiancé would care to take a turn in the Eversleigh gardens," Leah finally said, mischief shining in her eyes. "It would do you good to get some exercise after sitting in your coach for so long and then at tea."

"A capital idea," Alex agreed and rose.

Rachel thought most of the exercise involved would include their lips and tongues and stifled a smile.

"I think I shall go and take a nap before dinner," Cor told them and she accompanied the couple from the room.

Once the trio exited, Catherine said, "I heard Merrick's name brought up. What was said?"

"Alex is disappointed that Merrick did not accompany him to Eversleigh today. He begged off and referred to some unforeseeable business that had to be attended to in London." She paused. "He will not arrive until the day of the wedding."

"It's for the best," Catherine said. "Jeremy is very protective of you, Rachel. He means what he says. Do not speak to Merrick while he is here."

Rachel might not speak to him—but avoiding seeing him would be impossible.

RACHEL WATCHED AS Catherine herself dressed Leah's hair. The sisters had toyed with various hairstyles for the past two weeks, trying to decide upon which was most flattering with Leah's wedding gown. With the bride's long, golden tresses, it wouldn't matter. Everything looked good on her.

"No, you need another pin to secure it," Cor advised, sitting next to Leah and supervising Catherine's work.

Rachel believed Cor suspected something was amiss with her but her grandmother had never vocalized her concerns since their return to Eversleigh. In fact, she'd avoided being along with Cor because, if given the chance, her grandmother would get to the root of the problem better than any English officer interrogating one of Bonaparte's spies. Rachel couldn't let that happen. She couldn't ruin Cor's good opinion of her.

A knock sounded on the door.

"That better not be Alex," Rachel commented. "He knows he cannot see the bride."

She went to the door and opened it a crack. Sure enough, the groom stood anxiously in the hallway. Rachel opened it enough to slip outside.

"You cannot see Leah," she gently chided. "Go to the St. Clair chapel. Reverend Smythe is expecting you."

"I know I cannot see her. Can I just hear her voice?" begged the earl.

"I suppose so."

Opening the door enough to stick her head through, Rachel said, "Alex is here. He merely needs to hear your voice, Leah. I believe we have a nervous groom on our hands."

She jumped up, pins spilling everywhere, and rushed to the door. Rachel stepped back, leaving the door slightly ajar.

"Alex? Can you hear me?"

He stepped to the door. "I can, love. I just wanted to hear your voice and tell you I love you."

"I love you more," Leah proclaimed. She snaked her bare arm around the doorjamb and wiggled her fingers.

Alex caught her hand in both of his and kissed her knuckles several times. He released it and it disappeared behind the door again.

"I'll be waiting in the chapel," he said, love spilling from him. He looked to Rachel. "Thank you." He brushed a kiss upon her cheek. "I can go now."

She watched him jauntily walk down the corridor, a lump in her throat. Leah would be well loved by this man.

Entering the room again, she saw Leah seated once more as Catherine tried to repair the damage. Before long, Leah had been transformed. She now slipped on her gloves and slippers and was completely ready to be wed.

Another knock sounded.

"That better not be Alex again," Catherine murmured as Rachel again went to the door and opened it a few inches.

"It's Jeremy," she called over her shoulder and admitted her brother.

He went directly to Leah and said, "A wedding day is very special. Catherine and I wanted you to have something to mark the occasion." He lifted a narrow, rectangular box and opened it.

Inside lay a beautiful pearl necklace and a matching pair of earrings. Rachel recognized them as part of the family jewels.

"Oh!" Leah exclaimed. "It's too much, Jeremy. I cannot accept a gift so grand. These have to be St. Clair jewels—and I am no St. Clair."

Jeremy grew stern. "You may bear the last name Crawford, Leah, but you are every bit a sister to me, Rachel, and Luke. I am a duke and what I say goes. By wearing these today, the world knows that we claim you as one of ours."

Leah burst into tears and Rachel quickly found a handkerchief for her as she sobbed against Jeremy's coat.

"No crying, Leah," he said, taking the handkerchief Rachel offered and wiping the bride's tears away. "Today is a happy day."

Solemnly, Leah said, "I only hope Alex and I can be half as happy as you and Catherine are."

"I doubt anyone will ever be as happy as your sister and I." He grinned. "I'm betting you and Alford might come close, though."

Leah composed herself and said, "I know Alex will give me jewels over the years but I want you and Catherine to know that these will always mean the most to me."

"Here, let me help you," her sister offered and fastened the necklace around Leah's neck.

Once the earrings were in place, Jeremy said, "Carriages have been going back and forth to the St. Clair chapel for the past hour. I'm sure Luke is getting restless downstairs waiting for us to be the last conveyed."

Catherine took Leah's arm and led her from the room.

Cor rose and came to stand in front of Rachel. She cupped her cheek and said, "Your time will come, my dear. I have no doubt."

Rachel knew her time had already come—and passed her by.

Chapter Nineteen

The footman assisted Leah into the carriage and Rachel followed behind her, smoothing Leah's dress to keep it from wrinkling. Cor and Catherine were the other occupants as the vehicle took off for the St. Clair chapel.

"We like your young man," Cor said, patting Leah's knee. "You will make him a fine countess. Tell him I expect great-grandchildren sooner than later. I'm not always going to be around, you know."

Leah put her hand atop Cor's. "I'm glad you approve of Alex, Cor. That means the world to me. You do realize, though, that they won't actually be your great-grandchildren."

Cor looked at her haughtily. "Those jewels in your ears and around your neck show you are a St. Clair. You are as dear to me as my other grandchildren, Leah."

Leah lifted Cor's hand and kissed it tenderly. "Thank you, Cor." She paused. "Who would have thought two bastard daughters of an earl would find such happiness with an earl and a duke?"

Rachel thought back to how Catherine had tried to annul her marriage to Jeremy once she'd learned she wasn't legitimate. She hadn't wanted to embarrass or bring grief to the St. Clair family name. Fortunately, Jeremy had convinced Catherine that their love was stronger than any trite gossip. As a duke, he could behave outlandishly or even eccentrically and society would forgive him most anything. He'd used his immense power to make sure Catherine's cousin never divulged to Polite Society the secret of her and Leah's births.

They arrived at the chapel and, suddenly, Rachel's stomach twisted in knots. The moment she'd dreaded for weeks had arrived. While Lady Leah Crawford spoke her vows to Alexander Lock, Earl of Alford, Rachel would stand by Leah's side in support.

As Merrick would for Alex.

She'd refused to think of him by his Christian name, even when Alex had spoken to her of him. She'd tried not to think of Merrick at all. Of course, she'd failed miserably. In the weeks since they'd returned from Fairfield, Rachel had endured Leah's euphoria, pasting on a smile and holding her tongue from shouting what was in her heart—that she loved Evan Drake beyond what any woman had ever felt for a man.

Leah, bless her heart, hadn't a clue as to Rachel's misery. Privately, she'd joked to herself that if she wished, she could take London by storm by stepping onto any theatre's stage. No other actress could have pulled off the part Rachel now played as they climbed from the carriage and moved toward the chapel.

Jeremy and Luke joined them. Luke took Cor's arm and escorted her into the chapel. Jeremy did the same for Catherine, leaving Rachel standing with Leah.

Leah hugged Rachel tightly. "Thank you for being my sister. My friend. My confidante. My everything."

"Alex will play that role now," Rachel said. "Except for the sister part, of course. I reserve full rights to that."

"Should I be nervous?" Leah asked. "I don't feel nervous at all."

"No. You shouldn't be. Alex is the man for you. He's everything you've wanted. He will love and treasure you." She kissed Leah's cheek. "I'm going inside now. Give me a moment to reach the front."

Rachel steeled herself and entered the chapel. She went to the left and walked up the aisle next to the stained glass windows and took her place at the front, nodding cordially at Reverend Smythe. Deliberately, she turned and faced the doors, not glancing at the two men standing before the clergyman. Her heart pounded erratically and she began taking slow, calming breaths.

Leah appeared in the doorway, sunlight striking her golden hair. The bride had chosen not to wear a veil and the guests gasped in unison, noting how Leah resembled an earthly angel. Warmth filled Rachel, seeing the joy on her friend's face. Alex would take good care of Leah. She had no doubt about the couple's future together.

The organist began playing and Leah floated up the aisle, her gaze focused on her groom. She arrived at the altar and handed her bouquet to Rachel so that she and Alex could join hands. Rachel clutched the flowers tightly, once again looking directly at Reverend Smythe as he began the proceedings.

It didn't mean that she didn't sense Merrick's penetrating gaze. Though she hadn't looked at him, she was aware of his nearness. Rachel almost thought she could smell the sandalwood soap that he used. Still, she refrained from looking at him the entire ceremony, tamping down her growing nausea as things drew to a close.

The clergyman pronounced the pair husband and wife and Alex gave Leah a passionate, lingering kiss. The invited guests broke out in cheers.

"The wedding breakfast will be held at Eversleigh," Reverend Smythe shared. "I need the bride and groom and their two witnesses to come sign the papers to make everything official. Everyone else may return to the waiting carriages."

Rachel followed Reverend Smythe to a small room to the side and was the first to sign the register. She stepped back and embraced Leah, kissing her on both cheeks and doing the same to Alex.

"Congratulations to you both," she said.

Then Jeremy stepped up, blocking her from seeing Merrick. "Come along, Rachel. Cor needs you."

He swept her through a nearby door and she found they were

outside. She could feel her palms becoming damp through her gloves. At least she'd avoided making eye contact with Merrick.

Jeremy led her to the family carriage and handed her up, climbing in after her. The vehicle began moving once he closed the door and she breathed a sigh of relief. The worst was over. She might glimpse Merrick at the wedding breakfast but she wouldn't have to speak to him. Catherine had planned the seating arrangements and placed them on opposite ends of a long table where the bride and groom and the family would sit.

"You'll be the next one at the altar," Luke teased, causing tears to spring to her eyes. "I'm sorry," he said quickly. "Are you sad that you didn't decide to wed at Season's end?"

"No," she reassured him. "It's just that I'm so happy for Leah and Alex. Women cry all kinds of tears, Luke. Tears of joy are as common as those of sadness or anger."

"Hmm. Something tells me I still have much to learn about women," he quipped.

"You might be next," Rachel told him. "Nothing says I have to be the next St. Clair to marry."

Her brother looked horrified. "Why would I do something like that? I'm only twenty-three. I don't plan to settle down for a good decade. Maybe longer."

Cor cleared her throat. "Don't you want to give me great-grandchildren, Luke?"

"You already have three, Cor—Jenny, Timothy, and Delia. Let Jeremy and Catherine give you more. Or even Rachel. I don't want to think of little brats running around, hanging on my legs."

Catherine laughed. "You are impossible, Luke! You adore your nieces and nephew and let them hang on you all the time."

"That's different. I can play with them all I want and then give them back. I'm already having to be responsible enough, learning how to run Fairhaven as the Earl of Mayfield. I don't want the additional responsibility of a wife—or family—for a long time."

Jeremy chuckled. "Love strikes when you least expect it, little brother. Who knows? Next Season, you may find yourself hopelessly in love."

"Then I will avoid Almack's entirely," he proclaimed.

Rachel sniffed. "You're too much of a flirt and enjoy dancing far too much to skip the Season entirely. There aren't any pretty girls at your club. A man can only read the newspapers and play cards and drink whiskey with other men for so long before he seeks out the company of women."

Luke laughed. "When did you become so wise to the ways of men?"

An awkward silence filled the carriage and then Catherine cried, "We're here! Let's hurry. I have a thousand things to tell the staff before the others begin to arrive."

The St. Clairs exited the coach and returned inside. Soon, dozens of guests descended upon them. Rachel spent time going from group to group until the happy couple arrived. Everyone cheered again as Leah and Alex entered.

Then she saw Merrick slip in behind them.

He turned and kept along the wall, avoiding speaking to anyone as he made his way to his seat. Rachel supposed Catherine had somehow gotten word to him where he was to sit because he never looked at a place card before sliding into the chair assigned to him. As the newlyweds made their way to the center of the long table, she helped Catherine and Cor encourage others to begin taking their seats. Once most of the group found one, Rachel ventured to the head table. To Leah's left was Catherine, then Luke, and finally Rachel. On Alex's right was Cor, Jeremy, and Merrick on the end. She had Luke to protect her and Jeremy to prevent Merrick from even glancing her way. She should feel relieved.

Instead, Rachel's misery grew.

To be in the same room with Merrick was hard enough. To want him as badly as she did until she felt sick inside was unbearable. To know they wouldn't be able to speak hurt more than when she'd broken her arm when she'd been tossed from her horse years ago.

She wouldn't show it, though. She would play the role of a happy St. Clair. Her dearest friend in the world had just married the man she worshipped. Rachel would not let any shadow deflect Leah's happiness.

Though she'd helped plan the breakfast menu, Rachel barely tasted the courses of food that came out and couldn't have told anyone what she'd eaten. She let Luke guide the conversation, doing her best to concentrate on what he said. Now that he lived at Fairhaven and in London most of the year, with only short visits back to Eversleigh, she missed him. Maybe she could go and stay with him after Leah married. Anything to get her mind off her heartache.

Finally, it was time for Merrick's toast. Rachel thought if she didn't look in his direction, it would seem odd. She turned after he rose and thought to look to his left and not directly at him.

And couldn't.

Her eyes were drawn to his handsome face. It seemed haggard, as if he might have been ill recently. She pushed that thought aside and drank him in. Or she wanted to. Now that she actually looked at him, his dark blond hair needed more than a trim. The mesmerizing blue eyes looked bloodshot. His tall frame seemed to have shrunk. She almost wept at the sight of him.

He held a champagne flute in his hand and looked at the happy couple. Everyone stood with their own flutes in hand.

"Never has a man had a better friend than I have had in Alexander Lock, Earl of Alford. From boyhood, he has been a loyal, caring friend and the brother of my heart. In his new countess, Alex has found his perfect partner. These two complement each other more than any couple I have ever seen. It's obvious to all who see them to know how very much in love they are."

Merrick raised his glass high. "To the Earl and Countess of Alford—may they live long and love well!"

"Hear, hear!" the guests shouted.

As Rachel brought the glass to her lips, her eyes met Merrick's. He nodded deferentially and then tilted his flute back, downing the champagne in a single swallow. She took a sip and then set hers down. Though she'd only had a tiny bit, she felt lightheaded as if she'd drunk an entire bottle. That was how intoxicating merely looking at Merrick was.

Luke leaned down and murmured in her ear. "Merrick doesn't look well. I wonder if something has happened to him."

She looked and saw a rush of guests moving toward Leah and Alex, ready to congratulate them before they left for their honeymoon. Even Jeremy and Catherine were surrounded with well-wishers. Rachel made an instant decision as she watched Merrick set his flute down and do as Jeremy had requested.

Leave without a fuss.

She latched on to Luke's wrist. "Come with me," she demanded, yanking him along, snaking through wedding guests. They managed to escape the room and she hurried to the foyer, where the front door was just closing. Breaking away from Luke, she raced to the door and threw it open.

Stepping outside, she called out to the fleeing figure. "Merrick!"

He turned and their gazes met. His shoulders seemed to sag in relief at the sight of her. A genuine smile began—and then fell. Rachel sensed Luke coming to stand behind her.

"I see you've brought along your watchdog for protection," the marquess said, his face becoming a mask again.

"Have you been sick, Merrick?" she asked, not disguising her worry.

"Sick?" He laughed harshly. "I am sick of all of you bloody St.

Clairs. Of life in general. I am sick at heart that I survived while my men died on the battlefield and in the hospital."

His words slammed into her as if he'd slapped her. Rachel stepped back and bumped into Luke's broad chest. His arm came about her for support.

Merrick turned without another word and stalked away. It took everything she had not to pull away from her brother and dash after the man who would always hold her heart.

Instead, she forced herself to stay in place.

"What on earth has gotten into him?" Luke asked, a frown creasing his brow. "Merrick was an interesting, pleasant fellow at Alford's. I can't say I got to know him well but what on earth does he have against us St. Clairs?"

"He had words with Jeremy just before we left," Rachel said, the lie spilling from her lips even as guilt poured through her. "I'm not sure what it was about."

Luke snorted. "Well, good riddance to him." He kissed her brow. "Let's go back to the festivities. Leah will be needing your help soon."

They returned inside the house and saw Leah and Catherine heading up the stairs. Rachel parted from Luke and followed them. They returned to Leah's bedchamber and helped her change into traveling clothes.

"Did you get out of Alex where we will honeymoon?" Leah asked Rachel.

"No," she said ruefully, trying to push aside what had just happened and enjoy these final moments with her best friend. "I'm afraid I wouldn't make for a very good spy. I think Alex wants to surprise you and that's incredibly sweet. Besides, your wardrobe can take you anywhere."

Leah giggled. "It really doesn't matter. We'll be together." Her eyes twinkled. "I will definitely share with him Cor's expectations regarding great-grandchildren. He loves her so, not having any parents or grandparents of his own."

Rachel embraced Leah, hugging her tightly. A chapter was ending in her life, one she'd thoroughly enjoyed with this wonderful friend.

"I'll write to you both," Leah promised. "And Rachel, you must come to stay at Fairfield once we return from whatever mysterious place we are bound for."

The three returned downstairs, where Alex claimed Leah and led her to his waiting coach. Everyone waved goodbye to the couple and then a round of farewells began as their wedding guests departed. When the last one left, Rachel declared she was exhausted and ready for a nap. She retreated upstairs and fell asleep.

When she awoke, tears stained her pillow.

CHAPTER TWENTY

Five months later...

EVAN HEARD A distant pounding, a constant noise, much like the hooves of a galloping horse down the road. He tried to swallow but his mouth was incredibly dry. His head throbbed painfully, as if someone had laid it upon an anvil and a blacksmith struck it again and again.

In other words, another day of awakening as the Marquess of Merrick.

Nothing had been right in his life since the last time he'd seen Rachel St. Clair. He hadn't been fully sober since the day Alex and Leah wed, arriving at the ceremony having drunk half a bottle of whiskey that morning as a way to build up his courage to set foot upon Everton's estate. He'd left the wedding breakfast at Eversleigh with an empty flask in his coat pocket, guzzled between leaving the chapel and arriving at the breakfast.

He'd chosen not to go back to Edgemere after that October day because there were too many reminders of Rachel there.

Especially Calypso.

Instead, he'd come here to London and lost himself in drink and cards. Women, too. Evan had coupled with as many willing women as he could find, trying to free himself from the prison Rachel had encased him in.

Nothing helped. Nothing at all.

Alex had begged him to come and spend Christmas at Fairfield, his first after returning from his honeymoon with his bride. Evan refused. Seeing Leah would only remind Evan of Rachel. He continued to douse his constant heartache with alcohol until nothing seemed left of him. He lived in his London townhouse, where the only piece of remaining furniture was a long settee in the parlor just off the entrance to the house. That way he could stumble inside and fall onto it without having to climb the stairs to a master bedchamber he'd thought to share with his wife. The rest of the furniture had vanished after he carelessly left the front door open multiple times over several weeks. He supposed people came in and merely helped themselves to whatever they saw until the place had emptied out. It didn't matter. Nothing mattered to him anymore.

He did venture to the kitchen to bathe occasionally in a copper tub that had a hole in it and had a woman come in to collect the clothes he'd discarded on the floor. She washed and returned them the next day. For meals, he ate at one of his clubs—when he remembered to do so.

Evan wished for death. He didn't know why it hadn't come on the battlefield. That would have been preferable to the living death he now experienced every day.

The blasted knocking hadn't ceased. Evan could hear muffled shouts coming from outside. If only his unknown visitor knew he never locked the door. There was nothing left inside to steal so he left it unlocked. That way, he didn't have to fumble trying to fit a key into a lock when he came home too inebriated to accomplish that small task.

Evan pushed himself upright, groaning as his head split in two. He forced himself to his feet and stumbled from the parlor to the foyer. Pushing his hair back from his eyes, he spied the door and opened it.

"Good God Almighty, Evan!" Alex Lock proclaimed. "You're a wreck."

Blearily, he saw the Earl of Alford standing there, along with his beautiful countess. Her jaw hung open in shock.

Without waiting for an invitation, Leah stepped toward him and pushed hard against his chest. Evan staggered back as she swept in, followed by her husband.

"What do you have to say for yourself?" she demanded. "Bloodshot eyes. Half-dressed at half-past three in the afternoon. Hair that hasn't been cut in a month—or two." She sniffed. "And you stink. No, you reek of whiskey."

Leah went into the parlor. Evan shuffled behind her and saw her survey the almost empty room.

"This is inexcusable, Merrick. How are you going to win Rachel back in your current condition?"

Rachel . . .

He tried not to think of her and lost that battle a dozen times a day.

Carefully, he articulated, "Rachel St. Clair *is* the reason I drink." He stood there, trying to muster as much dignity as he could.

Obviously, he failed miserably as Leah snorted in an unladylike fashion. "She'll never accept you this way."

"What makes you think I want her?" he asked testily.

Her eyes narrowed. "Because you love her, you bloody idiot."

Evan froze. He opened his mouth to fire off a quick retort but none came to him.

"She's right, you know," Alex said, sympathy for Evan in his eyes. "You wouldn't have fallen into such ruin if you didn't love her."

"I've never been loved," he said stiffly, walking unsteadily to the settee and plopping down. "I've never been a part of a family. Rachel has a close-knit one and they all adore one another."

He raised tired eyes and gazed at Leah. "I don't know how to love."

The countess sat beside him and took his hand in both of hers. "Do you feel incomplete without Rachel by your side? Do you wish to wake up with her every morning and despair the times you're apart?

Do you yearn for her kiss? Do you believe no one in the world can understand you the way she can?"

"All those things," Evan wearily admitted.

"That . . . and more . . . is love," Leah proclaimed. "Each couple's love is unique to them. Loving Rachel—being with Rachel—will make you a better man." She eyed him, not masking her disgust. "The Season starts in one month. Do you want her dancing with other men? Having them steal kisses from her? Could you live with seeing her engagement announcement in the newspaper? Would life still be worth living if you didn't do your damnedest to march in and claim the woman you love?"

His hands tore at his hair. "She hates me, Leah. So does her entire family. I can't blame them."

Leah clucked her tongue. "Well, Alex and I are part of her family and we certainly don't hate you. Just what you've done to yourself."

He wiped his sleeve against his eyes, soaking up the tears that freely fell.

"It's not enough, Leah. I know you mean well but—"

"You're a coward," Alex said sharply. "Rachel has been miserable without you. Yes, she plans to take part in the Season. Yes, she'll probably choose a husband this time around. Why can't you understand that she needs you as much as you need her?"

A ray of hope filled Evan. "Do you really think I have a chance?"

"Better to try and lose her for good than give up and drink yourself to death without trying." Alex rested a hand on Evan's shoulder. "You came home from the war for a reason. *Rachel* is the reason. Be a man, Evan. Do whatever you can. You know the two of you belong together."

Shakily, he stood as Alex helped Leah rise.

"Help me," he begged, deep shame running through him.

"We will," Leah promised.

Evan found himself whisked into their waiting carriage. A man of about forty with kind eyes sat inside waiting.

"This is Dr. Gray," Alex said. "He will be examining you and making recommendations."

"I'm not sick," Evan protested weakly.

"You've been drinking heavily for several months, Lord Merrick," said the physician. "We only have a month to clean out your system. I'll be supervising your recovery at the earl's request. You will be watched every minute. I promise to do my best to help you return to the man you once were. It will take commitment and hard work on your part. Sometimes, it will seem impossible."

"What if . . . it's all for naught?" he asked softly.

Leah took his hand. "If you're meant to be with Rachel, it will happen. If you're meant to go in separate directions, then we'll face that when the time comes."

Evan felt totally overwhelmed. He crumpled in the seat, his head coming to rest in Leah's lap. As he wept, she stroked his hair and murmured soothing words.

Evan determined if he had any chance of a life with Rachel, it was a risk he was willing to take.

EVAN NEEDED ASSISTANCE from the carriage. Already, his hands shook and the headache still pounded away at his temples and the back of his head. Two footmen wound up carrying him upstairs to a bedchamber he'd slept in several times over the years. Dr. Gray ordered a bath for him as Evan perched on the bed, holding on to the bedpost so he wouldn't fall to the floor. Both Alex and Leah wore grave expressions on their faces.

"I want you to listen to me, Lord Merrick," the physician said firmly but gently. "You won't remember everything I say this first time but I will be repeating myself over the next few days. First, I will not leave you. I will be with you throughout the day and during the night if you need me. I will sleep in the chamber directly across from yours. I only need a few hours each night. When I am resting, my assistant will remain by your side. His name is Randolph. He should arrive when your bath does."

Alex said, "Dr. Gray is familiar with cases such as yours, Evan."

He gave his friend a rueful look. "You can say it, Alex. I'm a drunk. Dr. Gray helps those who are sots."

Dr. Gray said, "I have made a study of those who drink to excess, my lord. I have helped a great many people. You will never be able to consume any alcohol again once our time together is over. No port after dinner. No wine or whiskey."

He shrugged. "I wasn't much of a drinker. Before, that is."

The physician looked to Alex and Leah. "If I can have time alone with Lord Merrick. As we discussed. When I think he is ready to see you, you will be welcomed. Until then, I am solely in charge of him and his care, no questions asked."

"Of course," Alex said. He and Leah departed from the room.

Turning back to Evan, Gray said, "Everyone who begins drinking to excess has a reason why they turned to strong drink. What is yours?"

"That's none of your business," Evan spat out, his head throbbing painfully at hearing his voice raised.

The doctor eyed him steadily. "Everything about you from now on is my business, my lord. If you truly want to conquer this demon, you must give me full access to what troubles you. I demand total honesty from you and commitment to the work we will have to do."

"I can barely swallow. Can I have something to drink?"

"Soon. Talk to me."

Evan supposed he had nothing to lose. "I fell in love. Madly, passionately in love. I was foolish enough not to tell the lady. And then I found out that she didn't love me. A poor excuse to fall into my cups."

"No. I think it a much more admirable reason than some I've heard. Go on."

"She believes in love, Doctor. She wants to wed a man she loves and one that loves her. Obviously, I could never be that man."

"And yet here you are."

He shrugged. "My friends seemed convinced that she does harbor feelings for me. I would like to present myself to her one last time and reveal what I didn't before. If her feelings have changed, we might make a go of it. If not?"

"If not, you will have regained your sobriety and have a chance to live. You were an officer in the army?"

"Yes. I was a major."

"Wounded?"

"Twice."

"And before . . . you didn't drink much?"

"It didn't hold much appeal for me. I'd rather have a good plate of meat and something sweet to eat."

"That's good," Gray said. "We will need to build your appetite back up. Sots rarely eat much—and that is what you are, my lord. You must recognize it. Own it. And then fight it. You must destroy what drink has done to you before it annihilates you, body and soul."

Evan noticed that his hands shook. That was always a sign that he needed to pour himself another drink. If he was to conquer this, he would have to be strong.

The sudden urge to regurgitate overwhelmed him and he raced to the chamber pot, vomiting for a long time. The nausea remained, though, and he found himself sweating profusely.

"Any abdominal pain?" Gray inquired.

"Yes." His gut tightened. Bile rose in his throat and he forced it back down.

"You're sweating. Shaking. These are all signs that it's been six to eight hours since your last drink."

"That would be correct," Evan said, his teeth beginning to chatter.

A knock sounded at the door and it swung open. A burly man with a grim countenance stepped inside and waved a crew of servants forward. They set down a copper tub and added buckets of hot and cold water, leaving a few for rinsing. One woman left a towel and bar of soap and then the line of servants disappeared.

The strapping man remained. He looked as if he were no stranger to a street fight. His nose had been busted multiple times.

"This is Randolph," Dr. Gray said. "He will bathe you."

Evan found himself moved around as a puppet, with no control over his limbs. Gray's assistant stripped him and lifted him, placing him in the tub and scrubbing the life out of him. He thought he would be sick again but he only dry heaved. Randolph scrubbed his scalp, causing Evan regret when his head refused to explode and end everything.

Finally, the ordeal was over and Randolph wrapped him in the provided towel and lifted him from the tub. He carried Evan to the bed and placed him on it, retrieving a dressing gown from a wardrobe filled with gentleman's clothing. They must belong to Alex since none of his had been brought along. The dressing gown hung on him. He assumed all the clothes would, too.

"Staying clean and dressing is important. For now, you're to try and sleep. You will become anxious the longer you go without a drink. Strong drink gives you a sense of confidence. A feeling as if you can do anything. Once it is taken away, your mood shifts from elevated to plunging to depths you have never imagined. You will become depressed. Feel totally worthless. It's all a part of the process."

Already, Evan's body had begun sweating again, despite only being minutes removed from his bath. The nausea had never left.

"I'm still thirsty," he said.

"You will get broth soon. Right now, you're to try and rest. Some of my patients experience insomnia at this point, which might last for days. If you cannot sleep, you will at least stay in bed for several hours of rest." Gray smiled. "Trust me, Lord Merrick. I have done this many times. I know what you need and when you'll need it."

Evan closed his eyes, despair washing over him.

CHAPTER TWENTY-ONE

He stood at the garden party, anxiously awaiting Rachel's arrival. Sweat trickled down his back under his coat and shirt, making him aware of how nervous he was. He dreaded Everton showing up and keeping her from him. It had happened over and over.

He looked around and put his hands to his ears. The cacophony of voices hurt his ears, the shrill tone grating on him. Everywhere, people smiled maliciously, women raising gloved hands to their mouths and speaking behind them, tittering to one another as they stared in his direction.

Where was she?

Suddenly, a plump cloud descended from the sky. The noise ceased as all eyes turned upward. Rachel floated to the ground and stepped from the cloud. She wore a pale blue dress. No jewelry. Ribbons of the same blue ran through her hair.

She was the most beautiful thing he'd ever seen.

She reached out a bare hand to him. He also wore no gloves. Their skin touched and heat rushed through him. His hand clasped hers. He would never let it go. Never.

Suddenly, Everton appeared to his left. The duke appeared twice as tall as the others gathered and glowered at him.

"Rachel is not for you," he said sternly. "You are not worthy of her. You never were."

Panic filled him as her fingers slid from his. Sadness filled her face.

"I need a strong man," she said. "One strong in body and mind. A man not afraid to love."

"But I do love you!" he insisted, shouting the words as she turned away.

She looked over her shoulder, her face now full of pity. "It was never meant to be. Accept it."

With those words, she climbed atop the cloud again and it floated upward to the heavens. He ran and leaped, stretching out his arms as high as they would reach, trying to grab it and force it to return. His fingers swiped nothing but air. Dejected, he turned away, not having the stomach to see her slip away. Again.

The crowd gathered jeered at him, fingers pointing as they roared, entertained by his pain.

Everton's eyes narrowed. "Go away. You are not wanted. No one will ever want you. No one. Ever. Will want you."

Evan gasped and sat up, confused, looking about the room. Gray sat in a chair by his bedside, reading.

"Do your breathing, Lord Merrick," the doctor said. "It will soothe you."

He breathed in slowly, counting to four as Gray had advised, and held the breath a moment before exhaling, this time to a count of seven. In four. Pause. Out seven. Evan repeated the pattern several times until he felt in control again and collapsed against the pillows.

"Was it another hallucination?"

"Yes," he whispered, his throat dry. "I'm hot," he complained.

The physician stood and took his wrist, checking his pulse, and then placed the back of his hand against Evan's brow.

"You still have a fever."

He jerked, the convulsion one of many he'd undergone the last few days. His eyes ached. Every limb shook. The nausea remained. He'd had constant diarrhea.

And the insane delusions.

They were numerous. Every single one had involved Rachel in some aspect. Each pointed out his unfitness and unworthiness, plunging him into the depression that Gray had warned him about.

He spasmed again, lying there and letting the tremors run through him. Knowing he could do nothing about them. Gray said they would come to an end soon.

The doctor motioned Randolph and the assistant left. Within half an hour, servants arrived with water for a new bath and clean linens for the bed. Randolph placed him in the tepid water. Everything about the man annoyed Evan. Gray had explained that irritability was one of the signs of withdrawal. Evan began trembling violently in the bath water, locking his arms about his knees and holding on for dear life. He shook so much water splashed from the tub. His head dropped to his knees and he wept again for the hundredth time this past week. He was tired of the visions. They seemed so real. His body had never been wearier. His thinking was clouded. He could feel his heart beating erratically and thought, perhaps, death might be more welcomed than life.

Then the tremors subsided. Randolph gently bathed him and Evan felt soothed for the first time since he'd begun this journey with Dr. Gray. Randolph lifted him and dried him off as if he were a small child and took him back to the bed. The sheets felt cool against his fevered skin. He slept again.

AFTER ONE WEEK, the symptoms decreased, just as Dr. Gray had predicted. Evan had still felt feeble and slightly nauseous but experienced no more muscle spasms. His heart and pulse beat normally once more. The delusions and accompanying fever vanished.

Then the real work began.

The second week, he was allowed to be up and move about, although walking tired him. Frequent meals on a tray appeared at regular intervals in his room. Dr. Gray wanted him to eat to build his strength but Evan could only tolerate small amounts of food at a time, thus the frequency. It was nothing for a tray to be brought to him eight or ten times a day. Each time, he was able to eat a little more. Each day, he could walk a bit farther. He craved whiskey every second of the day. It took extreme willpower to force the thoughts away, knowing if he drank again, it would kill him—and ruin any chance he had with Rachel.

With the start of the third week, Dr. Gray allowed Evan the run of the house and encouraged him to walk as much as he could to build strength. The doctor or Randolph shadowed his every step. Evan still thought of whiskey but only in a vague way. It didn't seem as important as before. He hoped its grasp on him had lessened. He was allowed to eat three meals a day downstairs with Alex and Leah. It was the first time he'd seen the couple since Dr. Gray kept him in isolation through the worst of things. Now, Evan longed for their company.

No one knew he was staying with the Alfords. He began eating normally and the weight came back on. Alex had Evan's clothes collected from his townhouse, though Leah admitted most of them had to be burned due to stains and smells that wouldn't come out. She'd sent to Edgemere for more of his wardrobe and his tailor appeared one afternoon, fitting him for several new coats and shirts, as well.

He also was allowed to ride during that third week. Dr. Gray said besides walking, riding was the best exercise possible. Evan rode with Randolph each morning at six, well before anyone in the *ton* arose. They rode again between seven and eight at night, seeing no one of his acquaintance. He sensed his strength returning.

After dinner, Dr. Gray asked if he could address Evan, Alex, and Leah. They went to a small, intimate parlor, where Evan and Alex had played several chess matches the past week. Dr. Gray was a great believer in exercising the mind as well as the body. The first time Evan had been able to call out "checkmate" he'd almost wept.

The three sat and looked expectantly at the physician. Having come to know Gray well, Evan could guess what he wished to address them about.

"I know you had high hopes for Lord Merrick to reintroduce himself into Polite Society when the Season opened. I do not think it wise at this time." He looked to Evan. "What are your feelings, my lord?"

Evan took a deep breath. "As much as I would like to attend the Parkers' ball in three days' time, I'm not ready. I am getting stronger, both physically and mentally, but I still need more time. At this point, the thought of entering a ballroom crowded with people frightens me more than charging into battle. I'm afraid I would head for the nearest decanter and down liquid courage merely to keep standing."

He looked at his friends. "You have stood by me during this awful time. I'm asking for you to continue to do so for a little while longer. I think if I had two more weeks, I would be better able to manage myself."

Alex nodded. "It's only two weeks. You know Rachel. She would not commit to anyone so suddenly. Why, she spent all of last Season refusing to entertain offers. I can't see things changing." He placed a hand on Evan's knee. "A stronger you will have a better chance to win her back."

Evan sighed. "You know my fondest wish is to win her back. If I don't, I promise I won't sink to the depths that I did. Drinking oneself to death is a miserable experience. After working so hard with Dr. Gray to climb out of that dark hole, I would never voluntarily leap into it again. I still have the urge to drink, though. Dr. Gray says it will always be there. It will take everything I have for the rest of my life not to give in to it. Even if I lose Rachel in the long run, I haven't lost myself. Thanks to your intervention and finding Dr. Gray to work with me, I have a chance at a good life again."

Tears spilled down Leah's cheeks. She rose and came to sit next to him. She took his hand and placed it against her face and then lovingly kissed it.

"We will always be here for you, Evan. No matter what happens."

"Thank you," he said softly. "I am blessed to have the both of you in my life."

"Do you have any recommendations, Doctor?" Alex asked. "For the next two weeks?"

"I think Lord Merrick should leave London and return to his country estate. The fresh air will do him good. Riding his property. Seeing his tenants. Creating a bit of normalcy in his life."

Evan chuckled. "Rachel did see that I had a first-class cook. Mrs. Bridges' food tempts me as much as Mrs. Dunnavant's ever did."

"Should we come with you?" Leah asked anxiously.

"No. This is something I should do on my own." He looked to the physician. "I assume you and Randolph will accompany me?"

"We will, Lord Merrick."

"I think we should leave very early tomorrow morning," Evan said. "Can I borrow your valet to pack for me, Alex?"

"Randolph will take care of that," Gray said. "We could use your coach, Lord Alford, if that is available."

"Of course, Doctor." Alex rose and shook the man's hand. "You have already worked a miracle by bringing Evan back to us. I hope these additional two weeks will benefit him."

"They will. The more time he has to prepare for being out in society again, the better. Lord Merrick has proven to be my most determined patient. I have high hopes that he will have a complete recovery and not experience any relapses."

Evan stood. He kissed Leah and shook Alex's hand. "I'll say my goodbyes now. The next time I see you, I will be ready to accompany you to whatever *ton* event takes place."

With that, he left the room. He only prayed he had the strength and courage to keep to his current path.

CHAPTER TWENTY-TWO

RACHEL SAT IN the drawing room with Jenny snuggled against her and Delia in her lap. She read a fairy tale to the girls, who were enthralled as she used different voices for the various characters. Timothy, being a typical boy, wanted nothing to do with story time. He sat playing with a multitude of blocks on the floor. Cor and Catherine both sat with sewing in their laps.

They'd traveled to London three days ago. The new Season began in two days' time. Rachel had determined to take a husband by the end of it. She would start a prospective husband list, where she would write the names of potential candidates and list their attributes. The man with the most would win her hand.

She had to marry. If she didn't, she'd go mad. Merrick had stirred physical desire within her and she'd taken to pleasuring herself with her own hand after she'd gone to bed at night, which brought her no end of shame. Much of the last several months had been spent playing with her nephew and nieces. The pull of motherhood gripped her and she knew her life would be incomplete without children of her own.

Because of these things, she would wed. Plenty of men had paid court to her last Season. Not all of them had married. There would also be others who took part in the events scheduled this year that would be additions for her to meet. Somewhere, among all of those bachelors, Rachel was determined to find one who could kiss reasonably well and give her children. She didn't care about titles or number of properties. She wanted a good, kind man who knew how to use his tongue and would be an excellent father—and a decent husband. One that if he took a lover, he could be discreet about it.

Barton entered the room and said, "Lord Merrifield is here to see the duchess."

Catherine looked at Rachel. "Merrifield is here to see you, I'm sure." She turned back to the butler. "Please send the earl in, Barton."

"Yes, Your Grace."

"Should I ring for Sara to remove the children?" her sister-in-law asked, her eyebrows arched.

"Why? Merrifield wasn't expected. I'm not going to interrupt what I'm doing simply because he showed up without an invitation," Rachel replied.

"The Earl of Merrifield," Barton announced as the nobleman swept into the room.

"Ah, Your Grace," he said, going straight to Catherine. "It's lovely to see you again." Turning, he looked at Cor. "And Your Grace. Always a delight to be in your presence."

Cor snorted. "I thought you were calling me Cor. You did at Fairfield. Half of Polite Society does. You might as well, young man." She eyed him with interest and then glanced to Rachel.

Merrifield finally swiveled and bowed to her. "Lady Rachel. It's a pleasure to see you. And in the company of such lovely ladies."

"This is Jenny on my left and Delia in my lap, Lord Merrifield. And that's Timothy on the floor, playing with blocks."

He came to the girls. "It's very nice to meet you. Is your Aunt Rachel reading to you?"

Jenny nodded. "She's a good reader. And she draws with us. We got a puppy."

"You did? I'll have to see it sometime."

Merrifield crouched before Timothy. "What are you building today?"

"Castle," Timothy grunted. At two, he was already a man of few words.

"I've built a castle before with blocks. Might I help you?"

Timothy shrugged.

The earl asked Catherine, "May I discard my coat, Your Grace? Building castles can be hard work."

"Of course," she said, smiling indulgently.

Merrifield shed his coat, though it took some effort since it was tailored to him beautifully. Rachel couldn't help but admire the broad shoulders that had been resting under it. He cut an impressive figure. She would add that under his name on her list.

"Read, Auntie," Delia commanded. She was the bossy twin but quite loveable.

She kissed her niece's head. "Of course, darling."

Rachel continued reading the story with surreptitious glances at Merrifield over the next half-hour as he got down on his hands and knees to help her nephew. The earl was quite good with Timothy, guiding the boy and letting him do most of the work as he gently made suggestions.

Hmm. Good with children.

Something else for the list.

Just as she wrapped up the story, Jeremy stepped into the drawing room and quickly assessed the situation. He came and lifted Jenny, kissing her soundly, and then scooped up Delia, as well.

"Kiss me, too, Papa," she demanded.

He did and looked at the two on the floor. "What are you building, Timothy?"

"Castle. And a moat."

Jeremy asked Merrifield, "I suppose the moat was your idea."

"It was, Your Grace, though we have now run out of building blocks. Moats are quite large things and require a good number of blocks to complete. Perhaps I can bring some to young Timothy." He glanced at Rachel. "Tomorrow, possibly, if that is convenient."

She nodded.

Catherine rose. "Come, Timothy. It's time for your nap. Tell Lord Merrifield goodbye."

The boy did, throwing his arms around the earl. It surprised Rachel because Timothy rarely was demonstrative.

Catherine held out a hand and Timothy scurried to her. "We'll be back shortly," she said and she and Jeremy left with the children.

Rachel scooted to the end of settee and set the book beside her. She gestured for Merrifield to take a seat at the other end. He did so and then stood again, retrieving his coat.

"You'll never get into that by yourself," she said and stood, reaching out her hands.

He gave it to her and she held it open as he slid his arms into it. She lifted it and smoothed it over his shoulders. He smelled awfully good. And was handsome. More things to add to her list.

They both sat and she asked, "Shall I ring for tea?"

"Please. Moat building is hard work. I've built up quite a thirst."

Hmm. Also clever. Her list was growing by leaps and bounds. Rachel wondered if Merrifield had anything wrong with him.

Other than not being Merrick.

"How did you know I was already in London?" she asked.

"I didn't know for certain but I assumed you would be. With the Season about to start, I was sure you'd be meeting with dressmakers and milliners and all kinds of people to see you properly outfitted for the Season."

Cor snorted and continued with her needle.

"My grandmother doesn't quite approve of my intentions this Season," Rachel began. "I've chosen not to have a new wardrobe made up."

"Why so?" His brows knit together in puzzlement. "Every woman does. Especially those on the Marriage Mart. I'm assuming you'll be searching for a husband."

She shrugged. "Everything created for last year was worn only once. It seemed such a waste, especially when I liked so many of the designs. I decided to merely wear what I did last Season. The men I speak with will never notice and it will give the ladies plenty to gossip about."

Merrifield smiled broadly. "You're right about both gentlemen and ladies. I find it a clever idea."

The tea cart arrived as Jeremy and Catherine returned. They seated themselves and Catherine began pouring cups of tea for all.

Cor waved her away. "I think I'll follow the example of my great-grandchildren and take a nap before dinner. If you'll excuse me."

Jeremy and Merrifield rose. "I will see you again tomorrow, Cor," Merrifield promised.

They spent a pleasant hour over tea. Rachel discovered not only was Merrifield an entertaining companion but he knew quite a bit about livestock, which interested Jeremy. The two engaged in an enthusiastic discussion over goats.

Finally, Merrifield said, "I've overstayed my welcome. Besides, I need to go shopping for blocks."

"There's no need to, Lord Merrifield," Rachel said. "Timothy has plenty."

"Not enough to complete his moat. I will return tomorrow and we'll finish it." His eyes gleamed. "And perhaps we might ride in the park, as well, my lady."

"We haven't ridden since we've returned to London," Jeremy said. "Why don't the four of us go to Rotten Row?"

"I would enjoy that, Your Grace," Merrifield said. "Lady Rachel?" He looked at her hopefully.

She pushed away Merrick and locked him in a far recess of her mind.

"Yes, Lord Merrifield. That would be most enjoyable."

MERRIFIELD ARRIVED THE next day at the same time as he had the day before. Rachel played cards with Jeremy, Catherine, and Cor. When Barton announced the earl, she was glad to feel a small tingle of anticipation as he entered. As he greeted everyone, Catherine sent for the children. She'd allowed the partially-constructed castle and moat to remain on the drawing room floor.

Once the children arrived with Sara, Timothy broke away and ran to Merrifield.

"Moat today?" he asked eagerly.

"Definitely a moat. Today," Merrifield confirmed. He held up a large sack and then placed it on the ground. "Pull out all our blocks, Lord Timothy. I'll wager we'll use every one of them."

The boy dragged the sack to the construction area and meticulously began placing blocks on the ground.

Merrifield then handed Jenny and Delia two slim packages wrapped in brown paper. After Catherine prompting them all to say thank you, the girls ripped into their packages. Each had received a book of her own. While Jenny curled up in a chair with hers, Delia placed hers on a table and wandered to Merrifield.

"I'll help," she announced and took his hand, leading him to where Timothy now had all the blocks out of the bag. "Jenny, you help, too," Delia ordered.

Jenny put her book aside and joined the three on the floor. Rachel was able to study Merrifield more closely today. His hair looked freshly barbered. His clothing was impeccable as always. He laughed easily and frequently. Once again, he did more directing and allowed the children to build the moat themselves. It wasn't as neat as if he'd taken more of a hand in it but the three little ones beamed with their effort once the castle and moat reached completion.

In that moment, Rachel determined she would wed Merrifield at

Season's end.

She had no reason not to do so. He was handsome and titled. He kissed extremely well. He was friendly and amusing and very good with children. She believed he would make an excellent husband and father. Of course, she wouldn't tell him of her decision now. She would take part in the Season. Add the names of various gentlemen to her prospective husband list. In the long run, though, she doubted anyone would please her more than Merrifield.

Especially if she refused to include Merrick on her list.

"Papa!" cried Timothy. "See my moat?"

"Our moat," corrected Delia. "I helped. Jenny helped," she said stubbornly.

Jeremy went and sat cross-legged on the floor. He admired the structure and he and Merrifield talked at length about what a moat was for and why it was so important.

"Tell a story, Papa," Jenny begged.

"I'm not a storyteller. That's for your aunt."

Rachel came to where they gathered and eased down on the floor. She made up a tale of a kidnapped princess and the army her prince brought to save her. When the princess was rescued from the castle, the prince crossing the moat in order to save her, Delia clapped her hands gleefully and announced she liked the story very much.

"Time for your naps," Catherine told her children.

Rachel saw Sara hovered in the doorway. With little complaining, the three St. Clair children said goodbye to Merrifield and went with their nursery governess. Jeremy and Merrifield helped her to her feet and she and Catherine went to change into their riding habits. By the time they appeared downstairs again, Jeremy had their horses saddled and brought around and the four set out for Hyde Park.

Once they reached Rotten Row, she and Merrifield split off from Jeremy and Catherine, who followed at a discreet distance in order to still be seen as chaperoning them while giving them a bit of privacy.

They rode for half an hour and then slowed their horses to a leisurely walk.

"Thank you for the gifts you brought my nephew and nieces," Rachel said.

"I was happy to do so," Merrifield responded. "Perhaps next time I will bear a gift for you."

"That isn't necessary."

"Will you be at the Parkers' ball tomorrow night? It opens the Season."

"Yes."

He stopped his horse and reached over to her reins so she came to a halt, as well. "I heard last year that you wouldn't entertain any offers of marriage during the Season. Will you keep to that pattern this year?"

"I believe I shall."

"What if you had an offer before the Season even began?" he asked, and Rachel saw the heat in his eyes.

She bit her lip and then firmly said, "I will make a decision at Season's end. Not before."

"I see. At least tell me you will save the supper dance for me tomorrow night."

"I will not," she said and saw surprise on his face. "You will have to show up as every other gentleman does and sign my programme, Lord Merrifield. *If* there are any vacancies."

He grinned. "I have never been known for being early to a ball. It seems I will have to adjust my schedule."

"Do that," she said saucily.

The earl laughed. She liked his laugh. It came from deep within and didn't seem false in any way. Another thing to add to her list. Though Merrifield was the only name on it currently, he did reside at the top and would no matter how many names she added.

"What if I asked for more than the supper dance?" His eyes

gleamed with mischief.

"You do realize that any gentleman dancing with a lady more than once—especially on the opening night of the Season—will be scrutinized by the *ton*. They will say he is most interested in the woman he chooses to dance with twice."

"Let them talk. You didn't answer my question, Lady Rachel. If I arrive early enough and you have two places on your dance card, might I place my name down twice?"

Rachel smiled. "You most certainly can, Lord Merrifield."

CHAPTER TWENTY-THREE

RACHEL DRESSED WITH care. She thought back to this time last year and how excited she and Leah were to be finally making their come-out. They had planned their wardrobes for months and talked endlessly about the kind of man they hoped to meet and marry. Now, Leah would show up tonight as a married woman of six months with Alex on her arm.

Rachel pushed her feet into blue satin slippers and then slipped on her elbow-length gloves. She couldn't help but think where Merrick had been this time last year. At war. While she'd danced away nights with gentlemen of the *ton*, Merrick had been healing from his bullet wounds and then continuing to fight on. It made what happened in London tonight seem so shallow with their country still at war with Bonaparte.

She wondered where Merrick was tonight. If he would make an appearance at the Parkers' ball. If he did, would he ask to dance with her? She doubted it. Jeremy and Catherine would be in attendance. Her brother would search the crowd. If he spied Merrick at any point, all it would take would be a single look from the duke and Merrick would never approach her.

It didn't matter. He didn't love her. He never would. Besides, she already had a respectable gentleman interested in wedding her. Tonight, she might add more names to her list. She would keep an open mind and find the man best suited to her. One she would learn to love, thanks to all of his wonderful traits which she would mark down on her list.

Rachel went downstairs and found Jeremy pacing. He looked quite handsome in his evening clothes.

Taking her hands, he held them out and eyed her with appreciation. "You are the most beautiful sister. Every man there will fall under your spell." He paused. "If Merrick is present tonight, you know not to dance with him."

"Of course," she said, no nonsense in her tone. "I hope to dance with many men tonight and throughout the Season but he will not be one of them."

"What are your feelings regarding Merrifield?" he asked cautiously.

"I like him a good deal. It will take someone outstanding to knock him from the top spot on my list."

"Oh, you have a list, do you?"

"I do." She chuckled. "At the moment, Merrifield is the only one on it. I've listed his good qualities. We'll see where he stands after tonight."

Catherine sailed down the stairs and Rachel saw her brother's eyes darken. He greeted his wife with a tender kiss.

"I will be escorting the two loveliest ladies tonight," he proclaimed and then amended it when Cor came down the stairs. "Make that three ravishing beauties."

Cor's answer was to swat him with her fan.

The coach ride only took a few minutes. As they disembarked, Leah and Alex pulled up next to them. They waved and joined them, going inside and immediately to the receiving line. Once they went through it, Leah clutched Rachel's wrist and began dragging her off.

"Where are we going?" she asked.

"I must get to the retiring room."

Rachel saw Leah had suddenly turned white as a sheet and rushed her there. They barely got inside the door and to a chamber pot before

Leah lost everything she'd consumed at dinner.

"Are you increasing?" Rachel whispered.

"I am. I've never been more sick in my life the past week. It never comes early in the morning, as I was led to believe. For me, it starts around nine in the evening."

She hugged her friend. "You will make a wonderful mother, Leah. Alex, too, will be a doting papa."

"You think so?" Leah asked, some color now returning to her face.

"I know so."

Leah swallowed and frowned. "That awful taste. I hate it. This baby better be worth it."

"He—or she—will be. You'll see," promised Rachel. "Why don't you go home? After all, you've already landed a titled, handsome husband. There's no need for you to be here."

"You don't mind? We haven't seen each other at all since you arrived in London. I so wanted to catch up with you."

"There will be plenty of time for that. Go." She kissed Leah's cheek. "I came with Jeremy and Catherine. Luke is also here somewhere. Or he will be at some point. He can escort me home if they wish to leave early. Don't worry. I'll have people to talk with. I will call on you tomorrow and bring Catherine. Maybe even the children."

"Yes, I'd like that very much."

Rachel saw Leah back to Alex and said, "Take her home. She's unwell."

"I understand." He winked. "You do know you'll be godmother to our son or daughter."

She smiled. "I'd like nothing better."

It was only after the couple turned away that Rachel frowned. As Leah's closest friend, it didn't surprise her to be asked to be godmother. But what of Merrick? Would he become the child's godfather?

She accepted the programme handed to her and joined what she'd called the Three B's—Bethany, Betsy, and Bettina. The trio had been thick as thieves last Season and this one starting tonight seemed to be no different.

"Good evening," she greeted them.

"Rachel St. Clair, you look positively lovely," Bethany said, eying her gown. "Is that from last Season?" she asked loudly.

"As a matter of fact, it is, Lady Bethany," she said boldly. "It's something I loved and wanted to wear again."

"I'm sure no one will notice," Betsy assured her.

"I wouldn't have—and I notice everything," Bettina interjected.

"I hope I'm not interrupting," Rachel said. "Please, carry on with your conversation."

Bethany's eyes gleamed. "We were discussing the Merry Marquess."

Rachel frowned. "Who?"

"I've heard him called Major Marquess," Betsy said.

"No, you have it all wrong," Bettina proclaimed. "He's Major Merry to many. When he doesn't answer to the Marquess of Merrick."

Her gut clenched. "And why do you call him that?"

Bethany, the leader of the group, took Rachel's arm and leaned in to share the gossip. "Because he's made merry all over London. He arrived in late autumn and has been seen everywhere in town with various women."

"Usually drunk, I might add," Betsy said.

"I heard he keeps three mistresses," Bettina added, her eyes wide.

"Three? I'd heard it was four," Betsy giggled.

Rachel now thought she would be the one to be ill. So Merrick had left Eversleigh and come to London. Not Edgemere.

"His townhouse is in Mayfair, diagonally from ours," Bethany confided. "Can you imagine—he has no staff. Not a valet or cook or even a single maid."

"I've heard when he's done drinking for the evening, he gambles at his club," Betsy said. "What would cause a man so handsome and accomplished to do such a thing? He's ruining his life. No respectable lady will have him."

"No one has seen him for a few weeks, though," Bettina said. "He's probably lying drunk in some alley. Oh, is that Merrifield coming this way? I danced with him once last Season. He is heading toward us," she said excitedly.

"He's never seen this early," Betsy whispered. "Oh, I hope I get to dance with him."

Merrifield arrived and smiled at the group. "Good evening, ladies. I'm in a dancing mood tonight." He looked to her. "Lady Rachel, might I see your programme?"

"Certainly, Lord Merrifield."

She handed it over as he made small talk with them. As expected, he scrawled his name beside the supper dance and the one after it, as well. He then asked each of the Three B's for their dance cards, as well. Rachel thought he took the first three dances of the evening with them.

He looked back to her. "Is your grandmother here this evening? I grew quite fond of her at Alford's house party last summer. I would love the chance to speak with her."

Pointing to where several older women had seats so they could view the dancing, Rachel said, "She's over there, holding court as usual."

Merrifield bowed to them. "Until later."

He sauntered off and she watched Cor light up as she and the earl began to speak.

Other gentlemen approached her and her programme filled quickly. The dancing began and Rachel enjoyed every minute of it. She'd loved dancing from the moment she was introduced to it. She even added two names to her list. Both men asked if they could call tomorrow afternoon and she had agreed.

Finally, Merrifield claimed her and led her out to the center of the ballroom floor.

"Have you danced any more after engaging the Three B's?" she asked.

He laughed. "I like that. The Three B's. It suits them. No, I did my due diligence and retreated to the card room until now."

"Are you dancing any after supper?" she inquired.

"Only once. With you."

Curiosity impelled her to ask, "Why did you ask the Three B's to dance?"

"I thought it would be impolite not to ask them, especially with you standing right beside them. I want you to have a good opinion of me."

"I do," she confirmed and he smiled.

"I thought you would be with the Countess of Alford tonight."

"Leah felt ill and decided to go home early and rest."

"I gather she's with child?"

"She is. It's early yet and she's feeling especially rotten. If I were in charge, I would have women birth the first child and men the second. I doubt any husband would want to go through the process more than once."

He beamed at her. "That's what I like about you, Lady Rachel. You speak your mind about the most refreshing topics. By the way, did anyone notice the rags you're wearing?"

She laughed. "It was the first thing Lady Bethany remarked upon. I'm sure she's spread the news to half the ballroom by now. The female half, that is."

"No wonder so many people are looking at you," he quipped. "Or maybe at us. We do make a striking couple."

The music came to a close and Merrifield offered her his arm. They went into supper and he asked if she wanted to sit with her family.

"No. I see them all the time. You may choose our seats."

"I see one of my friends to the right. Actually, your brother, Luke, just sat down next to him with a very beautiful woman."

"Leave it to Luke to sniff out a pretty girl every time."

They joined the table and Rachel wound up having a delightful time. Four couples made up the group and she found herself laughing most of the time at the outrageous things being said. Merrifield brought her a dessert and she protested she couldn't eat another bite.

"Then share it with me," he said, lifting a spoon of it to her lips.

Rachel ate it and swallowed carefully, her gaze never leaving his. He ate a few bites and then told the others they were going for a bit of air.

She wondered if he would kiss her.

Linking his arm with hers, they strolled onto the veranda. The April night was somewhat chilly since it was already past midnight. The hour made her think of her many lessons with Merrick and the thought saddened her. She hadn't seen him tonight. After what she'd learned about him from the Three B's, he was probably at his club, gaming and drinking.

Or in the bed of another woman.

That thought hurt her more than she cared to admit. By now, they'd reached the end of the terrace and begun to turn. Rachel gripped Merrifield's arm.

"Kiss me," she said.

He looked at her a long moment. "Why?"

"Because I want you to do so."

His brows arched. "And why is that?"

She sniffed. "Can't a woman merely want to do something for the sake of doing it?"

He chuckled. "That's not very flattering."

"I did not mean to insult you, Merrifield. What I want to do is kiss you, though. You've given me the impression you'd like to do so. You've shown you're interested in me. We've danced together.

Supped. I enjoy our conversations." She smiled at him winningly. "I do think I'd enjoy your kiss. That you would, as well."

Rachel paused and thought he would act.

He didn't.

Frustrated, she asked, "Aren't you going to kiss me? I'm giving you permission to do so."

He thought a long moment and then softly said, "No, I don't think I shall."

His answer took her aback. "Why not?"

Merrifield cupped her cheek. Warmth spread through her. "I will kiss you when I think it's time. When I know you yearn for it. When it's something you constantly think about. Right now, you like me. You find me amusing. But I want more than that from you, Rachel. I want you to burn for me."

With that, he escorted her back into the ballroom.

Chapter Twenty-Four

Rachel tried to listen to the earnest young gentleman speaking and totally lost her focus. He was one of four men gathered for tea in the St. Clair drawing room this afternoon, along with Catherine and Leah. She would much rather be talking with Leah since they hadn't had any time alone since the Season began over two weeks ago. Rachel's afternoons had been taken up with men calling on her, left and right. It already grew tiresome.

She had added three names to her potential husband list. She didn't want more than five or six total to consider. As the viscount—or was he an earl?—droned on, she knew he would never make the cut. All he had in his favor was that he was a marvelous dancer. Period. It would take much more to make her list than that.

Merrifield wasn't among those present today. The earl had definitely courted her but hadn't pursued her madly. He'd danced with her twice at any ball they both attended. He'd taken her riding once and driving twice. He'd also offered his box to her, along with Jeremy and Catherine, and the four had enjoyed a night at the theatre. In her mind, Rachel could envision many such outings in the coming years. Merrifield got along so well with her brother and sister-in-law that she sometimes wondered why she even bothered to consider other men.

He hadn't kissed her yet. She wondered what it would take. Would it be something he saw in her eyes? Would it be the way she used her fan to flirt with him? She couldn't guess. Maybe he was waiting for her to ask him again for a kiss. That might be it. She was curious. It had been months since they had and she deemed it important in a future husband.

Perhaps she would request a single kiss tonight—and see if it turned into more.

"Don't you agree with me, Lady Rachel?" a voice pleaded.

She turned and saw it was the incredible dancer who questioned her. She hadn't bothered to remember his name because he was so bland.

"Yes, my lord. You are quite right."

"See?" he said, looking at the other three men triumphantly. "I knew Lady Rachel would understand."

Tiring of him and the others, Rachel put a hand to her temple. "I'm afraid I feel a slight headache coming on. I look forward to seeing all of you at tonight's ball and I fear I won't be able to make it unless I lie down for a rest."

They all began fussing over her and stating how she should do whatever it took to be in good health for tonight.

"Leah, would you stay? You know how soothing it is to me when you brush my hair."

"Of course, Rachel." Leah quickly raised her teacup to hide her growing smile.

The men said their goodbyes and filed out as Jeremy entered the room.

"Will we always have half a dozen or more of Rachel's suitors underfoot, Duchess?" he complained.

Catherine said, "There were only four today, Duke," and lifted her face for his lingering kiss.

"And how do you feel this afternoon, Leah?" Jeremy asked as one hand massaged the back of his wife's neck.

"Right as rain now," she said cheerily. "Until after dinner tonight. That's when I'll spew like a fountain."

"It does get better," Catherine assured her.

"I hope so," Leah said. "Until then, I'm able to eat throughout the day. In fact, I might try another one of those scones to help tide me over."

Rachel passed the plate to her.

Jeremy said, "I know how you two like to gossip and haven't seen one another alone to do so. Catherine and I will give you some privacy."

The duchess laughed merrily. "That's my husband's polite way of saying that he wants alone time with me."

Jeremy pulled her to her feet. "Are you going to give away all my secrets, Duchess?"

"I might," she said airily. "Unless you find some way to convince me otherwise, Duke."

His reply was to sweep her off her feet and carry her from the drawing room.

That was what Rachel wanted. A man who would continue to act romantically even after they were wed and had children. One who was both friend and lover to her.

"They are still so in love," Leah said softly. "I hope Alex and I will follow their example."

"You will," Rachel assured her. "The two of you are mad for one another. I cannot see that ever changing." She lifted the teapot and poured them both another cup.

"Let's talk about your Season. I only see you at events and you're always surrounded by many men."

"I have started a prospective husband list," she confided. "I have four names on it now."

"Oh? Do tell. Let me guess. The gentleman who was so eager for you to agree with him isn't on it, is he?"

She laughed. "He hasn't a chance. The only thing he has in his favor is that he is a wonderful dancer. Though I love to dance, I can't see going through my marriage only dancing when I'm around him."

"You don't even know his name, do you?"

"No. I know we were introduced but I've found if a man isn't going to make my list, I'm not going to invest time in him. That includes remembering endless names and titles."

"He is quite handsome and will be an earl soon."

Rachel shook her head. "Looks have never meant much to me. Neither do titles. I'm looking for excellent qualities from the men on my list. That gentleman is much too boring."

"What does it take to be added?" Leah asked. "I'm curious."

"All kinds of things. Kindness. Generosity. Intelligence. A sense of humor. Someone who can converse about more than the weather or food."

"Share with me the names you've accumulated thus far."

Rachel went through the three that ranked number two, three, and four on her list, saving Merrifield for last.

"I might have guessed Merrifield would be on it," her friend said. "He showed quite an interest in you when we were at the house party Alex held before our marriage. I suppose it doesn't hurt that Merrifield has good looks and wealth."

She shrugged. "He offers more, though. He's amusing. Witty. We talk about all kinds of things. He actually likes that I have strong opinions and express them freely."

Leah smiled. "You are so like Cor in that regard."

"Thank you. You couldn't have given me a higher compliment."

"Every woman wants to be Cor and every man enjoys her company, whether young or old."

"Cor likes Merrifield. So do Jeremy and Catherine. The four of us have had tea together. Gone riding and to the theatre."

"It sounds as if Merrifield tops your list," Leah said thoughtfully.

"He does," Rachel confirmed. "He's also a good kisser even though he hasn't tried to kiss me since last August at Fairfield."

Her friend's brows rose in surprise. "He hasn't? Why not?"

She felt her cheeks heat. "He says he will when the time is right. He says . . . that he wants me to burn for him."

It was Leah's turn to blush. "Oh, my."

"I know."

"Do you? Burn for him."

Rachel considered the question. "No. I like him quite a bit. I can see myself with him. I believe he would make for a good husband and father. I've seen him play with Timothy, Delia, and Jenny. He seemed so natural." She hesitated. "I remember he kissed well. He would make me happy in our marriage bed. Burn for him? No. Not yet, anyway."

"What of Merrick?" Leah asked softly.

Her throat tightened. "What of him?"

"I know you have said nothing could exist between you but I sense otherwise, Rachel. I know you, perhaps better than anyone. What are your feelings toward him? Have they changed since last summer?"

Tears welled in her eyes. She grasped Leah's hand. It took a moment to compose herself before she could speak.

"I loved him," she confessed. "The problem was, he didn't love me. I understand that he came home from the war scarred. Not just physically but emotionally. He was a joy to be with but Merrick wasn't in a place to commit. To me or anyone else. It's true, there was a huge physical attraction between us but, on his part, that's all it was."

"Are you sure?" Leah's penetrating gaze made Rachel uncomfortable.

"Yes." She released Leah's hand and wiped away her tears. "Besides, I have heard the *ton's* gossip. Merrick has become a womanizer and gambler. He hasn't bothered coming to any events of the Season so far. His needs are being fulfilled in other ways and places," she said harshly.

Anger rushed through Rachel again at the thought of Merrick

gallivanting through London with untold mistresses on his arm.

"I'd prefer you not bring up his name again to me, Leah."

Distress filled her friend's face. "Of course, Rachel."

They continued to talk, discussing the upcoming social events. Rachel inwardly chastised herself for admitting her weakness for Merrick to Leah. For a final time, she pushed him away mentally as far as she could, slamming and locking an imaginary door of steel that she hoped would separate them forever.

EVAN RODE IN his carriage with Dr. Gray and Randolph as his companions. They would return to Alex's townhome. Before he'd left, he'd asked Leah to see that his London residence had a thorough scrubbing and that they throw out the settee he'd slept on. It now stood vacant, an empty slate that called out for a woman's touch.

He prayed that woman would be Rachel.

She would be allowed to do whatever she wanted with the place. Choose the furniture she desired. Hire the servants she wanted. She could leave her imprint on it—as she had Edgemere. It had been hard being there, knowing what a hand she'd had in revitalizing his country estate. Everywhere he turned were reminders of her. She'd not only brought Edgemere up to snuff, she'd brought him to life again after years of turning off his humanity during the war.

He would see her tonight—and he still hadn't a clue how to approach her. If Everton was there, he would try to keep Evan from her. He wondered if he could ask Alex and Leah to somehow distract Everton and the duchess and decided against it. They'd already risked their relationship with the pair because of their support for him. He couldn't come between Leah and her sister.

Even if he did see Rachel—and hopefully talk with her—it might not make a difference. The Season was already in full swing. With her sunny disposition and great beauty, she would have drawn many men to her. What if she'd already given her heart to another man?

He would deal with it. Just as he had his drinking these past few weeks. They'd been miserable. Daunting. Yet he emerged from the darkness somehow stronger. More resilient than ever before. He would always crave drink but knew even without Rachel in his life that he had worth. He would never devalue himself again and slip into the familiar pit of despair. He'd learned that alcohol offered only fleeting comfort. He was now invested in himself and his future at Edgemere.

Please, God . . . let Rachel be a part of it.

The carriage slowed and Evan glanced out the window. He saw the Alford residence on his right. He used the breathing technique Gray had taught him and calmed himself. The physician caught his eye and nodded approvingly.

They disembarked and went into the townhouse. A footman saw to his trunk. He'd brought back clothes from Edgemere, ones that fit him once again, including evening wear for tonight's ball. Evan had barely stepped into the foyer when Leah flung herself at him, throwing her arms about him. He embraced her and kissed her cheek.

Her eyes conveyed hope to him before she ever spoke.

"I spoke to Rachel today," she said breathlessly. "Without revealing any confidences, I will only say that you must keep the faith, Evan. I believe you have a chance."

CHAPTER TWENTY-FIVE

As usual, Merrifield made his way to Rachel before any other gentleman did. It had almost become a game among the bachelors of the *ton* to see if they could reach her and claim a dance before the earl. Merrifield never allowed anyone to waylay him. He skipped receiving lines and ignored all who called out a greeting to him, letting no one get in his path.

"Good evening, Lady Rachel," he said pleasantly. "How are you tonight?"

"I am well, Lord Merrifield. And you?"

"Quite well, indeed. Might I examine your programme and claim a dance?"

"Most certainly."

She handed it over and he examined it before writing his name next to the supper dance. They had repeated the game several times now but on this occasion, he changed the course. Rachel watched as he penned his name a second time.

Beside the last dance.

Handing her dance card back, he said, "I hope you don't mind if I took two slots."

"Not at all, my lord. I'm merely surprised you didn't claim your usual dance after supper."

Rachel had thought that tonight she would ask him as they strolled outside after supper if he intended to ever kiss her again. She needed to kiss him badly. She wanted Merrifield to make a decent impression on her—so she could forget that night in the gazebo with Merrick.

And all those midnight kisses . . .

"I thought if we shared the last dance together that I might be allowed to escort you home."

"I see."

She wondered if he wanted her alone in a darkened carriage for their next kiss.

"I'm not certain that would be appropriate, Lord Merrifield. My brother and his wife escorted me here tonight and want me properly chaperoned at all times. A young lady cannot be too careful, according to Jeremy."

"Then I will speak to Everton and let him know I wish to see you home. We'll see what the duke says."

Anticipation filled her. She needed to kiss Merrifield again. No one on her list came close. She'd kissed one of the gentlemen on it already and his kiss had been sweet and reliable. Another who hadn't made the list tried to kiss her three nights ago. Rachel had turned her head so that his lips merely grazed her cheek. It was time Merrifield staked his claim and let her figure out whether or not things would progress between them—even if she already knew she would accept his inevitable offer.

"Very well. You do that," she told him and turned away to greet two gentlemen wishing to claim a dance from her.

Rachel danced three times in a row. One partner was tongue-tied and his attempts at conversation fell flat. The second nearly broke her toe with his awkward steps on the dance floor. The third had great possibilities. He was an earl from Scotland that had just arrived in London for the Season. He possessed a charming accent and a dimple in his chin. His conversation was lively. So far, he was the greatest challenger to Merrifield—and she'd only just met him.

She thought if she wed this delightful earl from Scotland, she wouldn't have to come to London. Though she would miss her family terribly, she could visit them at their country estates. Moving to Scotland meant, in all likelihood, that she would never lay eyes on Merrick again. Suddenly, this man she danced with appealed to her even more than Merrifield. Would it be so wrong to be a coward and wed this handsome Scot just so she'd never risk a chance of running into Merrick again?

And then she saw him.

Rachel stumbled, her feet entangling, and the Scot had to halt his own steps in order to right her.

"Are you all right, Lady Rachel?" he asked.

"Yes. I am," she assured him.

They resumed dancing but she gazed across the room. The Marquess of Merrick boldly stared at her. Without thinking, Rachel licked her lips.

He smiled.

Realizing what she'd done, she glanced up at her partner and said, "This is my third dance in a row. Would it be possible to stop and have some punch together?"

Her partner smiled. A very nice smile. "An excellent idea."

He released her and escorted her from the dance floor. They went straight to the punch bowl, where he claimed two cups.

Handing her one, he said, "To new friends . . . and new experiences."

Her mouth was so dry that she didn't acknowledge his toast. Instead, she downed the entire cup in a single swallow and held it out again. "May I have some more?"

"Of course."

Rachel drank a second cup and then said, "It was delightful to meet you, my lord, but I must visit the retiring room."

"Might I call upon you tomorrow afternoon, Lady Rachel?"

"Yes," she said, feeling she might faint at any moment.

She took off with her empty cup still in hand, weaving her way through the crowded ballroom. She hadn't looked in Merrick's direction since she'd left the dance floor and had no idea where he was. Getting to her destination without him intercepting her became her goal.

Joining a group of ladies, she managed to wriggle her way into the middle of them as they headed to the retiring room. She entered and went to a corner, leaning against the wall as she faced away from everyone. Seeing Merrick was as if someone had punched her in the gut. She couldn't breathe. She couldn't think. Bloody hell. Why had he come tonight?

And why did he have to look so impossibly handsome?

Rachel remained where she was, sensing women come and go. No one approached her, for which she was grateful. Still, she couldn't remain in here forever. Already, she had missed several dances and disappointed who knows how many men who'd sought to partner with her.

She was through with hiding. She wasn't some scared rabbit. She'd done nothing wrong. Nothing at all.

Except love a man who didn't return the same feelings.

She refused to give in to the fear that raced through her. She would not be afraid. She would return to the gathering. Dance. Laugh. Enjoy herself as all guests should. If she saw Merrick again, so be it. She would boldly look him in the eye and move on.

Emerging from the retiring room, she ran into Leah, who looked pale.

"Are you going to be sick? Would you like me to stay with you?"

"No. I was actually worried about you. You disappeared and no one knew where you'd gone. I thought to check here to see if you were all right."

"I was feeling a bit fatigued after exerting myself but I'm fine now," she lied.

Leah looked at her in disbelief. "You can out dance anyone in that ballroom, Rachel St. Clair."

She linked her arm through Leah's and pulled her back toward the direction of the music.

"Drop it, Leah. We're returning to the festivities. I'm fine. That's all you need to know."

Rachel urged her friend on and then she spied Alex and Luke. They joined the pair and then, out of nowhere, Merrifield appeared. "It's time for our dance."

"Good," she declared. "I've looked forward to it."

The music began and they took to the dance floor. Rachel made sure to concentrate on Merrifield's face. They chatted easily as they danced. Her familiarity with him made her comfortable. This is the man she would wed. Merrifield would never let her down. He'd never bring turmoil into her life. He was dependable. Likeable.

And kissable.

She looked into his eyes and asked, "What do you see tonight?"

He gave her a slow smile. "The most beautiful woman in the room. In my arms."

"Anything else?"

He cocked his head. "Perhaps a woman who wishes to be kissed, I think."

"I was right. You are astute."

"And handsome," he quipped.

"That, too," she agreed. "Good with children."

"Also, an excellent rider," he added.

She grinned. "And most of all, humble."

He laughed heartily. "Well, there is that. I hadn't thought you'd noticed."

"I think I've noticed most everything about you, Lord Merrifield—and then some."

His eyes gleamed at her. "I like hearing that, Rachel. Very much."

She noticed the use of her Christian name as the music came to an end. He led her into supper.

"I think tonight I'd like you all to myself," he told her and maneuvered her to a table for two. Seating her, he said, "I'll bring back something for both of us."

As Merrifield walked away, Rachel tamped down her panic. She was alone. If Merrick were going to approach her, this would be when it occurred. Her eyes darted around the room, searching for him.

He stood in the doorway on the opposite side of the room. Their gazes locked and he held hers hostage, as if she had no will of her own. Then he nodded deferentially and turned from the room.

Was he leaving? Without speaking to her? She glanced about and found Jeremy and Catherine. They were engaged in conversation with another couple. If her brother had spotted Merrick, he would have confronted him.

Should she go after him? No. She was with Merrifield. She'd already decided she'd done nothing wrong. She and Merrick had nothing more to say to each other. She waited patiently for the earl to return.

He brought back plates heaping with food. Rachel looked at it and thought she might be sick.

"I know how much you enjoy eating," he teased.

"Actually, I had a larger than usual dinner. I'm not as hungry tonight."

She attempted to eat something so he wouldn't press her and succeeded, even allowing him to feed her a few strawberries.

"I'm looking forward to the last dance tonight," he said, his voice husky.

"You are an excellent dancer. It's always a pleasure to partner with you."

Somehow, Rachel made it through supper and parted from Merrifield. She danced with several other partners and did her best not to look over their shoulders for Merrick. He had to be gone by now. He probably had spied Jeremy and decided it wasn't worth staying.

He hadn't looked drunk or disheveled. In fact, Merrick looked the exact opposite—the picture of health in finely tailored evening clothes. She should never have listened to the Three B's and their vicious gossip. Now, she doubted everything she'd heard from them. Merrick might spend some time at his club. He might play the occasional hand of cards for money. He certainly must see other women. It was sad that he was the object of such vile rumors.

Merrifield claimed her as the final dance of the night arrived. The strains of the waltz started as they took their places and began the dance.

The music was only a few measures old when Merrifield halted. Rachel looked to her left and saw why.

Merrick stood there, interrupting them.

"I must speak with Rachel."

Merrifield hesitated and then said, "A gentleman always avoids a scene in public." He slipped away and Merrick seized her, sweeping her into the dance.

The scent of his sandalwood soap struck her first. Then the warmth that radiated from him. Her body knew his touch and immediately ached for it. She wanted to fling herself at him and had to stiffen her resolve to keep from doing so.

"You need to release me," she said. "This is embarrassing. I want to leave."

"No. I won't let you go."

Stonily, she stared over his shoulder, not wishing to look at his face. He drew her a bit closer, enough so her breasts brushed against his muscled chest. She remembered his mouth on them, sucking at them, nipping, teasing, bringing shivers of delight.

Rachel sucked in her breath and held it, angry that her body was betraying her so. Then she made the mistake of looking at him—and the entire world faded away. She was caught up in the dance, in the arms of the man she loved. If only she could move heaven and earth and change things between them. Marrying Merrifield was out of the question now. She would have to wed the unsuspecting Scot and never cross the border into England again. She couldn't trust herself to be in the same country with Merrick. Ever.

The waltz ended—but he kept her in his arms. Rachel squirmed, trying to free herself from him, but his gripped tightened on her.

"I came to say something to you," Merrick began.

"Will you *let go* of me?" she hissed, sensing that others were starting to look at them.

"No. Not until I'm finished."

"Please, Merrick. People are staring at us. I'll let you speak to me. In private."

"No," he said more firmly, his voice raised. "What I have to say to you is something the entire world can hear because it's an eternal truth." He paused. "I love you, Rachel."

Her heart stopped. Her jaw dropped. Her mouth was so dry that she couldn't speak.

"I didn't want you to think I'd become confused because of the lessons. That last night I was about to tell you how much I loved you. How much I believed in us together. How you brought me joy and fulfilled me in ways I never knew existed. And then . . . it was too late."

He loosened his grip on her and captured her hands, bringing them to his lips and kissing them tenderly.

"I held my tongue because you declared you didn't love me. You said you'd never speak vows with a man you didn't love. There was no reason at that point to tell you of my affection."

"I did love you," she said earnestly, tears spilling down her cheeks. "I thought *you* didn't love *me*. You'd never given me any indication of your feelings. I didn't want you to feel trapped. Forced to marry me. I feared it would destroy us both. That's why I said what I did. I had to let you go *because* I loved you so much."

Rachel saw hope spring in his mesmerizing blue eyes. The same feeling grew within her.

"I know months have passed," he said. "You are Rachel St. Clair, the most noted beauty of the *ton*. Men fall at your feet for a single smile. I can't think that you'd still love me after all this time apart. It's more than I could ask for. I couldn't live another day, though, without declaring my feelings to you."

He knelt and pressed a fervent kiss against her hands. Looking up, he said, "I wish you all the happiness in the world, Rachel. Know that I will love you not only until the day they place me in my grave—but even in the great beyond."

Tears almost blinded her now. "Get up, you bloody idiot, and kiss me like you mean it," she demanded. "And it better be good. As you said before, St. Clairs always get what they want."

He rose, his smile blindingly bright. "I love you, Rachel. More than Everton loves his duchess."

She smiled radiantly. "That's quite a declaration, Evan Drake. Prove it."

His arms came around her and his mouth took hers. Hungrily. Possessively. Deliciously. She had no idea how long they kissed until he finally let her go.

"How was that for a start?" he asked.

Suddenly, she was aware of thunderous applause and glanced around, seeing that the entire *ton* had remained to watch this scene play out.

She wound her arms about his neck and said, "I suppose you understand that you've announced your intentions to the entire world with that display."

Evan grinned. "It's a story we'll tell our children. And grandchildren. I'm sure the *ton* will tell and retell it so many times that we'll become legends."

With that, he kissed her again and then swept her off her feet.

"Where are you taking me?" she asked breathlessly as she watched him look around.

Evan didn't have far to go. He carried her straight to Jeremy and Catherine, who stood nearby, as Luke hurried to join them. The front of Catherine's gown was soaked with her tears, ones that Rachel knew were happy ones. Luke beamed and winked at her.

It was Jeremy who concerned her. His face was a mask.

Evan eased Rachel to her feet, keeping his arm about her waist.

"Your Grace, I would like to ask your permission to wed Lady Rachel. I believe you know how highly I hold her in regard. I promise she will be the most loved and most cherished wife in the *ton*."

Rachel held her breath, waiting for Jeremy to respond. Slowly, a smile replaced the solemn look he'd held. He pulled Catherine close and asked, "Duchess, do you think Merrick can love my sister as much as I love you?" he asked.

Catherine pretended to consider his question. "You've set a high mark, Duke. I suppose Merrick can try. If he ever surpasses you, I'm sure you'll make it up to me."

She kissed him on the mouth, causing the crowd to titter.

Jeremy finally broke the kiss and turned back to them. "All right, Merrick. I'll allow you to wed Rachel. I'm warning you, though, you better make her happy. Always."

Evan looked at her, love shining in his eyes. "I plan to spend the rest of my life doing just that."

Chapter Twenty-Six

Euphoria filled Rachel when she heard Evan's words. She hadn't let herself dream of this kind of storybook ending and yet it magically unfolded as her new fiancé kissed her soundly again in front of the entire *ton*. She laughed against his mouth, thinking what a scandal the St. Clairs were causing tonight. Luke, rogue that he was, would have to do something unique to top tonight's gossip. Knowing her brother, he'd somehow manage to do that very thing.

Evan's lips finally left hers and he said, "I love you, Rachel St. Clair," so softly that only she could hear.

"I love you," she repeated.

As he released her and she saw looks ranging from glowing approval to outrage at the way they'd flaunted convention, she caught sight of the one person who'd been hurt tonight.

Merrifield.

He gazed at her wistfully, causing her throat to tighten. Turning to Evan, she said, "I must speak to Merrifield."

Evan nodded. "I understand."

Rachel stiffened her spine and courageously walked toward the man she'd thought would be her husband. He watched her approach, waiting patiently.

"I'm sorry, Merrifield."

The earl gave her a rueful smile. "I suppose it always was Merrick."

She nodded. "I love him. I always have." She reached and took Merrifield's hand, surprising him. "But I thought I would wed you. You would have made me a good husband. You're bright and witty. I think we would have laughed a great deal."

"I would have enjoyed that. I will miss our bantering."

"As will I. You are certainly made for entertaining sons and daughters."

"I do love children," he admitted and sighed. "I suppose I'll have to reenter the fray and see who else is available on the Marriage Mart if I'm to get those children."

"Stay away from the Three B's," she advised. "They're not good enough for you."

Rachel leaned over and kissed his cheek as she squeezed his hand and then released it.

"This may sound odd," he began, "but I still like you, Rachel. I even like Merrick. I wonder... if someday... we might all be friends."

She motioned Evan over. He slid an arm around her waist.

"I know you and Merrifield got along at Fairfield," she told her new fiancé. "I also get along with him. I think the three of us should be friends."

Evan's brows rose and he looked to Merrifield. "Is this your idea—or hers?"

The earl shrugged. "Both, I suppose. I know Polite Society will see me as a jilted suitor. I'd rather look at my situation as having lost a possible wife while gaining two very good friends. If that's even possible."

"I think you mean it," Evan said, surprise in his voice.

"I do. Maybe the two of you can help me to one day find the happiness and love that you share—with the right woman."

Evan offered his hand and Merrifield took it. Rachel heard the gasps and glanced around, realizing that many people continued to watch their little drama unfold. She ventured that no one would have guessed how tonight would turn out, with the two men who vied for her now friendly—if not true friends.

"We've certainly given the *ton* enough to gossip about for weeks, if not the entire Season," Merrifield said. "I am honored that you will accept my friendship, Merrick. You, too, Lady Rachel."

She chuckled. "Well, if we're going to be such good friends and help you find a wife, the least you can do is call us Rachel and Evan."

Merrifield smiled broadly. "I can do that."

"We'll find you a bride," she promised. "It might not be this Season but you are quite a good catch, Merrifield. Somewhere in London—or perhaps beyond—is the woman you will give your heart to." She turned to her fiancé. "Just as I have given my heart to this wonderful man."

"Don't think I'll ask you to stand up with me," Evan said, humor laced in his tone. "That's Alford's job."

"Of course."

"And I won't ask you to stand with me either on my wedding day. That's for Leah to do, although wouldn't the *ton* be shocked if I did?" Rachel mused.

Evan pulled her closer. His eyes seemed to devour her. "It's time to go home, Rachel. Goodnight, Merrifield."

He led her from the ballroom as every eye followed their progress. They reached outside and the cool air greeted them. She looked over her shoulder and saw Jeremy, Catherine, and Luke only paces behind them.

"You've certainly given the *ton* fuel for their fire," Luke joked.

"I know that look in your eye, Merrick," Jeremy said. "It tells me you'll be purchasing a special license tomorrow."

"Don't you want the banns called?" Catherine asked. "After tonight's performance, the entire *ton* will be expected to attend a grand wedding."

"I don't want to wait three weeks," Rachel said. She glanced at Evan. "Even three days seems like a lifetime."

"Then give me a week," Catherine pleaded. "I can put something lovely together in that time."

"What do you think, Evan?" she asked. "Can we wait a week?"

"Could you give us a moment?" he asked, leading Rachel away.

"Why do we need privacy?" she asked. "I'll marry you tomorrow if you wish."

"Let's give the duchess her week," he suggested. "But leading up to it? I think we should continue our midnight lessons."

A frisson of desire rippled through her. "Oh, really?" she asked coyly.

"You do realize what I'm asking?" he said, his face serious.

"I believe I do. You wish to initiate me into all the ways of love before we wed." Rachel grinned. "I think it's generous of you to allow Catherine her week to plan while we use our time wisely."

His hands cupped her cheeks. "It will mean leaving balls early. Not going to supper after the opera," he warned, his thumbs caressing her face.

"I will say that I'm wanting to rest up for my wedding day," she declared. "No one will be suspicious. You can come to me every night and teach me something wild and wonderful. Doesn't that sound delicious?"

He kissed her tenderly. "I cannot wait until midnight tomorrow."

Evan paused, an unusual and unreadable look on his face. Rachel's heart missed a beat as she tried to analyze this strange look. "What has you troubled?" she asked.

"Your brother. You know I'm still wary of angering him again. What if he catches us? He could break the wedding agreement! This might be a bad idea."

Rachel simply giggled. "He won't, silly. He's already agreed to our marriage. All my brother cares about is that I'm happy and have a love match. And he knows that is what we share. Rest easy, my love. The midnight lessons will continue!"

They returned to her family and Evan said, "We would like to wed in one week, Your Grace. I shall purchase the special license tomorrow. I can also check and see if St. George's could accommodate us so that all you would need to do is plan the wedding breakfast with Rachel."

Catherine sniffed. "That shows you how much you know about weddings, Merrick. There are clothes to be considered and, once chosen, the gown to be made up. Hats, as well. I won't bore you with all the small details." Then she smiled. "I do believe you'll be able to book St. George's, though. The Season is in its infancy. I doubt any wedding is scheduled to take place next week."

"Then I will call upon you and Rachel tomorrow and let you know what progress I've made."

When he finished speaking, Leah and Alex rushed over, both of them embracing her and then Evan.

"I knew it would work out," Leah proclaimed. "Alex and I believed in our hearts that the two of you were meant to be together as man and wife."

"As long as you're both here, will you commit to standing up with us at our wedding next week?" Rachel asked.

"Of course," they both said.

"May I call on you at ten o'clock tomorrow morning?" Evan asked Alex. "I fear I'm going to need your help navigating the waters. I've a special license to purchase. Wedding finery to be fitted for. A church to reserve."

Alex slung his arm around his friend. "Let this old married man show you the ropes."

Luke hugged Rachel. "See? I told you so. You are marrying before me. You can give Cor a half-dozen great-grandchildren to get me off the hook for another eight or ten years."

"We'll see," Rachel said. "I'm already supposed to look for a wife for Merrifield. I might look for one for you at the same time."

EVAN AND RACHEL accompanied Everton and his duchess to the theatre and had an enjoyable time. The duchess insisted that he call her Catherine since he was to be family. The duke looked straight through him, daring Evan to call him by his given name. Evan knew Alex had experienced the same problem. The Duke of Everton was a most intimidating man. Evan could see how much he loved his sister, though, and because of that he would summon up the courage and call the man Jeremy one day.

Just not tonight.

They said their goodbyes outside the theatre. Rachel told everyone how she was curtailing her late nights in order to rest up for her wedding next week. She'd been pleased that he'd been able to book St. George's for them and told him though she wasn't one of those women who'd always dreamed of her wedding since she was a little girl, she'd did enjoy attending ones at St. George's and was happy they would wed there. He could picture her coming down the aisle. She would be his in six days.

Evan went to his club for an hour. He was still staying at the Alford townhome and had been given his own key. He'd use it when he returned in the wee hours tomorrow morning. Though he longed for a tumbler of whiskey to steady his nerves, he refused to wallow in the particular mire that drink had cost him. He glanced up and saw Randolph still shadowed him. Gray's assistant was to keep a watch on Evan as best he could in order to prevent such an occurrence during this first week as he took his place in society once again.

When the clock chimed a quarter to midnight, Evan rose and exited the club. The streets were mostly deserted as his coachman took him to within two blocks of the St. Clair residence. He instructed the driver to wait at this distance until he returned. When the carriage stopped, Evan hopped from it and continued on foot. A ball was taking place tonight and its guests wouldn't venture home for another couple of hours. Others of the *ton* who'd attended the theatre or opera were now at supper, thus leaving the streets empty.

He headed to the right once he reached his destination. That side of the house was where Everton's study was located. It was through a window there that Rachel would let him in.

It began misting just as he saw a dim glow appear on the other side of the curtains. A slender hand drew the curtain aside and then slid open the window.

"Hurry," she urged, stepping back to give him room.

Evan climbed through and quickly shut the window. Turning, he saw she wore the silk dressing gown he knew so well. She took his hand, entwining her fingers with his as they sneaked from the study to the large staircase. He followed her up the stairs and down a long, carpeted corridor until they reached her room. She opened the door and he stepped in after her, closing it behind him.

Rachel put the lamp down and then rushed into his arms. Their kiss was urgent, his hands rubbing up and down her slender back as he tasted the woman he loved.

She was the one who unexpectedly broke the kiss and took his hand, leading him to her bed.

"Are you certain?" he asked.

In response, she untied the dressing gown and shrugged out of it, letting it fall to the floor.

She wore nothing underneath it.

Rachel had thought about this moment during the entire play tonight. She had no hesitation regarding what they were about to do. She wanted to be with Evan in the way a woman came together with a man. If anything, she was eager to begin this part of their life together.

Cor had prepared her at the beginning of last Season, explaining how everything worked in the marriage bed. She was grateful her grandmother had done so. She doubted every young woman was as informed as she and Leah had been.

Evan stared at her, enraptured. "You are perfection," he said huskily.

His hands cupped her face and he kissed her so tenderly that she knew how much he cherished her.

They kissed for a long time, each one deeper and more meaningful. Slowly, his hands began to caress her, sliding down her bare back.

Rachel broke the kiss. "I need my fingers to feel you," she said breathlessly. "I want my naked skin against yours."

"Then help me undress, my love," he said softly, his eyes shining with both devotion and desire.

She slowly unknotted his starched cravat, sliding it from his neck and dropping it to the floor. Her fingers went to his shoulders and pushed his wool tailcoat from them. He wriggled as she went behind him and pulled it from his arms. He worked on the buttons to his waistcoat while she began on those fastening his shirt. Both pieces came off and she took a step back, admiring his torso in the candlelight.

Stepping to him again, she brushed her palms from his shoulders down his bare chest, loving the feel of warm skin and muscles that rippled at her touch.

"If I would have known what you looked like under your clothes, I would have suggested you shedding them back at Fairfield," she quipped.

He caught her wrists and raised her hands, palms up, pressing a kiss into the center of each. "It was not the right time for us. It is now."

Evan led her to the bed and he sat. "I'll need help with my Hessians."

Rachel grabbed the heel and supported the top with her other hand. With one long, smooth jerk, she removed the boot. He lifted his other leg and she did the same.

"My, you're better than any batman I had in the war."

"Have you gotten a valet yet?"

"No. I suppose I won't need one . . . if I have you," he teased. "Of course, I can return the favor and serve as your lady's maid."

As she unbuttoned his fall, she snorted. "As if you have a talent for dressing hair."

What emerged from his fall fascinated her. He rose and removed his trousers quickly and she could better see his member, stiff and straight.

She chuckled. "You look as if you're saluting me, Major Merrick."

Evan wrapped his arms about her, pulling her close. "I plan to do more than salute you. I want to worship you, my lady."

"Does that involve kissing, my lord? I had a capable tutor once. His midnight lessons focused on kissing. In all kinds of places. Not just my mouth."

He grinned. "I plan on kissing every inch of you, Rachel St. Clair."

By the time he had kissed most of her, she burned for him. And then his lips trailed down her belly—and kept going.

"What are you doing?" she squealed.

Evan lifted his head, mischief dancing in his eyes. "What I said I was going to do. Kiss you. Everywhere."

"There?" she asked, fascinated by the idea that had come to her long ago.

"*Especially* there," he replied.

"With your tongue?"

He smiled wisely. "I see your former midnight tutor did a good job educating you. Lie back, Rachel, and enjoy."

His fingers and then tongue played with her so that he drove her into a frenzy. She writhed beneath him, the orgasm building and building until it slammed like a full force gale. Rachel cried out and

Evan's mouth was on hers, as she rode out the storm. She barely had time to recover when he pushed his cock into her, one swift motion that brought a moment of fleeting pain which dissolved almost instantly.

"Are you all right? It only hurts the once."

"It didn't hurt much at all."

He shifted and she sucked in a quick breath.

"Oh! I quite like that, Lord Merrick. Do that again."

"With pleasure, Lady Rachel."

Evan moved again and Rachel found herself responding. Somehow, their bodies took over, moving in unison, as if they had always been one.

And always would be.

They both reached a feverish climax at the same time. It was the most delicious feeling she'd ever had. Evan collapsed atop her, his hot flesh pressed against her breasts, which already longed for his touch again.

"I love you," he said, panting, his heart thumping wildly.

"I love you," she agreed, knowing her heart did the same.

He somehow turned and she found herself facing him, their heads sharing a single pillow.

"Will it always be like this? This good?"

Evan laughed softly. "It will only get better. I promise."

They dozed and then made love twice more, one time fierce and raw and primal, the other tender and gentle. As Evan cradled her in his arms, he said, "I must go. You need to get some sleep."

She touched his cheek. "You will come back tomorrow at midnight, won't you? I need midnight with my marquess."

He kissed her sweetly. "And I need every midnight from this one for decades to come with my marchioness."

"I'm not quite your marchioness yet."

His eyes gleamed possessively. "You're mine, Rachel. You're my fiancée. My almost bride and marchioness. My love and my life and my future wife. Mine always, my love."

Evan climbed from the bed and quickly dressed. She lazily drank him in, thinking he, too, was hers for all time, marveling at the revelation.

Once he was ready, he came to the bed and sat on it, drawing her up for a final kiss.

"Until midnight tomorrow."

"Don't forget tomorrow night's ball," she reminded. "I fully intend to have two dances with you. No, three, since we are now engaged. And then we will have another lesson at midnight. Think of something especially wicked to teach me, Lord Tutor."

"I promise you it will be beyond wicked."

Chapter Twenty-Seven

Rachel prepared for her wedding day in much the same fashion Leah had. Cor sat in a chair, supervising the proceedings. Catherine and Leah fussed over the bride. They had helped her to dress and had just completed arranging her hair. Leah now bent and helped Rachel into her slippers, mint green in color. They'd been dyed to match her wedding gown. Her groom's only request had been for her to wear green on their wedding day because he loved how her emerald eyes seemed to grow in size and color when she wore the shade.

"You are the most beautiful bride I've ever seen," Catherine exclaimed. Then a strange look crossed her face and her hand flew to her mouth. She hurried across the room and knelt beside the chamber pot, where she was sick.

Leah went to her sister and helped her rise, leading her to sit on the bed. Rachel quickly doused a cloth in water and brought it to Catherine, who wiped her mouth and then dabbed it on her face.

"I'm sorry," she told Rachel. "It won't happen again. Once and I'm always done."

"You're increasing," she said to her sister-in-law. "Does Jeremy know yet?"

"I was waiting to be sure before I told him."

Leah laughed. "You look and sound exactly like I have these past three months. Actually, I've had two days in a row when I've kept everything down. Cor told me I've turned a corner and it should get better from now on."

Catherine sighed. "She's right. I was sicker for a little longer with the twins. About four months. I suppose because there were two of them causing mischief inside me."

"When do you believe you are due?" Rachel asked.

"I think mid-December." Catherine took Rachel's hand. "I wanted to have everything with the wedding over before I said anything. I didn't want to take away from your day."

"I don't mind at all. I'm delighted to know I'll have another niece or nephew."

"Please, don't tell Jeremy," Catherine asked. "I want to share it with him. I'll do so tonight."

"Our lips are sealed," Rachel promised.

A knock sounded at the door and Leah went to see who was there. She admitted Jeremy. All four women smiled brightly and greeted him. Rachel noticed he carried a box similar to the one he'd brought to Leah on the day she wed Alex.

Her brother took her hand. "You have brought such joy to my life, little sister. I am fortunate that you are in my life. I'm also pleased that you didn't rush to take a husband because you've found a man worthy of you."

"You should tell Evan that," she said. "I think he—and Alex—are still wary of you."

Jeremy laughed. "Good. Then I'm doing my ducal job. Those two better always walk a straight and narrow path around me because they are entrusted with two people I love dearly."

Rachel blinked back tears. "You have been both a brother and father to me, Jeremy. And I know you will be an indulgent uncle to our children."

"I hope you and Merrick have many of them." He grinned. "Especially since you've already started work on that."

She gasped. "You know?"

One eyebrow shot up. "You do realize your bedchamber is next to ours."

She felt her face flame. "We—or rather, I—tried my best to be quiet. I suppose I didn't quite succeed."

He cradled her cheek. "No, you didn't. And I'm delighted that you've found a man you love so . . . thoroughly."

"Stop!" she cried, punching him in the arm.

"Watch it, now, or you won't get your gift."

She took a deep breath and looked at him expectantly. "Well?"

By now, Catherine had crossed to join her husband and linked her arm through his.

"Catherine and I are ready to present you with a lasting memory of being a St. Clair. Even when you become the Marchioness of Merrick, we hope you will wear these with pride."

Jeremy handed her the box and Rachel opened it. She gasped when she saw what lay against the crushed velvet.

"The St. Clair emeralds? Oh, Jeremy, I can't. Catherine should be wearing these and then they should go to Jenny. Or Delia."

"As you point out, I have two daughters and, hopefully, more will come. I am a duke, Rachel. One of the wealthiest men in the kingdom. I will simply buy new emeralds. This is part of your heritage. We want you to have them and wear them with pride."

She flung herself at him, hugging him tightly and then doing the same to Catherine.

"I can't thank you enough."

"The only thanks I ask is for you to wear them and live your life in love," he said softly.

Rachel went and sat, staring at the emerald and diamond necklace and matching earrings. Finally, she lifted one earring and fastened it to her lobe and did the same with the other. Catherine removed the necklace and placed it around Rachel's neck, fastening the clasp. She touched the jewels with her fingertips.

"They look lovely with your dress," Cor complimented.

"Evan will be mad for you when he sees you," Leah proclaimed. "Make sure he doesn't sweep you off your feet and run away before you speak your vows."

They all laughed and then Jeremy informed them it was time to leave for St. George's. Downstairs, they found Luke waiting. He grinned when he saw her.

"You're riding in the second carriage with me," he informed the group. "All these female relatives have fussed over you all morning. It's my time with you now."

He led her outside and helped her into the carriage while the others boarded the first one outside the townhouse.

Luke sat next to Rachel and took her hand. "You've been such a big part of my life."

She chuckled. "I'm not dying, Luke. I'm not leaving you. I'm simply getting married."

"I know. To a very good man, I might add. Still, I know how things will change now. Merrick and the family you create together will be your priority. I just wanted to tell you how much I love you."

Tears misted her eyes. "I love you, too, Luke. And I cannot wait to find you a bride so you can experience the same kind of happiness I've discovered with Evan."

"I think you should make Merrifield your priority. He's been publically rejected and has the sympathy of the *ton* now. He's also older than I am. He needs a wife before I get one."

"Hmm. That's true. All right. I'll focus on Merrifield first," she agreed.

"You do know the *ton* can't figure out your and Merrick's relationship with him. You've danced with Merrifield at two balls this past week. You and Merrick even supped with him and other companions the other night."

"We truly like him. I'm sorry I hurt him so but we get along well. Yes, it surprises me that Evan and Merrifield also get along. It just... works."

Luke squeezed her hand. "Both of them are lucky to have you in their lives. Merrick most of all."

Rachel smiled brightly. "I think so, too. But once I help Merrifield find true love, you will be my next project, Luke."

"Oh, look. There's St. George's." He grinned. "Are you properly distracted?"

She kissed his cheek. "For now, Brother. For now."

Luke helped her from the carriage. Catherine and Leah bent to straighten her gown but he waved them away.

"You don't need to be doing that in your condition, Leah," he warned.

"I'm not an invalid, Luke. I'm merely having a baby."

Rachel looked at her friend, whose belly was slightly rounded now. Her baby would arrive in November, while Catherine's would come sometime in December. Rachel brushed her fingers along her own stomach, wondering if she and Evan had already made a baby and that by this time next year, they might be parents. She wanted that very much. He'd grown up an only child, pushed away for some reason by his father. Since she'd grown up with loving siblings, she wanted Evan to experience the joys of family and hoped they had many children.

Luke finished arranging her dress and Cor nodded in satisfaction. Jeremy took Catherine and Cor's arms to escort them inside. Catherine looked back over her shoulder and blew Rachel a kiss. Luke held out his arms for her and Leah to take and brought them through the church doors.

Once inside, Leah said, "I'll go to the altar now. I'm telling you because I doubt you'll see me there. Your eyes will be on Evan, as they should be. When the time comes, try to remember to hand me your bouquet." Her eyes twinkled. "Don't forget when the music starts, you're to walk down the aisle."

Luke and Leah entered the chapel and Rachel went to stand at the doors. She saw every pew filled. Then her eyes found Evan and love soared within her. Vaguely, she was aware that Leah had arrived at the front but she only gazed at her beloved. Organ music swelled and she lifted a foot to begin her journey toward the man she was making a lifetime commitment to.

Then a voice called out, "Lady Rachel! Wait."

She turned, annoyed, ready to chastise whoever was ruining such a lovely moment for her.

From the shadows emerged an older man who looked somewhat familiar but she couldn't place him.

As he came toward her, he said, "I must stop you before you make the biggest mistake of your life."

It was the Duke of Winstead.

EVAN'S HEART FILLED with love as he caught sight of Rachel standing in the doorway, ready to come to him. She was lovelier than he could have imagined. The fact that she was here to pledge her life and love to him was overwhelming. The music began.

Rachel didn't move toward him.

Instead, she turned away from the door. Her back now faced it. Queasiness enveloped him.

Something was wrong.

Evan left the altar and strode down the aisle. The organ music died. The only sound in the church was the click of his boot heels against the stone as he moved toward his bride. He reached her and saw what had distracted her.

His father.

It had been many years since he'd seen Winstead. Time hadn't been kind to the duke. His brown hair was now completely gray. His nights of carousing had etched deep lines into his face. He seemed a shadow of the man who'd once terrified Evan.

"In all likelihood, he's not even my son," Winstead said. "You don't want to tie yourself to a man like that. Everton would be appalled."

He winced at the words. Even now, all these years later, his father hated him enough to come and ruin Evan's wedding day. He hadn't told Rachel that his mother might have been unfaithful in her marriage. He should have. He'd already told her about his drinking and how he would have to be vigilant the rest of his life. But it had never occurred to him that he should mention Winstead's suspicions.

Or the fact that his father had murdered his own wife.

Evan reached out a hand to touch Rachel. Get her attention. See if this could be resolved. Before he could, she attacked as fiercely as any guard dog on earth, her voice ringing in the narthex.

"You think I'm marrying Evan because he's a marquess? And that he'll become a duke someday? I don't care one whit for titles or wealth. I'm wedding the man I love, Winstead. If Evan cobbled shoes or swept chimneys to earn a living, I would still marry him. He is my soulmate. My life. My eternal love. You're a bloody fool if you think what you've told me would make an ounce of difference in my feelings for him."

Rachel glared at the old man. "Get out of this church. You were not invited to our celebration for a reason. No one wants you here, especially Evan and me. You turned your back on him long ago and I'm doing the same to you now."

With that, Rachel whirled around—and saw him.

A radiant smile lit her face. "Evan!" she cried.

He captured her hands as she balanced her bouquet and kissed them fervently. "I love you, Rachel St. Clair. Perhaps more now than ever before."

She beamed at him. "Would you care to escort me to our wedding?"

He offered her his arm. "I'd be delighted to, my love."

They began down the aisle. A few steps into their walk, the organist had sense enough to begin playing again.

"I wonder how much of the conversation the *ton* overheard?" she asked.

"Probably all of it," he replied. "What they didn't hear, they'll make up."

Rachel giggled. "We seemed to stir up gossip wherever we go."

Evan smiled at her. "We will definitely be legends in our own time. Not many can lay claim to that."

They reached the altar, where Rachel immediately handed her bouquet to Leah and then held on to him tightly. Evan nodded at the flustered clergyman, who began the ceremony, though his voice shook.

"I love you," Evan mouthed, looking at his beautiful bride.

"I love you more," she mouthed back—and winked.

Evan would later blame that wink for what he did next. While the good reverend continued speaking, Evan turned and kissed Rachel, then and there. He heard the collective gasp of the invited guests fill the church and smiled against her mouth.

Breaking the kiss, he looked to the clergyman. "Please continue."

Miraculously enough, the man never missed a beat after that.

They made their vows facing one another, holding hands as they beamed with joy. He blocked out everything except Rachel's face as he spoke from his heart. When the good reverend pronounced them man and wife, Evan made sure that their first kiss was long and satisfying—then he scooped her up and carried her to the room where they would affix their signatures on their marriage license.

"You really are giving the *ton* something to talk about," Rachel murmured into his ear, causing pleasant tingles to ripple through him.

"At least Everton will know he's got his work cut out for him," he replied. "His duchess will need her husband to make a grand gesture to prove to the *ton* that he loves her more than I love you."

"Mmm. I love a good competition," she said. "Especially if Catherine and I benefit from it."

He had to set her down as they signed the register and Leah and Alex did the same. His friend grinned from ear to ear and slapped him on the back, no words necessary. Once more, Evan lifted up Rachel and she looped her arms around his neck, giving him a lingering kiss. He carried her back into the church and saw absolutely no one had left yet.

"I suppose they want to see what we'll do next," she said.

They reached the first pew, where the Duke and Duchess of Everton sat.

The duke shook his head and growled, "You are upping the stakes, Merrick."

With that, he stood and pulled Catherine to her feet and then swept her up into his arms, as well.

"Jeremy!" she cried. "What are you doing?"

"Showing you—and the *ton*—how very much I love you," he replied and kissed her.

Rachel burst out laughing as Evan carried her down the aisle and out the doors of St. George's, Jeremy and Catherine following behind them.

Epilogue

Ten weeks later...

RACHEL DISMISSED HER lady's maid for the night and checked her image one last time in the mirror. Tonight was the first ball she and Evan would host. He'd presented her with his London townhouse, a blank slate, and told her to do whatever she wished with it, claiming she'd made Edgemere a home that brought him great satisfaction. It pleased her that her new husband trusted her enough to give her carte blanche to redo their London residence. She'd selected paints, carpets, draperies, and furniture for literally every room in the residence since it stood bare. She instructed the carpenters to knock out a few walls and they now shared a massive bedchamber, though each of them had their own dressing room. Evan had been more than pleased with what she'd accomplished and wanted her to do more of the same once they returned to Edgemere after the Season.

Though she loved the hustle and bustle of London, Rachel couldn't wait to return to the country. Not only was she ready to begin their lives at Edgemere but she was eager to be closer to Leah again. Her friend had retreated to Fairfield with Alex only two days after Rachel's wedding, longing for the fresh country air while she increased. Leah and Alex insisted that Rachel and Evan remain in their townhome during the renovations to their own. They'd moved in a week ago, with the staff she'd hired in place. That staff had to deal with finding locked doors in various parts of the townhouse throughout the day and night because Evan had decided they must christen every room by making love in it.

She placed a palm against her stomach. She had no doubt now that she carried a child and planned to tell him tonight once the ball ended. Her best guess led her to believe it would come in early March, as spring began and new life blossomed everywhere. The thought of her children and Leah's being brought up together in such close range was icing on the cake.

Evan entered, already dressed in his evening clothes. Her fingers itched to run her fingers through his thick, dark blond hair but she knew if she did, they might never make it downstairs to their own ball.

He came and kissed her where her shoulder and neck blended together, an especially sensitive spot he'd recently discovered. "Everything is in place. The ballroom's flowers and decorations are magnificent. You will be acclaimed the hostess of this Season."

"I suppose I shouldn't ask whether you will behave tonight."

He grinned. "Scandalous behavior seems to suit me." He paused. "I do have something to ask you, though. I know you're wearing your St. Clair emeralds but I thought you might like to start a new tradition."

"I'm intrigued. Go on," she urged, running her hand along his waistcoat.

"What if you wore the Drake diamonds each time we hosted a ball?"

"I would—if I had any Drake diamonds."

"You do now. As of this afternoon, anyway."

Evan reached and unclasped the necklace she wore. Rachel removed her earrings and handed them to him and waited expectantly.

"Oh, you think it's going to be that easy, do you?" he teased. "You'll have to find them."

"Can you give me a hint?"

"They're somewhere within this bedchamber," he said mysteriously.

Rachel glanced about the room, knowing there were numerous places the gems could be hidden. She didn't have long because they were due downstairs to greet their guests within minutes. She'd learned Evan was a romantic at heart and tried to think as he would.

And immediately knew where to find the diamonds.

She crossed the room to their massive bed, which was already turned back for when they came upstairs after the ball ended in the wee hours of the morning. Their marriage was rooted in love and they'd already spent many happy hours in this bed. Lifting her pillow, she found what she was looking for—and gasped.

The Drake diamonds lay against the sheets, gleaming with fire.

"They're dazzling," she said softly as her husband came behind her and slipped his arms around her.

"I might have known my clever girl would know where to look," he murmured, kissing the long column of her neck.

"I've never worn anything so grand."

He reached for the necklace and placed it around her neck, fastening it. She glanced down, amazed that she now possessed so fine a piece. He undid the clasp on the bracelet and put it around her wrist. She held her hand out, admiring the sparkling gems, and then slipped the earrings onto her earlobes.

"I want to see them," she said and seated herself before the mirror, where she observed the diamonds glittering. "They're beautiful."

Evan came and placed his hands on her shoulders. "No, love. You're beautiful. They merely add to your beauty. I plan to shower you with many gems in the years to come but I hope you'll always wear these Drake diamonds whenever we host an event."

His lips grazed her neck, finding her pulse and nipping lightly before he took her hands and helped her rise.

"One kiss," he said. "Then we better go downstairs."

He kissed her gently, reverently, so sweet and soft that she wished it would never end.

"Downstairs, my lady," he said when he broke it.

"Very well, Lord Husband."

They descended to the bottom floor so they could receive their guests. Rachel noted that even the usual latecomers arrived on time before the music began. She guessed they didn't want to miss anything exciting that Evan might spontaneously do.

Catherine raved over her new jewels when she and Jeremy came through the line.

"Those are stunning," her sister-in-law exclaimed.

Jeremy drolly said, "I suppose, Duchess, this means you will be receiving new jewelry soon. I can't let the *ton* think you aren't as loved as Rachel."

"I do think I would shine in diamonds, Duke," she replied sweetly. Looking to Rachel, she said, "It's proven useful to us for our husbands to carry on their little rivalry."

Rachel and Evan opened the ball, dancing the first measures of the beginning dance before other couples joined them on the dance floor. After that, she danced only sporadically, wanting to see to the needs of her guests. She found herself growing tired and motioned a footman to bring a chair so that it rested next to her grandmother, who sat with some of her friends.

Cor took Rachel's hands. "You are glowing tonight, Granddaughter."

"I am in love, Cor. Evan has made me happy beyond anything I thought possible."

"It's more than love, I'd say. Or diamonds." Cor leaned in. "How far along are you?"

"You know?" She looked around. "Do you think other people have guessed?"

"Women might have. Men are usually too dense to know until they're told. I assume you haven't mentioned it to Evan yet?"

"No. I was going to tell him when the ball ended."

"Do so now," Cor urged. "Let him enjoy every moment of it with you."

"So far, I haven't been sick. Judging by Catherine and Leah, that time will come soon."

Rachel rose and kissed Cor's cheek. "I'll go find Evan now."

She moved through the ballroom and spotted her husband, quickly joining him.

"I was about to announce it's time for supper after this dance," he told her.

"Let's dance for a moment," she said, lacing her fingers through his and leading him to the center of the room.

The song was more than halfway through as he took her in his arms and they began to move as one.

"Are you pleased with how the night's progressing?" he asked.

"I am. I checked the buffet a few minutes ago and it looks divine."

"I hope everyone will leave happy tonight."

"I have something to tell you." She paused. "You're going to be a father come spring."

Evan stopped. He stared at her as understanding dawned on him.

"A father. I'm going to be a father," he said in wonder.

His hands captured her waist and he began twirling her around, his smile growing larger with each turn. The music came to an end and Rachel smiled back at him, joy spreading throughout her.

He finally slowed and set her back on her feet. Looking out at the pairs on the dance floor who looked at them with interest, he cried, "I'm going to be a father!"

The ballroom's guests broke out in thunderous applause.

Evan swept her off her feet and kissed her.

"This is beginning to become habit with you," she said.

"I know." He said to the crowd, "A sumptuous buffet awaits you. Please enjoy the rest of your night. As for the Marquess and Marchioness of Merrick? We will be celebrating privately for the rest of the evening."

Their guests made way as he strode through the ballroom with her in his arms and out the doors to the stairs.

"We're *leaving* our guests in the middle of the ball we're hosting?"

"We are."

The clock chimed midnight.

"I thought rather than be with the *ton*, you might wish to spend midnight with me."

Rachel arms tightened about Evan's neck. "I will always want to spend midnight with my marquess."

THE END

About the Author

Native Texan and former history teacher Alexa Aston lives with her husband in a Dallas suburb, where she eats her fair share of dark chocolate and plots out stories while she walks every morning. She enjoys reading, Netflix binge-watching, and attending sporting events when she's not watching *Survivor* or *The Crown*.

Alexa's Medieval and Regency historical romances bring to life dashing knights and loveable rogues and include the series *The Knights of Honor*, *The King's Cousins*, and *The St. Clairs*.

Made in the USA
Middletown, DE
04 June 2019